MORE THAN A LAWMAN

Anna J. Stewart

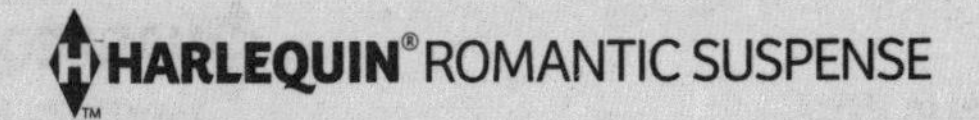

Recycling programs
for this product may
not exist in your area.

ISBN-13: 978-0-373-28204-3

More Than a Lawman

This edition published by arrangement with Harlequin Books S.A.

For questions and comments about the quality of this book, please contact us at CustomerService@Harlequin.com.

Printed in U.S.A.

Anna J. Stewart, a *USA TODAY* and national bestselling author, loves to spend a free weekend curled up in her favorite chair with Snickers, her cat, remote in hand, flipping through whatever streaming service her Wi-Fi will connect to. A geek at heart, she loves blow-'em-up action and sci-fi movies and has rarely met a superhero she didn't like. Anna writes both sweet contemporary and romantic suspense for Harlequin and believes that, when all is said and done, there's nothing better than writing about falling in love, with a little action thrown in for good measure.

Books by Anna J. Stewart

Harlequin Romantic Suspense

More Than a Lawman

Harlequin Heartwarming

Christmas, Actually
"The Christmas Wish"

The Bad Boy of Butterfly Harbor

Make Me a Match
"Suddenly Sophie"

Recipe for Redemption

For Eileen Rendhal

Thank you for your encouragement,
advice and friendship.

I want to be you when I grow up.

Chapter 1

Icy air shot through Eden's lungs.

She choked and dragged in breaths as fast as she could and moaned against the pain blazing across her shoulders. She lifted heavy lids and stared down at the yellowed laminate floor, nausea swirling as she swayed in the air.

Her face had gone numb with cold, freezing the terrified tears on her cheeks. Not just cold air. Arctic air.

Stale air.

A whimper escaped her throat as she twisted back and forth and kicked out, but the movement sent new waves of pain slicing through her, especially her arms. She'd never hung like a slab of meat in a freezer before, but she figured there had to be a first time for everything.

She licked her cracked, dry lips and forced her chin up and back. A solitary bulb blazed bright enough for her to look up and see the raw bruises forming around her chained wrists.

Panic set in, stealing what little breath she had. Her head pounded like a freight train had rumbled through her skull. She could hear the thudding of her heart in the tomb-like silence.

Hysteria clawed its way at her, but she ignored the terror as the image of the rusted metal hook that suspended her from the ceiling burrowed into her brain. Fear was useless. Fear wouldn't do any good. Fear wouldn't get her out alive.

She kicked harder this time, but only spun herself in a dizzying circle. She took advantage of the miscalculation and scanned her prison. And the bodies surrounding her in what could be her tomb.

No windows, only one door…

She whirled again as her mind caught up with her and questioned how she'd gotten here. The last thing she remembered was heading to Monroe's to meet Cole…

Cole. Oh, God. Cole.

Wait. Eden squeezed her eyes shut. She recalled getting out of the car. She'd heard footsteps, heavy shoes, quick steps, alarming enough for her to reach into her bag for her stun gun, but an arm had locked around her throat before she could grasp it. And then she was…here.

Stupid, stupid, stupid.

She'd let down her guard, fallen into a routine. Predictability was as much an enemy to her as the criminals she stalked. What had she been thinking?

Eden dropped her head back, let out a long breath and blinked her eyes open. No use dwelling on mistakes she couldn't change. Not when she had to figure out a means to escape. Her eyes adjusted to the dimness, even as she wished she could block out the sight in front of her.

Men and women, various ages, sizes and ethnicities, hung in similar fashion, only their arms were stiff at their sides, hooks pierced through what she hoped were their clothes. Every one of the eight bodies had the same horrified death mask. Icicles had formed on their extremities. Sheer, sharp blades of ice dangled from fingertips and noses.

Eden swallowed. How long had it taken them to die?

She wiggled tingling fingers. How long did she have?

Stop. Detach. Work it out. What do you see? What can help you?

Eden grasped at the calm she'd spent years honing as an investigative reporter. She couldn't think about these people—people who had once led full lives, had friends and families who cared about them, were missing them. If…*when*, when she got out, she would do something for them.

Starting with bringing the Iceman to justice.

Even though she was already so cold, Eden's blood chilled at the thought of the serial killer who had been preying in the Central Valley on and off for the past three years. They—the authorities—had believed he'd disappeared after leaving three frozen, mutilated corpses hanging in abandoned food storage facilities within the Sacramento region, but Eden always suspected otherwise. Her frigid companions proved her right. The Iceman had been stocking up; storing his victims for this one big reveal.

The killer probably thought of Eden as the candle on the cake.

"Okay…whatever God is up there…if I get out of this, I'll tell Cole he was right." He'd been saying for years that she'd go too far one day; push someone over the edge. The detective and longtime family friend might be a pain in the neck, but he was the only cop willing to give her the time of day when it came to her theories. She knew what it was like to live without answers, without justice.

She was not giving up. Not when she still had to have answers herself.

Her arms strained as she tried to pull on the chains and haul herself up. No go. The air was thinning. Breathing actually hurt.

In hindsight, perhaps she shouldn't have spouted off about the Iceman. On her blog, she'd called him every name she could think of. Her boss at the paper had accused her of becoming a liability and a danger to both herself and the reputation of the publication. Clearly, he'd been onto something. Karma may be paying her back—given the name of her blog, *Eden on Ice*, was currently more than just a play on words.

"Maybe it can be my epitaph." Eden shivered so hard she thought her bones might snap. She was so weak, and yet the monster that dwelled within Eden—the monster that had been birthed twenty years ago when her friend had been murdered—stirred to life. She would not surrender.

Not to one of *them.*

A searing pain soared between her shoulder blades as she hoisted herself up a mere inch. She bit her lip to keep from crying out. The movement sent blood rushing to her starved muscles. The strain on her wrists was unbearable, but she welcomed the sensation. If she hurt, she was alive.

Terror washed afresh. Wait. Why was she alive?

She turned her head to one side and then the other, as if her kidnapper was about to come through the metal door.

She had to get down. Now.

An image of Detective Cole Delaney exploded in her mind and she laughed. How would Cole handle this situation? What would he do?

"Cole wouldn't be in this situation," Eden chattered. "Cole would have taken out the Iceman the second he realized he was being followed." Oh, how she really, really wanted to live long enough to see if her instincts were right.

Eden might be able to shoot any gun, use any knife, topple any attacker—at least one she saw coming—but a fat lot of good those skills were to her now. All she had to work with was her body. And hanging in the middle of a subzero freezer wasn't exactly like a visit to her local gym.

Step one, get down. Eden shut her eyes and tried not to think about the red stains on the metal hook. She couldn't scoot off. The bend in the hook was too deep. She needed to find another way. But how…

Eden grimaced as the idea took hold. Not pretty, but if it worked…

Grunting, panting, inhaling as much air as she dared, she stretched out one leg, testing how far it was to the nearest corpse. She pointed her toe and missed making contact, but thankfully, she'd chosen to wear her pointy-toed ankle boots for the rainy spring day.

This would happen. It had to.

Eden looked down at the floor. It would hurt. A lot. The drop wasn't long, but the fact that she couldn't feel, let alone control most of her body, meant hitting the deck could do more damage than the meat hook.

The vow to dump every last pint of chocolate peanut butter ice cream in the garbage if she succeeded was on the tip of her tongue, but the thought only stoked her anger. "No way I'm letting this creep put me off ice cream."

Never mind the pain; she'd take the risk. Suddenly, she was grateful she hadn't given up the Pilates classes, even though they were costing her a fortune.

Eden locked her legs together and swung them back.

Then forward. Back. Forward. Until she got a good momentum going. With one final push, she tightened her stomach muscles and threw her legs up and over the shoulders of the closest body, then clamped her feet one over the other. She heard a sickening noise.

Bile rose in her throat. The chains dug deeper, rubbing away her skin. Blood beaded beneath the metal as she stretched and arched her back, dragging the links up toward the point of the hook. Two inches up, one back. Metal ground against metal.

With less than an inch to go, poised to yank the chain free and uncross her feet, Eden braced herself for the fall.

Click.

Eden twisted her head and stared wide-eyed at the door. She gritted her teeth, gave one last push and released herself.

The door slid open.

Eden dropped to the ground and rotated at the last second. She landed hard on her side, her shoulder taking the brunt of the impact.

She slammed her eyes shut, not just from the pain but the onslaught of light blazing into the freezer. The world blurred; darkness closed in.

"Eden!"

She heard voices…lots of voices, and for a split second she thought St. Peter himself was hosting her welcome-to-the-afterlife party.

Eden frowned. St. Peter sounded like Cole. She tried to breathe, but the fall had stolen the last of her air. She tried again, managing to inhale a shallow breath. It was enough to clear her mind as a warm, strong arm slid under her shoulders and hauled her into a sitting position.

Firm hands grasped the chain around her wrists and pulled her forward.

Eden screamed.

"It's okay. You're okay, Eden. I've got you."

Cole.

She tried to say his name, but the shivering prevented her from speaking. Next, he'd scooped her up, leaving the chains in place. He carried her from the freezer through a maze of hallways and out into the fresh Central Valley air.

Her eyes watered at the change in light. She turned her face into the soft leather of his jacket, forcing herself to inhale his spicy masculine scent as it seeped into her. Warmed her. Surrounded her.

She couldn't stop shaking. She could barely get her thoughts straight as Cole tightened his arms around her and bent his head to tuck her face deeper into the thawing effects of his jacket. His breath was reassuring against her cheek.

He was talking to her, his voice fading in and out, so she caught only a few phrases. "Scared the life out of... Don't ever... Kill you myself. First thing... GPS tracker around your neck."

Eden smiled. He was angry with her. Again.

It wasn't the first time he'd suggested the tracker, but it was the first time she didn't feel like clocking him in response.

She knew his concern was out of an obligation he felt he had to her brother, to the promise he'd made years ago to keep an eye on her. Still, it was nice to know Cole cared, and she decided to enjoy the moment. She'd avoided death, unlike her silent companions. Soon enough he'd change tactics, read her the riot act for being so careless, for putting her life at risk. Again. For not following the rules. Again.

And she, in return, would remind him, again, that

the rules didn't apply when it came to stopping killers like the Iceman.

Her stomach fluttered as Cole pressed his lips against her forehead and lingered for a minute.

Odd. No part of Eden St. Claire ever fluttered. Besides, Cole Delaney wasn't her type. He was a friend. Maybe her best friend. And if there was one thing she'd learned the last ten years, it was that cops and reporters did not mix. Especially not her—a journalist who was so not by the book—and him—a detective so by the book he recited regulations as if they were his nightly prayers.

That warm and fuzzy sensation she was feeling toward him was gratitude. Nothing more.

She felt Cole sit down, keeping her on his lap as he stretched his jacket around her still-shivering body.

"S-s-sorry," Eden finally managed.

"Shut up," Cole ordered and then shouted over her head. "Medic! She needs medical attention!"

"D-do n-n-not n-nee—" She smiled a little when she felt his body tense.

"I said shut up. Medic!" His bellow only made her headache worse. Eden heard racing footsteps and her memory flashed back to Monroe's parking lot. She shuddered and swallowed the fear.

"G-get th-th-these off me." Eden lifted her wrists and found the chains incredibly heavy. Where was that adrenaline now that she knew she wasn't going to die? She was so sleepy, and Cole was so safe, so comforting. If she could close her eyes for a few minutes—maybe her mind would slow down.

"Hey!" Cole's fingers gripped her chin to jostle her. "Stay with me, Eden."

"Huh?" Eden blinked. She truly hated him telling her what to do.

An older female EMT appeared. Eden anticipated the freedom, reveled in it as the paramedic examined the chains twisted around Eden's wrists. Smiling, Eden lifted her chin and looked at Cole.

"Hi there, handsome."

Eden enjoyed the surprise in his dark green eyes. She'd always thought him good-looking, although not in the fairy-tale-prince sense. His angular features, slightly pointed nose, his wide-set eyes and the faded scar that ran from his right ear to his temple evoked images of his Celtic warrior ancestry. The idea was only enhanced by his perfectly honed body—one that had allowed him to lift her off the freezer floor as if she weighed no more than a sack of potatoes.

A sack of potatoes. Eden giggled. She was a bag of veggies.

"Get this around her." A voice she didn't recognize came from above her. She focused on a second EMT holding out a thermal blanket.

"Haven't seen you before," Eden murmured to the young male EMT. "You new?"

"She's probably got hypothermia," the first EMT told Cole.

"You think?" Eden said and then gritted her teeth as the chains were pried off her raw, bloodied skin. "Son of a—"

"Ah. There you are." Cole's chuckle sounded strained, and, sure enough, when Eden met his gaze, she loathed the concern she saw reflected in his eyes. "We've got to take you to the hospital, Eden. Get you checked out."

Eden set her jaw. "I'll be fine. Please take me home." A long hot shower, a gallon of coffee, and she'd be on the other side of frozen in no time.

"These wounds need treating."

Eden concentrated on the female EMT and tried her best to appear steady. "I don't like hospitals."

"I bet you'd like dying less. Hypothermia can mess with your heart. You're going to be checked out and probably kept for observation." The woman gave Cole a stern look. "I can bring a gurney over."

New panic overtook the fear she'd experienced in the freezer. "No, Cole. Please." She knew she had no right to ask him to help her again, but she didn't have to explain—not to him. He'd understand she wasn't up to facing another of her demons tonight.

Loyalty to her and obligation to his job battled behind the tension reflected in his gaze. "Compromise. No ambulance, but you let me take you to the hospital."

Eden parted her lips, planning to negotiate, but his eyes narrowed.

"Take it or leave it," he said.

Heart pounding, she realized she was too tired to fight him. Eden nodded.

"As long as you accept responsibility for her," the EMT told him.

"I did that a long time ago."

Eden hid her smirk, but kept her mouth shut.

Once the EMTs were gone, Cole fixed the blanket around her. "Fair warning, Eden. As of right now, things have changed. And believe me, you're not going to like it." He lifted her in his arms and strode over to his car. "Not one little bit."

"Hey, Delaney!"

Cole turned, but continued walking backward as a patrolman called out.

"This is your case! You're primary!"

"Secure the scene," Cole hollered over to him. "McTavish is in charge until I get back here." Cole stumbled.

Eden locked her hands around his neck as he righted himself. He might be mad as all get-out at her, but he wouldn't let her fall. He never had. "You okay?" he asked.

"Yeah." The shivering had subsided, and while there wasn't a part of her that didn't ache or burn, she welcomed every pinprick of pain. "I'll be fine."

Cole nodded to the patrol officer who yanked open the door to Cole's SUV. It was only after Cole secured her seat belt and closed the passenger door that Eden realized she'd forgotten to ask him one very important question.

How had he ever found her?

Chapter 2

Big-city emergency rooms in the early morning hours on a Saturday were chaos personified. Add in a three-car pileup on the I-5, a collapsed back porch thanks to an overabundance of drunk partygoers, and the mass-testosterone-induced excitement of a road-trip bachelor party gone wrong, and Cole was looking at chaos in the rearview mirror.

"Detective Delaney, it would be better if you waited outside, please," the duty nurse said as she switched on monitors and ordered her staff about.

"I'm staying out of the way." Wedged in the corner by the door, he couldn't be more out of the way if he was in the next room. Cole kept his gaze pinned to Eden's. She was holding it together, but only barely. He was well acquainted with her aversion to hospitals and the medical profession in general. She'd be shaky under normal circumstances.

These circumstances were anything but normal. "I'm right here, Eden, okay?"

She nodded, once, sharp, and flinched as the nurse inserted an IV into her arm. That Eden pressed her lips into a tight white line told him she was either repressing a scream or debating verbally abusing her caregivers. He was tempted to advise the nurse to tie Eden's hands down, but he didn't want to borrow trouble. As long as he stayed in sight, as long as she knew someone who cared about her was here, she'd be okay.

His entire body itched to answer his cell. It had been buzzing on and off since he'd left the scene, but one glare from the nurse had him pocketing the device and riding out the endless minutes it took for them to evaluate and stabilize Eden's core temperature.

As much as he wanted to be at the crime scene, his place was here, with Eden. He'd vowed to her older brother, Cole's best friend, that he'd protect her. It had been eight years ago that Logan had left for—and never returned from—Afghanistan. Little did Cole know that oath would morph into a second job.

If there had ever been a time Eden St. Claire hadn't pushed the boundaries of good judgment, Cole couldn't remember it. Act first, worry later was her mantra.

But, he reminded himself, Jack McTavish was solid. Cole's partner would keep the crime scene clear and their superiors at bay. And when he couldn't, Cole would get a 222 text message.

Obviously it was past time to give Eden an emergency code. If for no other reason than to preserve Cole's sanity.

Guilt then stabbed at his gut. Cole should have known something was wrong when Eden missed their weekly confab at Monroe's Coffeehouse. Or he might have, if they hadn't had that rip-roaring argument last week when he'd told her she was being reckless with her reporting. Instead of worrying when she didn't show, he'd assumed she was trying to teach him a lesson and had ditched him. She'd done it in the past when she'd gotten too caught up in one of her stories.

His frustration boiled over. That crazy blog of hers had gotten out of control. *Eden on Ice.* Bad enough she'd gone to journalism school—as a cop, he wasn't overly fond of interfering reporters to begin with. No, she had to supplement her crime-reporter income from the *Sacramento Tribune* by running a blog that kept tabs on killers, serial and otherwise, who were reputedly in California, Nevada or Oregon. She'd quickly gained a certain reputation with law-enforcement agencies—and not necessarily for the better. If Eden felt justice hadn't been served or if one of these lowlifes was on the loose, watch out. Chances were the suspected killer featured in Eden St. Claire's database.

Not that she'd paid any mind to others besides the Iceman in recent months. Her fixation had almost done her in once and for all.

He watched as Eden's eyes drifted closed and her head lolled to the side.

Finally. She was asleep and Cole felt as if he could breathe. He sagged against the wall.

When was he going to learn that nothing good ever happened between 2:00 and 3:00 a.m.? His father had called it "the hour of the wolf," when evil lurked, waiting for the opportunity to strike.

And phone calls at that time?

It was never happy news.

What relief he'd felt when he'd seen her name on his caller ID vanished when the disguised voice on the other end told him to hurry…to find her…before it was too late.

Cole didn't know what was more unsettling. The fact

he hadn't known Eden was missing or that it was the Iceman himself who had seen fit to inform him where she could be found.

Oh, his lieutenant was going to love the fact a serial killer now had Cole's direct number.

Even worse? Tonight's events meant that Eden had been right all along. The Iceman hadn't left the Central Valley area. He was still killing, and, as of a few hours ago, had upped the stakes considerably.

Cole took advantage of Eden sleeping and slipped into the hallway. He kept one eye on the open door to her exam room as he answered the call from one of the evidence techs on the case. "Hey, Tammy. What's up?"

"Thought you'd want to know. The officers you had checking on Eden's house reported in. They found her car parked in her driveway. Her purse and cell phone are inside. Doors are locked, house and car keys were wedged under some kind of gargoyle on her front porch. No sign of a break-in."

A shiver raced down his spine. "He knows where she lives." And how she lived. That she kept her spare key in that hideously adorable creature was a long-running joke—and secret—between the two of them. She had an entire collection of creepy, ugly ornaments scattered about that porch and backyard.

Given the growing popularity of her blog—she had a massive following—the fact she'd captured the attention of her latest obsession and target didn't surprise him. What nerve had she struck that awakened the Iceman from his hibernation?

"Did they find any prints?" Cole asked around a too-tight throat. He saw Eden's feet move under the pile of blankets and shifted to be able to watch her more clearly.

"Running them now. So far all they've found are Eden's.

Looks like another dead end. Oh, wow." Tammy hissed in a sharp breath. "Wrong thing to say, sorry."

Cole found himself smiling thanks to that odd sense of humor most cops possessed. "It would have been if we'd gotten there any later. Thanks, Tammy. Let McTavish know, will you? I'll be on scene as soon as I can."

"Tell Eden when she's better she owes me a bottle of Cuervo."

Cole frowned. "Why?"

Tammy clicked her tongue. "She'll know. Just give her the message."

He'd better not find out Eden had been bribing his techs for information again.

"Detective Delaney?" A lanky middle-aged man in scrubs and a white coat headed toward him, the dark circles under his eyes made more pronounced by the thin wire-rim glasses. "I'm Dr. Collins. The nurse at the desk said I should talk to you about Ms. St. Claire before I examine her?"

Cole pocketed his phone and shook the doctor's hand. "I need to be in there when you examine her."

"Are you a family—"

"I have her medical power of attorney." Cole recited his argument from memory. "You don't have her file here, but suffice it to say she has a severe phobia when it comes to hospitals, and, no offense, to doctors." The fact Eden held no control over her fear had been a topic of late-night conversation on more than one occasion. "I'm not talking issues, mind you. I'm talking full-blown panic attacks. You want me there if you want her coherent and amenable to your exam."

"O—kay." Dr. Collins's grimace did little to reassure Cole that the physician understood the situation. "Has she considered therapy—"

"Preaching to the choir, Doc." Cole gave a slow shake of his head. "Been there, tried everything. As long as there's someone she trusts in the room, she pushes through. All the same, the sooner you get this over with, the better." He made a beeline for Eden, much to the frustration of the nurses in her room. "Eden?" He took hold of her hand. "E? You need to wake up, okay? Just for a little while."

He saw her tense, as if she were grinding her teeth, and her eyes opened so slowly he wondered if they'd been lined with lead.

"Sleepy."

"It's no wonder," Dr. Collins said as he stood opposite Cole and accessed her test results on the nearby computer. "Your blood count is alarmingly low. Have you by any chance been diagnosed with anemia?"

"No." Eden frowned as if it was difficult to concentrate. She stared down at her now bandaged wrists.

"I've done a preliminary exam and haven't found any internal issues, Doctor," the remaining nurse in the room said. "No swelling, no broken bones or fractures, and she's not complaining of any pain."

"We'll double-check all that. In the meantime, the saline should get those numbers up. Ms. St. Claire? Eden?" Dr. Collins, clearly taking a cue from Cole, kept his voice low and calm as he asked, "I'd like to examine you, if that's okay? Detective Delaney can stay here with you. We want you to be calm. We'll get through this, I promise."

Eden squeezed Cole's hand so tightly he almost lost circulation. "All right."

Cole blanked his mind as Dr. Collins kept his word, examining Eden with a thorough efficiency that made Cole wonder if the AMA should consider cloning him.

"Eden, the nurse said you told her you had not been sexually assaulted."

"That's right." Eden's voice was tight and her fingers went white around Cole's hand.

"But you were unconscious for a period of time." He hesitated. "I'd like your permission to conduct a sexual-assault exam."

Eden squeezed her eyes shut and shook her head, but a solitary tear slipped down her cheek. Cole swallowed and pretended not to notice. "Do I know how to show you a good time or what?" she joked in such a strained voice Cole's heart constricted. "Do it," she said.

Cole's admiration for Eden—and all women—amplified exponentially as Dr. Collins proceeded.

A few moments went by and Dr. Collins murmured to the nurse, "No indication of sexual assault." He gave Cole a quick nod of reassurance. "Now. Let's see what we have here." He skimmed his hands up her left arm, tangled with the IV line and needle poking into her skin, before checking Eden's other arm. "Nurse? Did you or one of your assistants attempt to put a line in on her right side?"

"No, Doctor." The nurse leaned over the bed and followed the doctor's gaze to the bruises forming in the crook of Eden's arm. "I did make note of a similar puncture wound in the side of her neck. Excuse me, Detective." The nurse circled around and gently held Eden's head to the side. "It's small, but there's a bruise forming."

"We'll get you pictures, Detective." Dr. Collins tapped away on the bedside computer. "Her first blood results are in and there are trace amounts of Propofol in your system. I want to run more tests, but we won't get the results until later this morning. Eden?" Dr. Collins rested his hands on the railing and bent down so she had no choice but to look at him. "Eden, I want to admit you overnight. We need to get your blood count stabilized."

Her eyes went wide before they drooped.

"I know you don't want to be here, but I don't like those marks you have. Give me twelve hours, Eden. That's all I'm asking for. And I can sedate you for most of them if you want."

"Wh-what do you think you'll find?" She sounded little-girl scared, a sure sign she wasn't herself yet.

"I can't be certain, but I need you to trust me. Just for a little while. Can you do that?"

"Cole?" Eden shifted and looked him in the eye. "Will you be here when I wake up?"

"Where else would I be?" He squeezed her hand as his heart started thudding an uneasy rhythm.

"'Kay. Put me out."

"When you feel up to it—" Cole bent close and whispered to her as the nurse and Dr. Collins discussed the amount of sedative "—you and I are going to have a very long talk about what happened tonight. You hear me, Eden?"

He ignored every warning blaring in his head telling him to keep an emotional distance, but this was Eden. There wasn't any distance to be had. "You're done doing things this way. Understand?"

"Mmm." She nodded as her face relaxed into a goofy smile. "I hear you. Don't agree, though. He's out there. Hunting." She groggily patted his hand as the nurse injected the sedative into her IV. "Gotta get him. Gotta get all of them. For Chloe..."

And then she was out.

"Doctor?" Cole placed her hand gently on the bed.

"Outside, please." Dr. Collins led him into the hallway and drew Eden's door almost shut. "I can't be certain, but given her platelet and red cell count, I'd say her blood's been drained. Enough that I'm seeing more signs of that than the hypothermia. I'll know more once those tests come back. If you'll excuse me."

Cole nodded, then caught the nurse as she came out of Eden's room. "How much of the sedative did you give her?"

"She'll be out for six, maybe seven hours."

"I'll be back in five."

Chapter 3

It was an hour before Cole pulled into the parking lot of the deserted warehouse off Parkway Boulevard in West Sac. At a little before 6:00 a.m. on a Saturday, traffic was nonexistent. Patrol cars from both his and the West Sac department sat scattered about, their lights casting eerie blinding beams into the still-dark morning. Yellow crime-scene tape cordoned off the area. Behind him, the gold silhouette of the landmark Tower Bridge loomed over the city. Two coroner vans, along with two dark sedans, told him more than one department superior was on scene.

As were several news crews. Irritation singed his nerves. Then he realized it was better to deal with them here than have them staking out Eden's bedside. The longer her situation remained under wraps, the better. Especially for Eden.

Eden.

He couldn't stop thinking about the icy blast of that meat locker or her frozen hands clutching at him as he'd carried her out of the building. Feeling her shiver, listening to her struggle for air… Cole didn't think he'd ever complain again about how high the temperatures were in the valley.

His breath escaped in short white puffs as he closed up his SUV and returned to the scene, carrying the tray of steaming coffee cups to his team.

The building was old, long abandoned and beyond neglected. Looking at it from the outside, someone would have had to already know there was a freezer on the premises. Perhaps that list of someones would give them their first lead in months.

The investigating unit had been busy. They'd set up portable spotlights in the four corners of the expansive main area and assembled their equipment. Besides the rusting steel and corroded machine parts, evidence of squatters and remnants of various rodent visitors lay about. A mishmash of footprints could be seen in the buildup of dust and debris on the floor.

Searching for usable evidence would be futile. If there had been any at all, it had been obliterated by him and his men in their rush to get to Eden. Something he'd bet the Iceman had counted on.

The pure joy that surged through him when he'd found Eden alive had nearly overwhelmed him. He'd expected the worst. What else could he think given he'd been taunted by a sociopathic serial killer? In so doing, the Iceman had flipped the entire case on its head.

With all the attention Eden had given the Iceman in recent months, the killer must have had enough; he'd decided to return the favor.

Bile rose in Cole's throat.

There was only one reason the Iceman hadn't murdered Eden.

He wasn't done with her yet.

If the Iceman planned to try again, he'd have to get through Cole first.

"Thought you'd call me with an update before you got here." Jack McTavish emerged from the freezer and grabbed the large paper cup Cole handed to him.

"Tried. My phone's been dropping calls since I changed carriers." He managed a tired smile. "So I drove faster."

"How's Eden doing?" Jack drank deeply and let out a long, satisfied sigh.

"Sedated, but good. I put two officers on her until I get back there." Which Cole was anxious to do, he realized.

Jack gave him a quick nod. His partner was Cole's age, but there were times he acted a decade younger. Thirty-two as of last week—a celebration that had resulted in a two-day hangover for half the squad—his buddy reminded Cole of one of those '80s TV cops with his good looks, sturdy stance and dedication that shone in too-wise dark brown eyes.

They'd been partners for a little over a year, ever since Jack had moved west from Chicago, but Cole was confident that Jack was a good cop. Solid. Dependable. One who would take this attack on someone Cole considered family as personally as he did.

"What have we got?" Cole asked him.

"I wish we could say it's a gold mine." Jack sounded as frustrated as Cole felt. "Other than eight corpses, and an agreement from the West Sac department for us to take the lead, not much."

"So he is still hunting." In any other circumstances, Cole might have smiled at Eden being a step ahead of them. "He was just hiding deeper underground." Cole walked into the freezer, his eyes immediately going to the hook hanging from the ceiling.

Fresh rage descended and he gritted his teeth. He scanned the line of bodies and saw the pale copper-blond hair of a young woman. For an instant, he envisioned Eden's face on the corpse. He attributed the unease to the arctic freezer temps, rather than dwell on the fact that he easily could have been too late.

He'd seen a lot during his ten years on the force, especially in the last two, serving as a detective. The crimes, the victims, the aftermath of what human beings were capable of inflicting on one another were like slash marks on his soul. Was it any wonder some cops lost their faith in…everything? But when the victim was someone you knew, someone you cared about… The breath he exhaled may as well have been fire, given the anger behind it.

Cole's eyes burned as he blinked the vision of Eden away, but he couldn't stop the image of her hanging in this place. What had been going through her head? Had she been awake? Screaming?

No. Eden wouldn't have screamed. She'd done exactly what he would have expected her to do: she got herself down.

"Eden was lucky," Jack muttered as if sensing where Cole's thoughts had taken him.

"I doubt luck had much to do with it," Cole said. Their killer had wanted Eden found. "Glad to see Hendrix is on scene." He inclined his head toward the older silver-haired woman standing in front of a row of gurneys. The medical examiner headed up the entire forensic division, as well she should, given her nearly twenty-five years on the job.

"They're taking bets," Jack said. "This big a development, odds are it's less than twenty-four hours before the Feds arrive."

Not one to pass on a sure thing, he said, "Give me ten on twenty-three. Mona," Cole acknowledged the coroner and stepped over to greet her and hand over the last cup of coffee. "Any idea how long they've been dead?"

"Won't know for sure until the bodies thaw out." Mona Hendrix gazed upon the first two that had been removed, her laser-like blue eyes widening behind thin wire frames. "But these aren't recent kills. I'd say anywhere from a few weeks to a few months. So, Cole, tell me, what do you see?"

He hated this necessary game, but at least the frozen corpses didn't have that sickly sour stench that crept into his nostrils and settled in the back of his throat. Instead the stench had been partially obscured by the frost.

"Their clothes are all still intact," he observed, blanking out the fact that these people had once been living, breathing members of society. "And so are the bodies. No mutilations visible. Strange." The previous three victims had been cut open, organs left exposed. These bodies didn't have that. "A change in MO? Or are you saying it's a different killer? This isn't the Iceman?"

Mona glanced at him, disapproval evident in her face. "You know better than to put words in my mouth, Detective. I asked for what you see. I didn't say tell me what I was thinking."

Cole circled the gurneys, checking for differences, any variances from the first three victims' files he'd memorized, a necessity a month back after realizing Eden had the Iceman in her sights. She might be used to working alone, but she wasn't a cop. Somebody had to be her backup. "Like the original three victims, there doesn't seem to be any racial, physical or gender-specific commonalities, but how they were found and where…"

The Iceman had led him to this spot. Brought Eden here. Eden… She hadn't been focused on anyone other than the Iceman for ages. Who else could it be?

"What about their blood?" he asked and gave himself a mental pat on the back when Mona blinked wide eyes at him. It took a lot to surprise her.

"Their blood?"

Cole bent close and examined the side of the neck of one of the victims. "We need to take another look at the previous bodies." He did the same check on the present victims, pointing to round puncture markings near the jugular in each case. "Eden's doctor found these same pinpricks and bruises, only smaller, and on her arm, too. He believes whoever took her also took a significant portion of her blood."

"Is that so. Well, it's good to have a starting point, but it'll be a few days before I can confirm that."

"How about prints?" McTavish asked.

"We've got in one of those fancy new digital scanners. We'll see how well it works. In the meantime, I'll pull the files of the previous victims and go through them again. Interesting. Given their injuries, any blood loss would have been attributed to those markings, but you're suggesting the blood itself was what he was after? I'll take another run at the photos, too, see if I can find any more wounds similar to these. So, is it him?"

"Going by the evidence in front of us?" Cole cast doubtful eyes to Jack, who shrugged. "I can't say for certain. But my gut tells me it is. There's a reason we didn't get anything from him in almost two years. If he's changed MOs, that could explain it. I'll have Dr. Collins send you a sample of Eden's blood to have something to compare."

For the first time, he felt a crack, however thin, appear in the case.

"Sounds good." Mona returned to the freezer to supervise the removal of the rest of the victims.

"What game is he playing?" Cole couldn't wrap his brain around the scene. "There's so much that's wrong. If I hadn't gotten that call from him, I might not even believe it myself." And hesitation, as Cole knew all too well, could be a cop's worst enemy.

"Buck up, Delaney." Jack shifted on his feet. Cole turned. "Boss is in the house."

"And he's brought a friend. Looks like I should have bet on a shorter time." Even Cole wouldn't have guessed the FBI would turn up within a half hour. "Lieutenant." Cole nodded at Kevin Santos, a cop with twenty years' experience, most of it in homicide, despite the fact that he looked like a computer geek. Three years behind the lieutenant's desk hadn't dulled his detective skills one bit. Nor had it affected his capacity to detect what Cole's grandfather would have called nonsense.

"Detectives Delaney and McTavish," Lieutenant Santos greeted them and approached them with a guarded look in his eyes. He gestured to the man behind him. "This is Agent Anthony Simmons, our new local FBI liaison. His office is suggesting we establish a task force on the Iceman investigation."

"Shoot," Jack muttered. "Missed it by two hours."

Cole noted his lieutenant's arched brow and wondered if his superior had entered the betting pool himself. "Sir, while we value the FBI's willingness to help—"

"We do?" Jack choked on his coffee.

"Respectfully, Agent Simmons," Cole said, as politely as possible, "nobody knows this case better than my team."

"That may be true." With dark, tired eyes, and a wariness that spoke of too many years on the job, Agent Simmons gave a slow nod. "But you have to admit, given this morning's developments, one has to wonder if you and your team should have known he'd surface again."

Whatever congeniality Cole might have been willing to extend to Agent Simmons evaporated. "I don't have to admit anything." Cole stretched his lips into a wide smile as his coffee churned in his stomach. "Someone did know, but that someone isn't a cop."

"Delaney." Santos's voice held that hint of warning that set cops' hearts to thudding.

"That would be Eden St. Claire, the woman found alive in the freezer?" Agent Simmons asked. "I'd like to interview her as soon as possible."

Cole's eyes narrowed as he sipped again. "I'm sure you would."

"I brought you here for introductions, Agent Simmons. Not to get into an argument with my detectives." Lieutenant Santos put his hands deep into his pockets and rocked back on his heels.

Cole cast a sideways glance at his partner and tried not to smile. Their boss had a long fuse, but the "pocket rock" was a definite sign Agent Simmons had lit it in record time.

"Unless the FBI is officially taking over the case, Delaney will remain in charge. You're welcome to stick around, sit in on the meetings and interviews, even work it with his team, but we make the calls. Understood?"

"A task force is just that. A force," Agent Simmons replied with something akin to a growl in his voice. "I would like to be present when Ms. St. Claire is able to be questioned."

Cole wasn't letting this guy anywhere near Eden; at

least not until he had the chance to talk to her himself.

"She's been sedated for at least the next twelve hours," Cole lied. "They aren't sure of the emotional trauma the attack might have had." He ignored the surprise that flashed across his lieutenant's face. Santos—along with the rest of the Sacramento PD—was well acquainted with Eden and her...proclivities. Emotional trauma tended to have the opposite effect on Eden. If anything, it made her more obstinate, more focused than normal.

Agent Simmons's nod of sympathetic understanding only proved he hadn't done his homework when it came to the Iceman's most recent target, and the woman who'd spent the last year and a half tracking him.

"I'll officially request to be notified when she's conscious," Agent Simmons said.

"You do that." Cole smirked. Why did they always have to be so adversarial? "Sir, with your permission, I'd like to get back to Mona and see if she has any new information."

"Certainly," Santos said. "But first, a moment if you don't mind, Agent?" Santos grabbed Cole's arm and moved him out of Simmons's earshot. "I don't know what's going on with this guy, but there's something we aren't being told. I'll stall Simmons as long as I can, but he's up to something."

"The Iceman made a mistake taking Eden," Cole said, not caring about anything else right now, including police politics.

"You mean because he's angered her even more?" Santos's thick eyebrow went up a good inch. "If he meant to deter her—"

"By taking Eden he confirmed what she'd been saying. Leaving her alive is probably his way of telling us he can get to her—to anyone—whenever he wants, which means her years of working on her own are over."

"Glad we're on the same page. Watch out. The both of you," Santos told him and gestured to Jack. "At some point we'll have to update the press, but the chief will take care of any official statements. I'd prefer to keep all of us, Eden included, away from the cameras. Do me a favor?" Santos's mouth quirked into an amused smile. "Let me know when Agent Simmons plans to question Eden. That's a conversation I do not want to miss."

Chapter 4

Had Eden's body not been throbbing, she might have woken with a smile on her face. The drug-induced haze that welcomed her to the conscious world was almost intoxicating. Any other time, she might have actually enjoyed the ride.

The second she moved her head, however, her entire body screamed and she realized where she was. Monitors beeped, cords and tubes were attached to her, and the bars on either side of her bed may as well have been made of barbed wire for all the peace they brought her. That the dull, beige-colored walls, the scribbled-on whiteboard and the dingy sea-foam-green curtain gave her none of the privacy promised bothered her enough to shove herself into a sitting position.

Out. Out. Out. She dug at the IV in her arm. Not in the hospital. Never in the hospital. The walls seemed to close in and the weight of the past descended on her…

"Eden?" Cole's voice drifted to her from across the room. Blinking sleep from his eyes, he leaned forward in his chair, and the mere touch of his fingers against her arm stilled the terror inside her. "It's okay. I'm here. Just like I promised. Lie back. Be calm."

He squeezed his hand around her arm, didn't push, didn't press, but shifted closer so she could see he was there and that he understood.

"I didn't see you," she managed and did as he'd said, collapsing against the flimsy pillows as the squeaky mattress eased under her. Her right shoulder both ached and burned. "Thought I was alone."

"I told you I'd be here when you woke up," Cole said. He scrubbed a hand over his face. "Since when don't you believe me?"

"It's been a rough night." She searched for the humor even as she stared at her bandaged wrists. "A few things might have shifted in here." She poked a finger against her temple. "What time is it?"

"Almost noon."

"On Saturday?" Her brain and mouth felt fuzzy. The drugs.

Cole nodded. "Doctor Collins should be by in a little while with your test results. You hungry?"

"What?" He sounded weird, as if he were speaking under water. Her brain was not cooperating. She sighed and dropped heavy arms onto the mattress. "Yeah, actually." The stent patch in her arm pinched and her stomach turned. Then again…

"They were warm when I bought them." Cole pulled a paper bag from the counter beside her and handed her a cinnamon raisin bagel from Schofield's Bakery.

She smiled, forgetting for a moment what had put her in the hospital in the first place. "My favorite."

"I wanted to make sure you'd eat." He gestured to the three containers of lime gelatin on her table. "I didn't think those would do much for you."

"Is that color even found in nature?" She broke off part of the bagel and popped it in her mouth, the spicy flavor exploding against her tongue as her stomach growled in eager response. "I owe you," she mumbled behind her hand. "Thanks."

"Don't thank me yet." Cole pulled his chair closer. "We have a lot to talk about."

"Not here." She could barely swallow at the thought of being surrounded by medical personnel and machinery. "Later."

"Not much later." Cole didn't look surprised. "Fair warning. I called Simone and Allie."

Eden choked, sputtering bagel onto her chin. She wiped the crumbs away and Cole passed her a cup of water.

"Why?" she squeaked. Her eyes teared, and she drank. "Why would you call them?"

"Because they're your best friends and I didn't want them reading about this on the front page over their morning coffee."

"What front page?" Surely her own paper wouldn't have featured— Who was she kidding? Of course they would. "How bad is it?"

"For you?" Cole shrugged, but Eden could see he was keeping his temper at bay. He was angry, frustrated definitely, and she must be in pretty bad shape if he was willing to hold things in check until a later time. "You're breathing, so I'd say you're in better shape than the other eight people they found in that locker."

"Eight." Eight lives. Eight souls. Turn eight on its side and it became infinity. Infinity… A killer like the Iceman would keep going unless he was stopped. Unless she stopped him. "Who were they?" She'd made them a promise. One she intended to keep.

"We should know in the next day or so. In the meantime—"

She shoved another bite into her mouth and jostled the railing. "In the meantime, I need to get out of here before—"

"Too late. I'm here." The sharp feminine voice shot through the doorway and preceded Simone Armstrong's pristine white form into the room. The woman wore white as effortlessly as a bride and more elegantly than a queen.

The bride she'd been for all of three months a few years back. A queen? It was probably on her list of things to do. Eden once considered submitting Simone's photo to Merriam-Webster's dictionary so they'd have a visual display of professional perfection.

"You didn't have to come down," Eden mumbled as she picked at a loose thread on the blanket. They might be the same age, but at twenty-nine, Simone was most certainly the eldest. "Aren't you getting ready for the Denton trial in a few weeks?"

"Denton's not going anywhere. He's on ice."

Cole snickered. Eden glared at him and he shrugged. "Tell me that wasn't a little funny."

Simone flicked a latch under Eden's bed and lowered the bar before sitting beside her. Eden caught the familiar, comforting scent of Simone's perfume. Some kind of flower. Eden didn't do flowers.

"Thank you for calling me, Cole." Simone took hold of Eden's hand and squeezed, and only then did Eden feel the fear trembling through her friend. Eden had scared her. Again. Not that Simone would ever admit to such a thing in public.

"I wasn't going to deal with her all on my own." Cole's grin didn't quite reach his eyes. "You know the way she gets."

"*She* is getting that way right now." Eden felt a puff of relief as Allie Hollister flitted into the room like the dark-haired pixie she was. "Finally. Someone reasonable. Allie, please tell them— What. Is. That?" Eden angled her eyes to the sad-looking one-eyed panda bear tucked under Allie's arm.

"Pathetic, isn't he?" Allie walked over and plopped the bear on Eden's lap. "Looks like he's been kicked around a bit. Found him on the top shelf of the gift shop. Discounted by about a million percent and it still cost me ten bucks. He reminds me of someone I know. Can't imagine who. I also stopped by your place and got you some clothes." She dropped a plastic bag on the bedside table. "Ooooh, bagels. May I?" She snatched the sack and snagged the second one. "I missed breakfast. So, how was your night?" She fluttered her lashes innocently at Eden—as if she didn't know.

"Okay, okay. I get it. I was stupid. I even told myself that when I was hanging in that meat locker."

"Gah." Allie's mouth twisted as she dropped the bag. "Thanks so much for that image. At some point we're going to have to discuss this annihilation wish you seem to have."

"Stop analyzing me, shrink."

"Criminal psychologist, please." Allie held up her hand much like their fifth-grade teacher had when correcting a spelling error. "I worked hard for those degrees."

"Excuse me." An unfamiliar voice accompanied the

knock on the door frame. Eden lifted weary eyes to the cautious-looking blond man wearing dark green scrubs. "I'm sorry to interrupt. I need to draw some more blood before they remove your stent, Ms. St. Claire." He held up a plastic-handled container one might carry cleaning supplies in. "It won't take but a minute."

"Yeah, sure. Whatever." Eden squinted to read his badge as he drew closer. "Glen."

"Careful—she bites." Allie grinned.

"Shut up." Eden shifted and focused on Cole. The expression on his face seemed odd, caught between concern and confusion. But the smile he gave her was pure Cole and took her breath away. Where would she be without him?

"All done." Glen gathered up his supplies.

"That's some touch you've got, Glen." Simone patted Eden's knee in comfort. "She barely flinched."

"Have a good day." He gave them a quick wave on his way out.

"So which one of you is going to fill us in on what happened?" Simone asked as she looked between Cole and Eden.

"Didn't you read the paper?" Cole asked.

"I only read the paper if I'm featured," Simone said with a sly smile. A lie. Simone never read the paper, not even Eden's articles. "You finally did it, then, Eden. You're solidly in some maniac's crosshairs just like you've always wanted."

"No fair picking on the sick girl," Eden said.

"She must be desperate if she's playing that card." The other railing went down as Allie perched at the end of the bed and rested her hands on Eden's feet.

The monster inside Eden settled, curling up and falling into hibernation once more. She had her friends—her family—around her. She was safe. Even in a hospital, she was home when she was with them.

"Do you remember anything?" Allie asked.

"Creep got me in the parking lot at Monroe's," Eden explained and tried to clear the last of the cobwebs. "Thought I had time to get my Taser, but..."

"Wait. You were at Monroe's last night?" Cole's entire body tensed, and he came toward her.

"Of course. We had a meeting, remember?"

"I thought you'd ditched me. Because of our fight."

"If I ditched you every time we fought we'd never see each other," Eden teased him. "I got there right after seven. I was late, sure, but—"

"Hang on." Simone squeezed Eden's hand and addressed Cole. "What aren't you telling us, Detective?"

Cole's expression turned cold. "We found your car at your town house, Eden. Your purse and phone were inside. Your house keys were under the gargoyle."

Whatever fear she'd managed to push aside roared back. "But I live more than a half hour from Monroe's."

"If you two didn't meet up," Allie said, and Eden saw the logic gears begin to turn, "how did you know she was missing, Cole? How did you know where to find her?"

"I meant to ask you that last night," Eden said, and for the first time she could remember, she dreaded Cole's answer. The silent seconds that ticked by only increased her apprehension.

"He contacted me. The Iceman," Cole said, proving to Eden that no matter how bad things got, he would never lie to her. "He told me where to find you."

"The Iceman has your phone number?" Simone frowned for a flash only, as if remembering they caused wrinkles.

"I thought it was Eden calling." Cole locked his gaze on Eden's. "He used your phone."

Only a fraction of a second passed before she made the next connection. "He knows where I live, then." Not to mention what else he'd have gleaned from her phone. Served her right for not using a passcode.

"So it would seem," Cole said. "Which brings me back to that discussion we're going to have. Now seems the right time. You're going into protective custody, Eden. No arguments."

"No arguments needed because it isn't going to happen." Whatever fear she should have felt didn't materialize. Not under the anger, not under the triumph circling inside her like an eagle finally diving for its prey. "Don't you see? It's personal now."

"Doesn't get more personal than a serial killer having your address," Allie said.

"No, I mean he's messing up. I'm getting to him." The adrenaline inside her surged. "I'm not about to run and hide when he's afraid. We've got him cornered."

"*We* do not have him cornered," Cole said in too calm a voice. "*We* don't have the first clue who he is. We don't even know why he's doing what he's doing. And trust me, Eden, you're either doing this my way or you'll find yourself in the hands of the FBI under witness protection."

Eden balked. "You wouldn't."

"Try me. Special Agent Anthony Simmons, our new FBI liaison, is more than anxious to help with the case. And talking to you is definitely on the top of his list of things to do. Give me a reason, Eden. One excuse, and I won't hesitate to turn you over."

"You do that, Cole, I'll never forgive you." He knew how important her work was, how she lived and breathed finding every last killer she could in order to bring them to justice.

"You'd be alive, though," Cole said and pushed to his feet. "Guess which means more to me?" He kissed the top of her head. "I made a promise, Eden, to keep you safe. No matter what it takes."

"Hold on. No, Cole, please—" She grabbed for him as he moved away. "We can talk about this. What about—"

"Eden, I'm wiped. I need a couple more hours' sleep before I can even think about going to the station. I'll be back later."

"To take me home, right?" Eden asked.

"You can't be serious," Simone demanded before Cole could. "Eden, for heaven's sake, a serial killer knows where you live. Cole? Tell her she can't go back there."

"I'm not putting anyone else in his sights," Eden mumbled around gnawing on her thumbnail. That she barely flinched probably told Cole he had his work cut out for him with her. Independence was one thing. Reckless disregard for her own life, she guessed, was another. Which meant she needed to find a compromise. "I'll get the locks changed," she offered. "I'll look into an alarm system. Maybe I'll get a dog."

As if she had time for a dog.

"Don't worry, Eden, I'll take care of it." Cole squeezed Simone's shoulder, brushed his fingers over Allie's and gave them a silent smile goodbye.

"Take care of what?" Eden called after him. "What did he mean by that?" she asked.

"If I had to bet?" Simone said with a hint of frustration in her voice. "It's that somebody's getting a bodyguard. Oh, snap out of it, Eden. There are worse things than being put under house arrest by Cole Delaney." Her attempt to placate Eden didn't work. If anything, the idea of spending extended time in close quarters with Cole only made Eden's stomach do giant Olympic pool–sized belly flops.

"He's worried about you." Allie reclaimed her bagel. "He has reason to be. I read your test results. Sedative aside, another few hours in that freezer, you'd be dead. As it was, you went in there with only two-thirds your normal blood supply. Not sure if that might help with the investigation or not." She arched a brow.

Eden rubbed her arms and shivered. "The Iceman took my blood? Why would he do that?"

"The only person who can help you answer that just walked out the door." Simone got to her feet and took Cole's chair, crossed her legs and waggled her fingers at Allie. "Gimme. I'm hungry."

"That's what happens when you live on pea shoots and sesame seeds." Allie handed over the last half of her bagel as Eden stared ahead.

"Uh-oh." Simone nibbled on a raisin. "I know that look. Eden? What are you thinking? Do we need to buy Cole a flak jacket?"

"He already has one. And I'm not thinking anything. Yet." But she was starting to. Something between her and Cole had changed. They weren't wholly off-kilter exactly, but she could sense a difference in their relationship, as if something had become lodged between them. Or maybe dislodged. One thing was for certain.

It was time for her and Cole to come to an understanding.

About a lot of things.

Chapter 5

"I don't suppose you're going to listen to what the doctor said and take it easy." Later that afternoon, Cole shut the door to Eden's town house off La Riviera Drive, but not before casting an accusatory glare at the silent gargoyle. The ugly thing was partially hidden by overflowing camellias and should have been protecting Eden's home.

"I don't take it easy, Cole, remember?" She pulled off the sling her doctor had given her and tossed it onto one of the chairs.

"Some things I don't need reminding of." He'd taken her at her word and had her locks replaced. A security system would take longer, but motion sensor lights would do in the meantime, which Jack had installed this afternoon. None of that meant Cole would be leaving her alone, but, for now, he knew how to pick—and plan—his battles. She wanted to stay in her house and play more games with this maniac? She'd be staying on Cole's terms. And under his watch.

Eden paused long enough to settle the sad stuffed panda from Allie behind the framed photos and keepsakes she had lined up on the narrow china cabinet. It was one of few pieces of furniture he recognized as having belonged to Eden's parents. She brushed a reverent finger over the edge of the simple black frame depicting her mom and dad, another over the butterfly trinket box Simone had given to her on her sixteenth birthday. College graduation day for her, Simone and Allie. She hesitated a second longer over the photo of her brother.

Cole looked away. That familiar moment of grief struck whenever he saw Logan St. Claire grinning at him. Even with the filthy face and too-long hair, surrounded by his comrades, eyes slightly tarnished by the reality of their time in Afghanistan, Cole could almost hear Logan's laughter. Except Logan's laughter—along with his friends'—had been silenced forever by a mortar attack.

Cole missed his best friend; the boy he'd learned to ride a bike with, the teen he'd competed with for dates. The young man who had devoted his life to Eden after their parents' deaths in the car crash that had nearly killed Eden, as well. Cole had found his own way to grieve, to get through, to move on. But Eden?

Cole's fists clenched as if he could fight her ghosts and his own. He knew Eden considered death her personal nemesis.

The sound of a drawer being yanked open in the kitchen drew him through the living room that housed a meager DIY couch, a small flat-screen TV and an antique Tiffany-style lamp that looked oddly out of place. Half a dozen cardboard boxes sat wedged against walls, some opened, most with a thin layer of dust on top. Boxes that he knew for a fact hadn't shifted an inch since she'd moved in.

When he rounded the corner into the kitchen, he found Eden with her head in the freezer. "What are you doing?" He stepped forward and grabbed her arm to yank her back. "If this is some half-baked plan to try to remember what happened to you..." He trailed off, suitably silenced by the sight of the spoon in her mouth and the pint of ice cream in her hand. "Really?"

She popped the spoon free, the irritation and defiance in her eyes an oddly attractive combination. "He almost made me hate ice cream." Eden took another huge bite before she sucked in a breath and pinched the bridge of her nose. "Nobody makes me hate ice cream. Ah! Ice-cream headache!" She bounced on her toes and replaced the lid. Aiming her spoon at him like a gun, she then quickly dropped it into the dishwasher.

Cole tossed his keys onto the counter and pushed her aside to open the fridge. "You need to eat."

"What I need is to get back to work." Her gaze skittered toward the padlocked door in the small alcove. "Besides, you brought me a bagel at the hospital, remember?"

"You ate half a bagel, and you need protein, preferably with some iron for all that blood you lost." He bit his tongue and put his frustration into something productive. He dug around until he found eggs, spinach and a good-sized chunk of cheese. At least she hadn't forgotten to shop for groceries. "You're not working until tomorrow. Now sit."

"I'm not entirely sure I like you right now, Cole." She surprised him by doing as he ordered and hopped onto one of the two stools on the other side of the breakfast bar. "I'm supposed to be the bossy one, remember?"

The fact she was still as pale as a hundred-year-old

ghost no doubt meant she had the energy of a flea, but Cole wasn't about to challenge her on that. As much as he hated to admit it, he needed her fighting spirit back, if for no other reason than to convince him she'd be ready for anything.

Having a serial killer on her trail would be enough to keep him awake for the near future. He'd already spent most of the morning distracted by worrying about her. The fact that Simone had texted him almost as soon as he'd left the hospital to let him know she'd stay until he returned had eased his mind temporarily. Hip-hip hooray.

"You'd best get used to it." Cole shrugged out of his jacket and draped it over one of the kitchen chairs piled high with files and photos. "You're stuck with me for the foreseeable future."

"Won't that cut into your *personal* time?" Eden surprised him yet again by reaching for one of the bananas in the bowl, then snapped it open. "What's the latest one's name again? Tiffany? No, Tawny. Thelma?"

"Thandie." Cole cringed as he rolled up his sleeves. "And there hasn't been any *personal* time for a few months."

"Huh." Eden broke off a chunk of banana and swallowed it. "Maybe it would help if you didn't live somewhere that required a life vest."

Cole cracked eggs into a bowl and heated up the only pan she owned. "Don't go dissing my boat." Refurbishing the 1960s gentleman's river cruiser had kept him sane the last few years. "And that's big talk from a woman who hasn't unpacked in, what?" He stepped back from the counter and gestured at the boxes in the living room. "Just how long has it been since you moved in?"

"Three years." Eden shrugged. "I've had other things on my mind. Besides, I unpacked the essentials."

"So if I were to head upstairs to your bedroom, I wouldn't find your clothes tossed over unopened boxes or piled up in the corner?"

Another shrug, but this time her gaze skittered from his. "Don't criticize my organizational style, Cole. It works for me."

He dumped the eggs and spinach in the pan and went to work on the cheese. "Home should be a respite, Eden. A place to escape."

"Given my front door may as well have a giant bull's-eye painted on it, I think we can agree that's no longer an option." She got up and opened the hand-carved bread box on the counter—a Christmas gift from him years before—and pulled out a loaf of sliced sourdough. She dropped a couple of pieces into the toaster. "So what's the plan? You moving in?" She leaned her arms on the counter and watched him stir the eggs. "If so, my guest room will need some, um, fixing up."

When he glanced at her she grinned and batted her lashes at him.

"Don't do that, Eden." Cole shook his head and switched off the stove to let the residual heat finish the eggs.

"Don't do what?"

"Pretend as if what happened last night didn't scare you." It sure had scared him, and Cole didn't scare easily. "It's me, remember? I can read you like a book. You're spooked, which means you're doing what you always do when you get scared. You deflect with humor and sarcasm, and when that doesn't work, you'll start insulting me and anyone else who tries to help you just to drive us away."

She inclined her head, her thick sandy-blond hair falling around her shoulders in a way that shouldn't tempt him as much as it did. Intense blue eyes sparked like the center of pure fire, where the oxygen barely kissed the air. "What kind of book am I?"

The kind he couldn't put down. The kind that kept him up nights. The kind he shouldn't be reading. He pulled the pan off the heat and faced her, moving in so she was forced to straighten and step back. For an instant, he found himself at the warehouse again, looking down at her on that frozen floor. It had been the longest moment of his life, waiting for her chest to rise, and when it did, he'd almost wept.

Now here she was, standing in front of him, defiance personified, licking her full lips and forcing herself to meet his gaze as he took one more step closer.

"Cole." She pressed a hand against his chest, the warmth of her touch seeping through his shirt and reminding him that she, that he, was still very much alive. "What're you doing?"

"Not sure I know." But he wanted to find out. He'd almost lost her, almost lost this chance with her he'd been thinking about for so long… He skimmed his fingers over the bandage on her wrists, unable to erase the image of the chains that had been there.

Cole lifted his hand, cupped her chin in his palm and leaned down, his eyes scanning her face as she searched his, confusion marring her brow as he dipped his head, and after he heard a soft sigh escape her mouth, he kissed her.

Fire and spice. The heat of her, the feel of her mouth touching his was everything he'd have thought it would be, if he'd let himself dwell on it long enough. She didn't shrink from him, didn't withdraw. Instead she ran her hand up his arm until her fingers gripped his shoulder, kneading as he deepened the kiss and tasted her.

The sound that erupted from her throat reminded him of a cat on the prowl, hunting, claiming, and as his lips teased hers, for that moment, everything he had to worry about faded.

"Cole," she murmured against his mouth when he raised his head.

"Hmm?" He pressed his forehead against hers, closed his eyes and held on to the feeling for as long as he could.

"Thank you for saving my life."

"Yeah." And there it was. Gratitude. The conciliatory acceptance and silent confirmation that their kiss had been nothing more than the aftereffect of a potentially life-changing event. "Well..." He cleared his throat and stepped away. Well, hadn't that just been a mistake of epic proportions. "You did your part. You stayed alive."

"It's what I do." The smile she gave him seemed strained. "Which is why you don't have to worry about me."

"I will always worry about you," Cole said as he pulled two plates out of the cabinet and dished out the eggs. "I made a—"

"I know. You made a promise to Logan to always look after me." Was it his imagination or was there a trace of bitterness in her voice? Hard to tell since she'd turned to retrieve the butter from the fridge. "After last night I'd say you've more than lived up to your end of the bargain. Whatever your plan is for protecting me, if it includes moving in here—"

"I didn't say I'm moving in." The idea of sleeping on that backbreaker of a couch of hers was enough to have him reevaluating his career choice.

"Oh." Her shoulders straightened and her grin returned as if they'd done nothing more than talk these last few minutes. "That's a relief. You and I both know I can take care of myself."

"Open your freezer and say that again," Cole snapped. "I meant what I said. After you finish eating, you're going to go upstairs to pack and then you're coming home with me."

"To the boat?" Eden squeaked. "I hate the water. You know that. And that...*boat* of yours is a death trap. Besides, I bet you don't even have internet access out there."

"As if that's what you should be worried about right now." If it wasn't for that stupid blog of hers she wouldn't be in this situation in the first place. All the more reason to lock her away...

"Oh!" She snapped her fingers. "That reminds me. I totally need to post an update to let everyone know I'm okay."

"Eden—"

"He's not driving me out of my home." She actually sounded...hurt. "I realize it's not much to look at," she continued. "That to you it's a jumble of boxes and junk, but this is my space. *Mine.* Leaving would be admitting he's won, and neither you nor I would ever do that."

"This isn't about winning or losing, Eden. And it's not about forcing you out of your home. This is about your life." His phone rang and it instantly drove the rest of his lecture from his mind. She smirked as if she'd been saved by the bell. "We're not done, Eden. Hey, Jack. What's up?"

"Agent Simmons is here." Jack's voice had lowered to the point that Cole had to strain to hear. "Something about you absconding from the hospital with the witness in an ongoing investigation."

"My investigation," Cole muttered. Unless something had changed. "My witness." He glanced at Eden, who made no pretense about eavesdropping as she sat at the counter and propped her chin in her hand. “She needs food and a good night’s sleep.”

“Says you,” she grumbled and returned to the toaster.

“Yeah, well,” Jack said. “That sounds fine, except our friendly FBI interloper is about ten seconds from demanding Eden’s address. So if perchance you’re inclined to bring her in, and she can give her official statement—”

“Tell him we’ll be there first thing in the morning.”

Eden glanced over her shoulder, her grin fading as her eyes narrowed. “Bring me where first thing in the morning?” she asked after he had hung up.

“The station. To make an official statement. Don’t let me forget to stop for doughnuts on the way. Half the department is covering for us right now by playing up the damsel-in-distress story. Not so much butter, please.” He plucked the knife out of her hand and snagged his toast.

“What damsel-in-distress story?” She shot to her full height and pinned him with that testosterone-draining stare he’d become immune to years ago.

“The one that kept the FBI from questioning you in the hospital.”

“You mean the FBI really is involved?” She blinked. “That wasn’t a bluff?”

“Some things I don’t bluff about.” Suddenly, putting her in a room with Simmons didn’t seem like such a bad idea to Cole. If he couldn’t get through to her about the danger she was in, maybe the FBI agent could. “I don’t get it, Eden. It’s like you want this maniac to come after you.”

“Maybe I do.” She stuck a butter-covered thumb in her mouth. “Maybe that’s the method to catch him. I hit a nerve, Cole. Pushing him like I did got a reaction and now we have new evidence to work with.”

"Is that your way of saying last night was worth it? Or is it a warning you're about to let him know what your next step is? Allie's right. You do have an annihilation fantasy."

"Allie's biased."

"Allie's a smart woman," Cole countered. "And she's not wrong. But I was."

"About what?" Was that excitement in her eyes?

"It's not the Iceman I have to worry about." He dumped the dirty pan in the sink, his resignation matching decades of pent-up frustration and concern. "The only person I have to protect you from is yourself."

And that would be the far more difficult task.

Chapter 6

"Your talents do not extend to sarcasm." Eden took a small bite of toast to ease her queasy stomach as she carried her plate to the breakfast bar and claimed a stool. Diving into the ice cream face-first hadn't been her best idea, but she'd made a promise to herself. "This is my job, Cole. It's what I do."

"Taunting serial killers isn't exactly on the Fortune 500 list. Any normal person, even a reporter, would take being abducted as a sign to back off or at the very least ask for assistance. If for no other reason than to do what you have to in order to stay alive."

"I haven't been normal since I was nine years old." No matter how much time passed, the pain never diminished. She hated the familiar silence that followed as Cole no doubt tried to find the words that would make things right. But those words didn't exist.

"Not everything in your life has to circle around to

Chloe, Eden. Nothing you or Simone or Allie do will ever bring her back."

From anyone else she'd loathe the sympathy, even challenge it. No one, save the people left behind, could ever understand or contemplate the emotions the murder of a nine-year-old conjured. Those left behind included Chloe's parents, her siblings and the three friends who had to go on without her. But this was Cole; the same Cole who had tugged on Chloe's pigtails to pry a gap-toothed smile out of her when the classroom bully taunted her on the playground. After he'd given the bully a taste of his own medicine. He'd also witnessed the aftermath of Chloe's murder, stood silently behind Eden along with Logan, Simone and Allie when they'd been told their friend was no more. Even still, he'd never truly gotten what that night—and ensuing days—had done to them. Done to her.

How could he when Eden hadn't been honest with anyone, not even Simone or Allie, when it came to that night. Eden's shame, the guilt, the insurmountable grief had become a part of her, settling inside her as her constant companion.

Instead of admitting the truth, of accepting responsibility for her part in the tragedy, Eden had refused to spend her life being afraid of whatever—and whoever—lurked in the shadows.

Whoever she was supposed to be before Chloe's death would forever remain a mystery. She didn't possess Simone's patience or logic to venture into law. Eden lacked the compassion and curiosity Allie exemplified to spend her life exploring behavior and treating the aftereffects.

Instead Eden had found solace in true-crime books, in crime journals and newspapers, in blogs with a leaning toward justice for victims. Words became her weapon of choice. Pushing for answers, speaking for those who had lost their voice, demanding justice through whatever media she had available to her had become as essential to her life as the oxygen she breathed. If Cole didn't understand that…

"I'm well aware Chloe's gone, Cole." She chose her words with care. "I see them lowering her casket into the ground every night before I go to sleep." When she did sleep. She flipped chunks of spinach free from the cooling eggs, clenching her fist around the fork when her hand shook. "The fact her killer is still out there drives me every moment of every day. Cases like hers shouldn't be cold. They shouldn't be forgotten. As far as your precious law enforcement is concerned, her case and dozens of others are as dead as the victims. And yes, it's a gamble whether I learn anything new, but sometimes, like last night, sometimes I hit the jackpot."

"You winning the jackpot shouldn't include me having to identify your body in the morgue."

"Wow." She swallowed hard and dipped her chin to hide her cringe. "Melodramatic much?"

"Only when it comes to you. Now eat." He tapped his fork against her plate.

"It's cold."

"Then you should have stopped running your mouth. These people, these *killers*, they aren't worth your life, Eden."

"Maybe not." Or maybe they were. "But it's not your decision, is it?" She forced herself to stare into the handsome face that had been a presence in her life for longer than she could remember. "It's my choice. This is *my* life, and as far as I'm concerned, catching this guy is worth any price I have to pay. The sooner you accept that, the better. I'm going to take this upstairs with me.

I need a shower." And about ten hours of sleep to kick the sluggish feeling still swamping her head. "And then tomorrow I'm getting back to work."

She didn't wait for him to respond. Anything he said would only continue the circular argument they'd been having for the better part of a decade. The one that had started when she'd announced her plans to double major in journalism and criminal psychology months before she'd even graduated from high school. About the time Cole had entered the police academy. How long ago that all seemed now.

Eden headed upstairs to her bedroom, dashing the final steps into the bathroom before she slammed and locked the door. She rested her forehead against the wood, reaching to set the plate on the sink, but she missed. As she turned, she watched—as if in slow motion—the plate drop and shatter, splattering eggs and bits of spinach on the black-and-white-checkered tile.

She clenched her fists and pounded them against her thighs, the little she'd eaten swirling in her stomach like a sickening cyclone.

She stumbled to the shower and wrenched open the faucet, setting the water to hot as the first sob erupted from her lips.

She ripped the clothes from her body and shoved them into the trash, boots, underwear and all, before she stood underneath the water. Eden slid down the wall to the tiled floor as her body revolted, endless hours of pent-up fear and rage bubbling to the surface. The harder she fought, the more painfully her muscles contracted. Curling her knees into her chest, she closed her eyes and tried to focus on the sound and heat of the water coursing over her. Instead all she felt was that jab of the needle followed by the darkness.

Even in the steam of the shower, she could feel the dry, icy air of the meat locker coating her skin, the stinging pain rocketing through her extremities. The image of dead eyes staring at her, lifeless gazes, parchment-thin discolored faces and mouths contorted in a silent shriek only she could hear.

She jumped at the sharp knock on the door.

"Eden?" Cole called. "Are you all right? I heard a crash."

Eden squeezed her eyes shut as tears leaked from the corners. She cleared her throat and swallowed. "I'm fine." The two words scratched her throat raw. "Just dropped the plate. I'll be out in a bit." Her body drained with the effort it took to call to him.

"Okay." A moment of silence. "I'll be downstairs."

Doubt clung to his voice. He didn't believe her. She didn't believe herself. Cole was right. Simone and Allie were right. She'd been reckless, stupid even, drawing attention to herself by taunting a killer. She'd been pushing boundaries for months—years. With one killer after another. How could she be surprised she'd eventually have to answer for it?

Reality had shifted in the last twenty-four hours. This killer was different. The Iceman wasn't someone who had murdered out of passion or revenge or even for money or power. He didn't have any motive except whatever cause sat in his psyche. This one was…smart. He knew where she lived, knew her routine, one she'd become lazy in varying. He'd been to her house. Her stomach dropped. He'd touched her things, her purse, her phone, her car…stood in her yard.

She scooted forward on the shower floor, placed her head under the steaming spray and forced herself to keep calm. "Control," she repeated. Control was all that mattered; it was what kept her sane. She'd had it, she'd maintained it, hanging in the locker, trapped in that hospital bed and even for those terrifying few seconds it had taken to make herself walk through her front door less than an hour ago.

She'd done it all until…

Eden shoved her fingers into her wet hair. Until Cole had kissed her. No. She couldn't deal with this now. Didn't need to or want to and yet…

"Stop it! Just stop it!" She struggled to her feet, turned down the hot water and braced her hands on the wall of the shower. She'd deal with this—the consequences of her actions—as well as she could. If that meant checking every lock in the house a hundred times, if it meant installing a security system or even digging her brother Logan's old service pistol out of its lockbox from the guest room closet, so be it.

Serial killers, criminals, the darkness of the human mind? Those she could deal with.

But Cole Delaney kissing her?

That was something else entirely.

"I'll be done in a minute." Eden's fingers had gone numb from clutching the pen so hard.

When whoever opened the door to the interview room at the police station didn't respond, Eden glanced up and found a tall, older, distinguished man watching her.

She caught a slight hint of irritation on the man's face. His solid jaw was clenched, his posture forcibly relaxed as he leaned against the door frame and slipped a hand into the pocket of his well-tailored navy suit pants. "Let me guess." She ducked her chin, noting the power-red tie. "Agent Simmons? I'm just finishing my statement now. Would have taken me half the time if they'd let me type it." Cole and his addiction to procedure. One day if he didn't bend, he'd snap. "Not to mention it would have saved me from carpal tunnel. Cole said you wanted to question me?"

"Feeling better, Ms. St. Claire?"

Ah, passive-aggressive. Check. "As well as one can after having her blood drained before waking up hanging in a meat locker." She scribbled her signature, dated the bottom of the yellow lined paper and clicked the pen shut. "Cole said the FBI was taking an interest in the case. Now." She pushed to her feet. As much as she appreciated Cole's desire to give her some privacy as she relived her ordeal, being on this side of the two-way mirror didn't exactly calm her nerves. "Coffee?"

She didn't wait for an answer before she walked out of the interview room. "Here you go, Bowie." Eden handed over the yellow tablet to the uniformed officer at the desk next to Cole's. The young man had been assigned to the major case division a few months back. He still had that whiff of youth and eagerness, his nickname a tribute to the British rock star his father idolized. But even with that blue-eyed baby face of his, she picked up on his determination to make a difference. Much like most of the officers Cole worked with. She'd never admit it out loud, but she felt at home here, in the bustle of law enforcement. It reminded her of the hours she spent working at the *Tribune*, where the energetic buzz of discovery and revelation was contagious. "Is Cole around?"

"Said he had an errand to run." Bowie eyed Agent Simmons over her shoulder. "He asked that you wait for him."

"As I'm stuck without my car for the time being, that's a given. Thanks." She jerked her chin toward the pink bakery box she'd deposited on Jack's desk on her way in, making the other cops in the division swarm like bees to honey. "Better get your maple bar before it's gone."

"It'll wait. I'm the only one who likes them," Bowie said with a wistful look on his face. The transplant from Vermont may as well have had a bottle of syrup branded on his arm.

"Sure about that?" Eden arched a brow.

"You like maple?"

"I like doughnuts. Save me from myself, will you?" She glanced at Agent Simmons, who was watching the exchange with more interest than she thought necessary. "I'll be in the break room." Being interrogated by a federal agent. This day was shaping up to be great.

As she and Simmons sauntered inside, the few detectives and officers parted like the Red Sea, giving Simmons a wide berth while murmuring words of welcome and relief to her as they passed. Somehow the break room had been neglected in the recent remodel of the station. With its mismatched chairs, chipped tabletops and crooked blinds covering the windows, the space reminded Eden of an out-of-date coffee shop. The air was saturated with the smell of overpopped popcorn and continuously brewing coffee. Funny how the familiarity relaxed her.

"Odd," Agent Simmons said as she handed him a chipped mug. He motioned to the officers who had just left. "They like you."

"Odd because I'm a reporter?" She added a good dash of cinnamon to her cup before taking a seat by the window. "Or because I'm me?"

"In my experience reporters and cops don't tend to get along."

"It's my charm." Her friendship with Cole went a long way to bridging those professional gaps. "They know I want the same things they do. Doesn't mean I'm their favorite person." She'd spent plenty of time being frozen out of investigations. Eden cringed and added more sugar to her coffee. Great choice of words. Personally, she accepted their trepidation as a badge of honor.

"They circled the wagons for you." Agent Simmons took a seat across from her, cupping his hands around the mug. "That tells me a lot about them. And you. It's funny. I was led to believe Detective Delaney was keeping me away from you because you were..."

Eden sipped, looked at him over the rim of her cup and silently dared him to finish his thought.

The strained smile that stretched his lips caught her by surprise. "Not important."

"Cole can be a bit—"

"Overprotective?"

"Determined." And yes, overprotective, thanks to that oath he'd sworn to her brother. An oath she felt certain hadn't included kissing. She shifted on her chair and veered off that track with a ferocity that could leave skid marks. "Cole's radar goes up if he thinks I'm in trouble, which I often am, according to him. He also gets testy when he thinks someone's trying to home in on his case."

"I'm here to advise, that's all."

"Why? I didn't think the Iceman case was even on the Feds' radar."

"On the contrary, it's a case we've been following for some time." He drew his gaze around the room. "As I told the lieutenant and Detective Delaney, I'm here to lend any assistance you might need."

"So that wasn't you raising a ruckus when you thought he'd— What was the phrase he used?" Eden kept her eyes on his face. She found Agent Simmons difficult to read. He didn't give much away, barely a twitch or a flicker of his dark eyes. This was a man who was used to being in control. And getting what he wanted. If what he wanted was to steal this case from Cole—from her—she certainly wasn't going to help him do it.

"I don't like being lied to. And I don't like the idea that this case might have stalled thanks to your—" he paused and inclined his head "—excessive interest."

"This department's had its fair share of disappointing interactions with your agency," Eden felt compelled to explain, or maybe defend. "And the last thing a case does with me is stall."

"I'm not the agency," Simmons said. "But I took the lieutenant's advice and did a little research while I was waiting. On Detective Delaney's record with this case. And on you."

Here we go. "Find anything interesting?"

"Aside from a couple of misdemeanor arrests—"

"A girl has to have a hobby." She'd learned the most important lesson when it came to breaking and entering a good decade ago: don't get caught.

"You've done good work, Ms. St. Claire. You've helped reopen at least three cold cases both here and in Oregon, all murders, in the last few years. Cases law enforcement had given up on." His temper didn't catch, not even with her baiting him. Interesting. "Worthy of a badge, some might say."

"Bite your tongue."

"Not a fan?"

"Of them?" She glanced through the blinds and chose her words carefully. "Absolutely. I admire them. I just prefer not having the...restrictions they do." Cole needed those boundaries to stay sane. Eden fought them for the exact same reason.

"That doesn't mean you don't need some. Calling out

a killer the way you did has consequences. Which brings us to last night. Did you see him? The Iceman?"

Ah. There it was. Put the witness at ease with small talk before you hit her with what you really want to know. "I did not." Anger bubbled in her blood, not at Agent Simmons's curiosity but at her own carelessness. Not checking her surroundings, not parking under a light. "One second I was getting out of my car and the next..." She rubbed a hand over her bandaged wrist where the pain had subsided to a dull ache as ghostly footsteps echoed in her memory. "I woke up in an air-conditioned igloo with a third of my blood missing." Her ears buzzed as the fear crawled back into her throat.

"So there's no hope of a description."

Fragmented images flashed through her mind. Like jagged puzzle pieces with no way to fit together. "Not from me." And didn't that just burn. "Maybe the lab will have some luck with my phone."

"Strange, don't you think? That he broke pattern like that? Potentially exposed himself by calling a police detective and telling him where to find you. You've been on his trail long enough. Why do you think he did that?"

Strange? Strange was the tip of the iceberg, wasn't it? "Killers like this aren't exactly known for their grasp on reality." Personally, she didn't appreciate the increased level of anxiety she had to adjust to thanks to his changeup, but she didn't have anybody but herself to blame after that last blog post she'd run. "The Iceman has spent three years being invisible. No one's come forward with any information of having seen him, let alone a description. There's been no indication as to how he targets his victims, how he transports them—only that he seems to have an unhealthy fascination with vivisection and deep freezers. Now we can add blood to that list." Her palms itched to get to her files and notes. "Aside from the missing persons' reports, there's been nothing to track. His abduction pattern has always been erratic and meticulous, and we've never found a common thread among the victims. At least not the first three victims."

"More victims give us more data to work with."

"But that's the sad thing. Like Cole's superiors, I wanted to believe he'd stopped, but that's not the norm with these types of killers, is it? The Iceman is confident. Smart. Organized. Until..." She cleared her throat and drank her coffee, the warm spice of the cinnamon bathing her tongue. "We still don't understand how he's choosing his victims, and if he isn't, if they're completely random, we might never catch him." That was what she needed to figure out: the connection between the victims. "Somehow he was aware enough to know their routines."

"And yours. The coffee shop where you were abducted. Is it your habit to meet with Detective Delaney at that particular time and place?"

"Yes." Eden frowned, realizing Agent Simmons had turned her questioning into a conversation. "And don't think that hasn't been bothering me." It was one thing to be predictable; it was another to fall into a careless routine that had nearly gotten her killed.

"And yet he went out of his way to make sure you survived. Seems...inconsistent to me."

"Makes me an outlier," she mused, agreeing with him. "Something he can't quite figure out or control." Except what he'd done had been an attempt to regain that control. She would have noticed if someone had been following her. Or had she gotten lazy earlier than she realized and stopped paying attention? She took a deep breath, sat back in her chair and looked at the FBI agent, grudgingly appreciative for making her look at the case in a different way. "He knew his victims' routines going back to the first three killings. Pam Norris disappeared on her way home from school before a three-day weekend. Her parents were away and didn't report her missing until they got home on Monday. Elliot Scarbrough, single, junior partner in a local law firm who had started working from home. Last place he was seen was leaving the gym four days before anyone realized he was gone. Denise Pageant—her husband was on a business trip that got extended. Her car was found abandoned in her neighborhood grocery store almost a week later. He knew when to grab them. He knew they wouldn't be missed for a while. That puts him somewhere in their lives."

Agent Simmons twisted the wedding band on his finger and dropped his chin. "You know their names."

"Of course I know their names." She didn't even try to hide her offense.

"Why?" He looked honestly perplexed. "Why do you do this? And please don't disillusion me by telling me this is about fortune and fame."

Eden crossed her arms over her chest. "I thought you wanted to question me, not analyze me."

Again, he didn't rise to the bait. "Why risk your life to go after him? To go after others like him?"

Eden couldn't remember the last time she'd been asked such a simple yet complex question. Her answer shouldn't matter. Not to the FBI. Not even to Cole or Simone or Allie. The only person who deserved an answer to that question was herself. And for her, the answer was simple. "Because their victims mattered."

"That's all?"

"Isn't that enough?" She didn't want to talk about herself; *she* didn't matter. Stopping the Iceman before he hanged anyone else in a deep freeze had to be her focus.

And then she'd move on to the next one. Because there would always be a next one. "Here's what's really odd about what happened last night. Not that he targeted me. Yeah, that's creepy and all—" and would give her nightmares for the rest of her life "—but why would he want me found?"

"He can't take credit for something no one knows about." Cole strolled into the break room with that cop look in his eyes that revealed confidence, obligation and a touch of annoyance as he bit into an apple fritter. Just seeing him eased some of the tension that had settled around her.

He was Cole. Her friend. Her best friend, and yet every time she laid eyes on him it was as if she was seeing him in a different light. A light she shouldn't want turned on.

"Bowie is typing up your report now," Cole said and poured a cup of coffee. "Sticky maple fingers and all. Should be ready for you to sign in a bit. Agent Simmons, I thought we agreed you'd wait until I was present before you spoke with Eden."

"It's fine." Eden sighed. "I don't need you hovering, Cole. We'll only kill each other that much sooner."

Agent Simmons's sad smile knocked against an unfamiliar soft spot on her heart. "You two sound like me and my ex-wife." Eden glanced down at his wedding band. He shook his head. "Long story. Suffice it to say obsessing over a case you can't crack destroys more than the victims' lives. Did Forensics give you anything?" he asked Cole.

"Only confirmed what we already knew." Cole sat on the edge of the counter and crossed his ankles as he polished off his doughnut. "No prints other than yours and people you know, Eden, and no prints on your phone. Dr.

Collins sent over the final lab results from your blood work. We might be able to trace the sedative he used—"

"That's good news," Eden interrupted.

"Remains to be seen. Propofol is popular on the black market, but we'll run it to be safe. Other than that, we're coming up blank. Again. He must have been hermetically sealed given the lack of forensic evidence. He drove your car, Eden. That should have given us something."

"All you have to do is watch TV crime shows to know how to evade forensics," Eden muttered. Nothing like television to turn those with twisted behavioral tendencies into master criminals. "How am I supposed to drive my Bug again?" She loved her neon green VW, the first new car she'd ever bought. "Not to mention use my phone." She shuddered.

"I'm afraid a new car is out of my budget, but the phone I can fix." Cole reached into his jacket pocket and held out a shiny smartphone. "It's the same make and model as your old one. I had Tammy transfer everything over."

"So that was your mystery errand. My hero." Eden smiled and accepted the phone with reverent hands. "Thank you." She tapped open her text app and noted the number of messages from her boss at the paper. "I'm going to have to make another stop on the way home."

"If you're done with your questioning?" Cole said as if dismissing Agent Simmons. "We can send you copies of all the reports. Keep you in the loop."

"I'd appreciate that," Agent Simmons replied in what sounded like a rehearsed tone. He'd surprised her, as congenial and curious as he'd been, but not around Cole. Clearly the mistrust between the agencies went both ways. "If you do happen to remember anything else about your abduction, I'd like you to let me know. In the meantime, I'll let you know if anything pops on our end with those reports. Thanks for your cooperation."

"Considering what you told me about Simmons," Eden said as the FBI agent left and she finished her coffee, "that didn't go at all as I expected."

"Maybe not for you." Cole walked to the door and watched as Agent Simmons stopped to talk to Lieutenant Santos. "I bet if you were to ask Simmons, it went exactly as expected."

Chapter 7

Cole clicked off his phone as he spotted Eden heading out of the *Sacramento Tribune* offices full steam ahead. Mouth set, eyes piercing, the slightly pink tinge to her skin told him she'd either just been given the exclusive of a lifetime or…

She wrenched open the passenger door of his SUV with enough force to rip it off its hinges. "Do you know what that sanctimonious boss of mine did?" She threw herself into the seat and slammed the door shut. "He put me on indefinite leave." She slumped and crossed her arms. The look had Cole spinning back to a particularly nasty temper tantrum she'd thrown when some boys in school told her she couldn't play football with them because she was a girl.

"Can you believe that? He says I've been traumatized, that I need time to recover." She rolled her eyes but he caught the slight shiver. Her pink cheeks were already draining, as was the energy in her eyes. She might be fighting it, but exhaustion was taking over. "He's already assigned Wonder Klutz to the crime column for the foreseeable future."

Cole started the car. "Wonder Klutz being?"

"Benedict Russell, who has trouble putting one foot in front of the other let alone structuring a sentence. Probably because one of them is always in his mouth or stuck up his—"

"Isn't he the reporter who covered the Panteras murder case?"

"One and the same."

Ah. "The one who called Simone an ineffectual, pedantic political scapegoat." Eden's outrage wasn't just about being temporarily replaced; Russell had done the unforgivable. He'd gone after one of her best friends.

"He's a toadstool." Eden smothered a yawn. "As if Simone's getting the guy for manslaughter rather than risking an acquittal was a bad thing. And *then* that cretin boss of mine has the nerve to suggest we run my blog articles on the Iceman as an exclusive feature while I'm out." She put air quotes around *out*. "He's the one who passed on the story idea to begin with and now he wants to print them."

"Have you ever called your editor a cretin to his face?"

"No." Was that a pout? "I should, but I'm not ready to lose my paycheck just yet."

Yeah, that was a pout all right. Cole had only met her editor on a few occasions, but he'd been unimpressed. Then again, Cole had no doubt Eden wasn't exactly the easiest of employees to deal with. "He's been the editor at the *Tribune* longer than you've been alive, Eden. Maybe he recognizes burnout when he sees it." Or, maybe, like Cole, her editor didn't like the chances she took.

"Russell's cheaper. In more ways than one. I'm not burned out. I'm angry. And I'm cold and tired, and yes, right now I sound like a two-year-old who needs a nap."

"We can agree on that." He turned right onto J Street. "Dinner's on me. What do you feel like? Other than your nails."

"I'm not hungry." She yanked her finger out of her mouth and hugged her arms around her waist. "My stomach's all in knots."

"It's probably trying to tell you something. Italian or Mexican?"

"How about Thai?"

"You got it." He made another right toward Broadway. "What did you say about the feature?"

"I said I wanted time to think about it." Eden flipped on the heat and the seat warmer.

"You did?" Cole didn't know whether to laugh or frown.

"You sound surprised."

"I thought you wanted to move into features. That's been your goal, hasn't it? To be the lead reporter at a major paper? This could get you national exposure. Maybe even job offers." The idea of Eden leaving town, moving on to bigger, better and probably more dangerous things, tied his own stomach into knots.

"I want to get there on merit," she said. "Because I'm good at my job. Not because some psycho left me hanging from a hook in a freezer and turned me into a headline."

He wouldn't put it past her to say no to running the stories just to be contrary. "Look at it this way. You got your wish. All your attention can now be focused on the Iceman." Which meant Cole needed to call his lieutenant. If Eden wasn't going to be safely tucked away at the

Tribune's offices for most of her days, he'd have to make some changes to his own work routine. "You can sleep in tomorrow and come at everything fresh. After you eat."

"What is it with you and my feeding habits?" She turned in her seat. "And while we're at it, what was with that kiss in my kitchen?"

"What kiss?" Grateful for the late-setting sun, he winced behind his sunglasses. *What kiss?*

"Really? We're friends, Cole. Friends who argue about anything and everything. That doesn't usually constitute a kiss like that."

So he hadn't been the only one to feel the spark. "Maybe I wanted to find a new way to win an argument." Or maybe he'd finally given in to the impulse that had been driving him mad for…longer than he cared to admit. Too bad he was the king of bad timing.

"Are you thinking about doing it again?"

"We're going to get into this now?"

"Trapped environment. You can't get away. I've got a lot going on at the moment, so if I need to schedule some wild crazy sex time in this—"

Cole gnashed his teeth. Who scheduled in sex? Eden did, of course, and he scoffed. He knew she wasn't a romantic, but… "Sure. Next Friday at seven work for you?"

He glanced over in time to see a flash of insecurity cross her face. She wasn't pretty, not in that classic, Hollywood beauty kind of way Simone pulled off. Eden's eyes were a little too wide, her mouth a little too small, and that button nose of hers got stuck in far too many places where it didn't belong. But somehow, along with all that strawberry blond hair framing her round face, she looked perfect to him.

"We could park near the restaurant and climb into the backseat—"

"Don't joke, Eden." His hand tightened on the steering wheel. He didn't want to joke about that. "And don't make light. If you aren't interested, say the word and we'll forget it ever happened." As if putting Eden out of his mind would be so simple.

"I didn't say I wasn't interested." He didn't often hear uncertainty in Eden's voice, but right now, it rang louder than a police siren. "I don't want to lose this. We're friends, Cole. I don't have many. I need to keep the ones I have."

"We'll always be friends." He shuddered slightly as it occurred to him he'd almost lost the chance to see if there could be more. The possibility it might just take a little extra push on his part…

She chewed on her thumbnail, something she only did when nerves got the better of her. He'd just never expected to be the cause of them. That felt promising. He pressed on. "About that guest room of yours. No way am I sleeping on your couch again."

When she glanced at him he focused on keeping things matter-of-fact. "I've brought the bag I keep in my locker at work," he said. "Another couple of days' worth of clothes, the essentials."

She nodded. "There's a bed. And a TV. I think. If it's really necessary that you stay."

He pulled into a spot around the corner from the restaurant and parked. This time he faced her and he waited until she looked at him before he spoke. "We aren't going to have this discussion again, Eden, so hear me. He knows where you live. He knows *how* you live. You're careful, usually overly so, and if he managed to get his hands on you, that means he's more thorough than we thought. You poked the bear and he bit back. Until this guy is caught, until I know with one hundred percent certainty that you are safe, I'm not going anywhere. You want to stay at your place to prove something to yourself—"

Her spine stiffened. "That's not what I'm—"

"Sure it is. And I get it. But you need to understand, I will do whatever it takes to keep you alive. If that means you leave your home, you leave. If that means I move in or if it means I send you to the FBI, I'll do it."

"Let me guess. Because you promised Logan."

His heart skipped a beat. Was that resentment he heard?

"I will always feel an obligation to your brother, Eden. He was my best friend and I loved him. But—" He reached over and caught her chin in his fingers when she ducked her head. "But that doesn't mean there aren't other reasons for wanting to keep you safe." To prove his point, he pressed his mouth to hers. A brief, soft kiss that he hoped conveyed what he couldn't put into words.

She surprised him by wrapping her hand around his wrist, keeping him close. She whispered, "I don't know what to do with this. I don't know how to do this."

"Neither do I," he told her. "We'll figure it out together. After we get you something to eat."

Eden jolted awake.

Bathed in sweat, despite the ceiling fan's spinning blades, she shivered. What was that noise? She kicked to untangle her legs from the jumble of covers and stared into the darkness.

Moonlight shone through the slats in her curtains and she climbed out of bed, walking over strewn clothes and tossed shoes to peer outside.

Nothing. The pressure in her chest eased. She could have sworn she'd heard—

Squeak.

She froze. There it was again. She grabbed her phone and her grandfather's old billy club, which she kept on the dresser, and accidentally knocked the ceramic music box to the floor.

Eden jumped as the tinny ballet tone exploded into the night.

Chloe's music box...

She bent down and clicked it shut, frowning as she picked it up. This was supposed to be next to her bed. Had she moved it the last time she cleaned? Glancing around the messy room told her that would have been ages ago. Maybe Allie had moved it when she'd gotten those clothes for her to wear home from the hospital. Yeah. That had to be it. Eden set the box on her nightstand, a new bubble of unease pressing in on her.

Squeak. Squeak, squeak.

She peered into the hallway.

The guest room door was slightly ajar. She could hear the hum from the refrigerator downstairs. Eden bit her lip. Should she wake Cole? No. What if this was just her mind in overdrive? The noise was probably nothing. Her mind never did its best work in the middle of the night. Maybe she'd imagined…

Squeak. Squeak.

Okay, *that* she didn't imagine. She headed downstairs, careful to avoid the creaky steps. She set her phone on the banister and tightened her hold on the club. Chills raced down her spine, bordering on the same terror she'd felt when she'd opened her eyes in the freezer. One of the things she loved most about this town house was the number of windows allowing for endless natural light. Teeth chattering, she resisted the urge to shrink against the wall. Now she felt so…exposed.

Squeak.

She darted into the kitchen. The sliding door was locked, and the round wooden rod she'd wedged in the frame for added security was in place. Her hand hovered over the light switch that would illuminate her small, overgrown backyard. Easy for someone to hide in those weeds and watch her through the windows or door. Easy for someone to sneak in…

Squeak, squeak, squeak.

"What are you doing up?"

Eden turned and swung like she was going for a home run. Cole's hand locked around the club before it plowed into his upper arm. She let him wrench the club out of her hands as she stumbled back against the counter. "Cole, I heard noises. I think there's someone out there."

In an instant he set the club on the table and pushed her down behind the counter. Standing in a stream of moonlight, he pulled his sidearm out of the waistband of his jeans and pointed at her with his other hand. "Stay put."

She peered out and saw Cole as he flicked on the light, unlatched the lock, pried up the rod and opened the back door.

Squeak. Squeak, squeak.

She heard him exhale, followed by the sound of him kicking through knee-high weeds as he reached the far gate. He rattled the latch.

Eden scooted around and stayed low, watching as he did a quick survey of the yard. He stopped and stared at the oversize gnome-encrusted windmill she'd found at a yard sale. He bent down and twirled the blades.

Squeak. Squeak, squeak.

Heat rose to her cheeks. She stood up and stepped outside, her bare feet chilling instantly against the cool brick patio. "Ah. That's new," she managed when he glared at her. He reengaged the safety on his gun and stood up. "I guess I didn't realize it made so much noise." And this was why she hadn't wanted to wake him up.

She tried to distract herself, but seeing a shirtless Cole Delaney return to her kitchen, heading for her coffeemaker, his hair mussed, his body ripped thanks to time spent at the gym, had her skin prickling in an entirely new way. How had she not noticed before now…? "Aren't you going back to bed?"

"Are you?"

She blinked at his question. "Am I what?"

His brow arched. "Going back to bed."

"Um, no." She'd already slept seven hours, three more than she was used to. Besides, something told her the farther away she stayed from a bed right now, the better. "No. I'm wide-awake. Might as well get an early start, right?" Eden walked over to the fridge and reached up for the key she kept in front of the gnome cookie jar. Mmm. Cookies. She brought the jar down and beheaded the creature, stuffing a lemon sandwich cookie into her mouth. Yeah, that should help take her mind off Cole and his…

She unlocked the padlock on the basement door. "My office," she mumbled around crumbs.

"The inner sanctum, you mean." Cole braced his hands on the counter and watched her. "Do I finally get to see it or am I banned?"

"I never banned you," Eden told him, but had to acquiesce. "Yeah, okay, I guess I kind of did, but seeing as you're my unofficial partner now, I can't exactly keep you out."

"Partner? Really?"

"I am familiar with the concept." Did he have to sound so surprised all the time? She wasn't impossible to work with or deal with. Difficult maybe, but not impossible. "I'm making a preemptive strike and avoiding another argument."

"Afraid I know how to win now?" Forget his sidearm. That grin of his should be considered a lethal weapon.

"Put some clothes on and bring me my coffee." She clicked on the basement light. "We have a killer to catch."

Hopefully before anyone else had to die.

Chapter 8

While the coffee brewed, Cole went upstairs to shower and change. Back in the kitchen, he flexed his hand that was a bit sore from catching her Babe Ruth swing. "Bet she's good in a batting cage." He poured their coffee, forwent the leftover Thai in the fridge and settled for two of her gnome-stashed cookies, before he headed downstairs.

It had been far from a perfect start to the morning, but time spent with Eden was anything but boring. The steep staircase reminded him of every horror movie he'd ever seen. Chipped, worn paint, rugged walls and the promise of stone-cold cement waiting at the bottom of the surprisingly well-lit basement. Leave it to Eden to make what could be considered a seriously creepy space into her office. He stopped short on the second-to-last step and sloshed coffee over the backs of his hands.

He gaped.

After three years she still had half her belongings in boxes upstairs, but down here? The NSA could take lessons in organization from her. Two large metal filing cabinets lined the far wall. A sturdy antique desk sat in the middle of the space with neat stacks of files on one side, photos on the other, laptop and assorted office supplies arranged to perfection in between. She'd set up a desktop CPU connected to not one but two large flat screens beneath a collection of maps, one of which was dotted and outlined with various colored strings. The ancient-looking printer seemed as if it were about to sputter and die as it spit out page after page. And there, in front of a trio of industrial-sized whiteboards displaying dozens of notes and photographs of familiar faces, stood Eden, hair knotted on top of her head, glasses perched on the tip of her nose and bare toes curling into the freezing cement.

"I'm going to have to start over."

"This is…" He took the final step down and held out her coffee, which she accepted without giving him a second look.

"Thanks." She drank and set the mug down, then tapped a finger against her teeth. "This is what?" she echoed.

Disturbing. Scary. Enlightening. "Efficient." He wandered toward Logan's old oversize leather sofa wedged under the stairs with wadded-up blankets and pillows strewn over it. A stack of paperback crime novels sat on the floor next to it. A small table at the end displayed a solitary battery-operated tea candle and a framed photograph.

A picture he hadn't seen in almost twenty years.

He glanced over his shoulder before he picked the photo up. Taken in Simone's parents' elegantly manicured backyard—Eden, Simone, Allie and…Chloe, all grinning at the camera, innocence and promise shining on their eight-year-old faces. His heart twisted, his mind flashing to those dark days after Chloe had gone missing. She'd been such a cute kid: round face, freckles and razor-straight red hair. Green eyes that would have made the Irish hills jealous. She'd loved wearing overalls and bright T-shirts, along with the mismatched sneakers that had become her trademark look.

He frowned.

They'd found her purple shoe first.

"Has Allie been down here?" He set the frame on the side table and took in the rest of the space. At least she'd added some color with a pair of bright lamps and a throw rug, but he'd bet that was more for practicality than decor.

"What? In my office? No. She'd probably have me committed."

Cole's mind eased. Seemed she realized the picture she painted. An unfamiliar sadness washed over him.

This was where Eden lived.

This was where she breathed. Upstairs was cursory, where she could chase her demons and write her blog, but this was Eden's world.

"I'm printing off every article I've published on the blog regarding the Iceman, along with all the comments." She gestured to the printer as it continued to chug away. "I thought maybe you could read through those. I'm too close."

"I'll take another look, but nothing stood out to me."

She jerked, eyes widening in surprise. "You've read them?"

"The articles? Yeah. I've read everything you've ever published." He pulled the pile of papers free and headed for an empty table. "You're a good writer, Eden. A great one."

"Why do I always hear a *but* in your voice?" She wrenched open one of the desk drawers and pulled out a pair of dark fuzzy socks.

"I just wish you'd put your writing skills to better use."

"Better being…?" She sat down and tugged on the socks, the strap of her tank top dropping off one shoulder.

"Less confrontational. Maybe you could write a novel." He glanced up at the beams in the ceiling. "Something tells me coming up with crimes wouldn't be too big a stretch."

"Hmm. Maybe. Someday."

"If you're not careful, someday is never going to come." Okay, now he sounded preachy. He scanned the responses by date, counting forty-three before he had to return to the printer.

She returned to the whiteboards and snatched off pictures to place on her desk. "I'm going to try rearranging these this time. How close are we to identifying the victims from the freezer?"

Cole wondered if she heard the catch in her own voice. He grabbed a lightweight sweatshirt off the back of one of her chairs and tossed it to her. "Put that on, will you? Your goose bumps have goose bumps. I'll check with Mona in a few hours. She was hoping the fingers might thaw enough by today to try to run their prints."

"I don't suppose I could get a look at evidence files from the case?"

"I'll talk to Jack about getting them together for us."

"There has to be a connection between them." She flipped on the portable space heater. "How does he find them?" Using her cell, she snapped pictures of the notes she'd scribbled on the boards before she wiped them clean. "And why them? What do they have in common?"

"Working with three victims didn't give us much data." He grabbed the chair she wasn't using and sat down. "Now we have eight more."

"Not my favorite way to increase the data flow." She drew two thick lines and divided the board into three sections, assigning a victim to each one. Filling out their names, occupations, addresses, relatives… The soft squeak of dry-erase markers against the board became background noise as he sat at the desk and started with her initial post, uploaded just over eighteen months ago.

She hadn't started focusing on the Iceman until well after the third victim had been identified. She'd treated each posting as if it were one of her articles for the *Tribune*, citing her sources. He assumed "officials close to the investigation" referred to himself, but she'd saved those mentions for important details, like the fact that a witness had come forward saying she'd seen Denise Pageant, the third victim, leave a local farmers' market a few blocks from the parking lot where her car had been found on the day they suspected she'd been abducted.

Eden's earliest posts tugged at his heart. She was so good at talking about the victims, bringing them back to life in a way that anyone who read couldn't help but understand the loss the families felt. If there was one thing Eden excelled at it was tapping into the empathy that most human beings possessed.

Those that didn't possess it were the ones they had to worry about.

"How closely do you read the comments?" Cole asked.

"Closely enough. Mostly, I skim." He thought that was what she'd say. Hard to tell given she had two pens sticking out of her mouth and a fistful of documents. He stood up and went to the bank of computer screens, clicking on the archives.

"Do you get a lot of return readers?"

"Yes. I even set up a subscription service. Anytime I post a new blog they get an email."

"We'll want a list of those subscribers."

"Sure." She abandoned her task and joined him, leaning over to tap in her access information. Cole sat back and watched her face scrunch into that familiar expression of concentration. A thick strand of hair dropped loose from on top of her head and brushed down over her arm. He reached out, tucked it behind her ear and felt her freeze under his touch. His finger tingled where it had stroked her skin, but he didn't say a word and returned his gaze to the screen in front of them.

"You can access both the comments and the mailing list from this portal." She backed away, clearing her throat as she returned to her whiteboard. Nice to know he could distract her as handily as she did him.

"Makes cross-checking screen names and email addresses easier," he said as he printed out the pages.

"Do you have credit-card information for the victims in the files?" Eden jotted down the rest of the first three victims' employment information. "Records of their purchases and where they'd been?"

"Going back six months before their deaths, I think. We can request more if we need them."

"Six is a good place to start. Especially once we can get ahold of the last eight's records, as well. Should help us fill out the timelines for their last days."

"We went over the backgrounds of the original victims with a fine-tooth comb," Cole reminded her. The process had gone more smoothly than expected given the potential logistical nightmare of the bodies being found in various areas of the valley. Other departments had been willing to lend a hand on the grunt work, but more than happy to let Cole and his team take the lead.

"I don't suppose you inventoried their homes after they were identified?" Eden asked.

"No." He looked up. "But we did take pictures. I'll add the photos to the list of things for Jack to track down. With this much evidence to go through, it'll take more than the two of us to make any kind of dent in it."

"We can organize what we have for now."

And so went their day, Eden staring at her newly tidied whiteboard and Cole digging through the umpteen comments on her increasingly popular blog.

When Eden's doorbell rang, they both jumped.

"Who would that be?" Eden reached for her coffee, which she frowned at. "Empty. What time is it?"

"It's after one." Cole stretched his arms over his head and stood up. "I'll go and hunt up lunch while I'm at it."

"Lunch. Awesome." She ducked back into her work like a turtle pulling into her shell. "You know what? If they want to run my articles in the *Tribune*, I'm thinking I might let them."

"Really?"

"Why not?" She nibbled on her thumbnail. "More readers might get us more information. Besides, maybe I can work out a deal so I can afford to quit. Go on, go on." She waved him upstairs. "I have a call to make."

It took him a full count to twenty before he realized an unemployed Eden meant she'd throw herself completely into this case, not to mention any others that might come down the line. "One day at a time," he muttered to himself as he headed upstairs. He left their mugs on the counter and answered the door. “Hey, Jack. You running a delivery service now?”

Jack grunted at him and hefted a file box into his arms. “Thanks, partner. Come on in.”

Jack picked up another box and followed him inside. “LT rallied the troops and got you everything you asked for on the first three vics. Speaking of asking for, Mona should be able to run prints this afternoon. Results will be in around five.”

“Great. Let me see if I can bring Eden up from the depths of—”

“Hey, Jack.” Eden stepped into the kitchen just as they set the boxes on the counter.

“Eden. Nice place. Cozy.” He glanced around the room.

“Jack thinks any place without high beamed ceilings is cozy,” Cole joked.

“Said the man who lives on a ship in a bottle.” Eden rolled her eyes.

“Ship in a bottle?” Jack sputtered and shot Cole a surprised look. “Hasn’t she seen the…?”

“You want lunch?” Cole cut him off. No, she hadn’t seen his boat since he’d finished restoring it. “We’ve got leftovers from last night.”

“Well, isn’t that nice.” Jack slapped a hand on his shoulder. “You almost sound domesticated. Uh-uh, Eden, not yet.” He pushed her hands away as she pried open one of the box corners. “Give your brain a rest. Cole said you’ve been at this since before dawn.”

“The curse of the gnome windmill,” Cole joked. “Hey, that can be the title for your first murder mystery, Eden. Now that you’ll have all that spare time.”

She glowered at him.

“You writing a book?” Jack asked.

"If I did it wouldn't feature killer gnomes." She pulled out a stack of paper plates from the cabinet. "I've got coffee, beer and water, Jack."

"Water's fine, thanks." Jack set the boxes on the floor and took a seat at the counter. "You guys come up with anything new yet?"

"Big fat nothing," Eden replied.

"I've got a couple of names I want to run checks on." Cole's statement earned a raised eyebrow from Eden. "You were right. I didn't find anything in your posts. The comments were another story."

"Nothing raised any bells for me."

"The more you focused on the Iceman, the more frequently a few of your more enthusiastic subscribers commented."

"That would be the purpose of a blog, Cole. They want a forum to be heard. I don't engage them. Not directly, anyway," Eden countered. "A few of them have had some good ideas, ideas I've looked into, but none of them produced anything. Other than proof our educational system is sorely lacking these days. Why? What did you find?"

"Aside from some pretty vehement opinions on why the Iceman is killing?"

"Oh, you're talking about 221BB, aren't you?" Eden waved away the comment as Cole set containers in front of Jack, before snagging one of the veggie spring rolls for himself. "I visited his website. He's a conspiracy nut. Hangs out on a lot of crime message boards. He's harmless, Cole."

"Forgive me, but you're not one to judge harmless. Remind me, again—who was it who tried to adopt a stray raccoon?"

"When was this?" Jack chuckled as he served himself.

"I was seven," Eden reminded Cole in that "shut up

before I shut you up" tone. "And the poor little guy had been attacked by Mr. Johansen and his shovel-wielding wife."

"Probably because he was a *raccoon.* Angry little creature."

"You survived," Eden said.

"Barely. Logan almost lost an arm."

"Oh, please. It was a scratch and I don't care what you say. Ricky was adorable."

"Ricky Raccoon?" Jack grabbed two spring rolls. "That's…unique. What happened to him?"

"I was told they released him out by the American River," Eden replied, and when Cole opened his mouth to tell her the truth—that her adorable little guy had gotten away from them and was run over by a car—she held up her hand. "And I'm going to continue to believe that until my dying day. If you want to follow up on any of my subscribers, feel free, but I'm telling you it won't get us anywhere."

"As a conspiracy nut is pretty far removed from a raccoon, I appreciate your permission." Cole brushed his fingers over the back of her hand as they reached for the spoons at the same time. She jerked, her gaze flying to his. "Sorry."

Jack pinned Cole with a silent, curious look before he plowed into his lunch.

"Okay, Jack." Eden stood across from Cole's partner and twirled her fork into the rice noodles. "You wanted my mind off this case for a while. How have you been? And how's the dating game going?"

Jack choked. Cole grinned. Now, this was going to be entertaining.

Chapter 9

"Knock, knock!" A familiar lilting voice chimed down the basement stairs. "Anyone home?"

"Allie?" Eden capped her pen and raced to the foot of the steps. "What are you doing here? Who let you in?" She peered up as Allie's all-knowing gaze absorbed Eden's office in one fell swoop. A flash of white behind Allie had Eden frowning. "Simone?"

"Cole let us in on his way out." Simone stooped down, took one look at the basement and wrinkled her nose. "I'm not coming down there. Pizza and wine. Upstairs. Now." She spun on her four-inch heels and stomped away.

"I don't know what surprises me more. That you two showed up unannounced or that she brought something as simple as pizza for supper." Eden attempted to push Allie up the stairs ahead of her, but Allie put a hand on Eden's arm, gave an almost imperceptible shake of her head and stepped into Eden's space. "I know what you're thinking." Instead of joining her, Eden sat on a step, waiting for the barrage of observations to begin.

"Do you?" Allie's cheery pink capri pants and matching tank top cast a stark contrast to the darkness that, despite the lighting, blanketed the basement. "Would you like to talk about what I'm thinking?"

"Not particularly, no." Eden flinched. "I never wanted you to see this place."

"I can't imagine why not." Allie's tone was as even-keeled as ever. She strode around the room, skimming her eyes over Eden's scribbled notes, her blinking computer screens and the tidy piles of photos and files she and Cole had spent the rest of the afternoon reexamining. "It's so...you."

"That would be why."

"You're profiling the victims." Allie gestured to the whiteboard before circling around to the sofa. "Find anything interesting?"

"Not yet. We're hoping the new victims might give us more data to work with." Eden leaned over and gripped the banister above her, then poked her head down as Allie brushed a reverent hand over their childhood photo.

"Hard to believe we were ever this young...or innocent." Allie's sad expression chipped at the wall Eden had built around her heart. While the four of them had been inseparable, Allie and Chloe had been two peas in a pod. So much so Allie had even dyed her hair that last summer to match their friend's color. The Wonder Twins, Simone had teasingly dubbed them.

For what felt like the millionth time, Eden wanted to tell Allie the truth about that night, but the words remained lodged in her chest. After so many years, would it make a difference? Or would it do damage she could never repair?

Allie shot Eden one of her trademark patient-and-understanding smiles as her friend flicked the tiny tea light off. "I think maybe you've had enough for today."

"It always amazes me how your suggestions end up sounding like commands."

"They teach us that in therapist school." Allie stopped in front of her and held out her hands. "Let it go for tonight, Eden."

Eden opened her mouth to argue, but realized she didn't have the strength to. Not with Allie and certainly not with Simone, who was probably working up a good lecture even as she poured the cabernet.

She got to her feet, smiling a little at the comforting if not pushy hands of her friend on her back. Allie turned off the light and closed the door as Eden accepted a filled wineglass from Simone, who was waiting for them.

"Now this." Simone dangled the padlock on her index finger. "Lock it away." The mingled expression of concern and determination silencing any protest Eden might have made. "Until tomorrow."

Eden slapped the latch closed and clicked the padlock in place. If only turning off her mind would be as easy. "Cole put you up to this, didn't he?"

"Funny enough, we didn't need him to. We know you, Eden," Allie called over her shoulder as she headed into the living room. "But he did call Simone to let her know he needed to go to the station for a while."

"He thought you'd appreciate our smiling faces rather than a pair of patrolmen sitting on your front porch." Simone guided Eden out of the kitchen. "He did ask us to leave him some pizza."

"Fat chance of that." Allie kicked off her ballet-slipper

flats and curled her feet under her in the corner of Eden's sofa. "I brought him his own."

"So you ordered, Allie?" Eden couldn't hide the relief in her voice.

"You think I'd leave pizza ordering to birdseed girl?" Allie looked horrified. "Please." She reached over and flipped open the box. The aroma of baked dough, roasted tomatoes and fennel-laced sausage wafted into the air.

"Chia seeds, not birdseed." Simone darted into the kitchen and returned with plates and napkins—and a second bottle of wine. "And you could both do with some."

"Please, no more lectures," Eden said as she sat on the floor on the other side of the coffee table and sipped her wine. "I've suffered enough the last couple of days. And enough with the white, Simone. Do you always have to look as if you've just walked off Mount Olympus?" Eden would probably keel over in shock if Simone ever wore any other color.

"I like overseeing you mere mortals. You, on the other hand, look like crap," Simone said as she popped off her heels, discarded the shimmery white sweater and took a seat next to Allie. "Good crap, but still."

"Clearly this visit wasn't meant to be an ego boost." Eden flopped a slice of pizza onto a plate and picked off the mushrooms. "How long have you known me and you still put fungus on my pie?"

"Gives you something to do in place of obsessing about a killer," Allie said.

"I thought we had locked that away for the night?" Simone sighed as she dislodged a handful of sausage chunks from her own piece. "Can we please just maybe not discuss serial killers, politics, news or court cases for one evening?"

"I doubt it, especially not with those reporters parked

outside." Eden sank her teeth into her pizza. Her taste buds exploded with the promise of more.

"What reporters?" Simone leaned over to look out the window. "I didn't see anyone other than your neighbors."

"Maybe Cole scared them away." Allie grinned. "He has that effect on people where Eden's concerned."

It also didn't hurt that he hated reporters with a passion. At times, herself included. "Whatever. Did he say when he was coming back?"

"Cole?" Simone's eyebrows shot up, but Eden didn't miss the knowing look she sent Allie. "He wasn't sure. He did say the prints came in and he wanted to help notify the families."

Eden nodded. Cole might be stubborn, opinionated and positively infuriating, but no one had a bigger heart when it came to victims and their loved ones. Cole took that responsibility very seriously.

A gleam off a passing car's window had Eden jumping to her feet to close the too-thin curtains. "Did he say anything else?"

"No," Simone replied. "Why? Should he have?"

"No, of course not. Not to you, anyway. I was just—" Eden's mind was ping-ponging back and forth. "Well, since this isn't serial-killer stuff, here goes." She sank down on the floor again and took a deep breath. "He kissed me."

"Cole?" Simone smiled widely. "Interesting."

"Is it?" Eden looked between her friends. "Not exactly the word I would have used."

"Definitely interesting." Allie put her pizza down, smiling. "About time, too. So?"

"So what?" Eden focused on her slice.

"She always did suck at the girl talk," Simone said. "So how was it?"

Words failed her. Just like they'd failed her the three times she'd attempted to update her blog today. For most of her life, words had been her salvation, her coping mechanism. Her livelihood. But now, just like earlier, her brain short-circuited and shut down, her entire body going cold as if she'd been thrown into the deep freeze again. "I don't know," she said finally.

"How can you not know how a kiss was?" Allie looked flummoxed.

"Because it was Cole," Simone cut in. "And Cole has always confused her."

"Confused can be a good thing." Allie shrugged. "It's when you start thinking too much about things like kissing that gets you into trouble."

"Speak for yourself." Simone winked. "There's nothing better than turning your brain off and just having at each other."

"Obviously you two don't need me for this conversation," Eden joked. "Just keep going. I'll let you know when you land on something that applies to me."

"Tell me something." Simone shifted to the edge of the sofa and leaned forward. "Does Cole still do that thing with his mouth, that twitch in the corner of his lips—"

"Simone!" Allie smacked her arm even as she laughed.

Eden's face flushed and thawed out the rest of her body. "How do you know about that?"

"I guess that's a yes." Simone reached for her glass and drank. "Put those daggers back in your eyes, honey. We were fifteen and seventeen respectively and I was curious. Cole—"

"Volunteered to satisfy your curiosity?" Allie asked. "Why didn't I ever think of that?"

"Because you were a late bloomer," Eden answered. When had all these knots in her stomach shown up? "And because you never would have asked."

"There was never anything to it, Eden," Simone told her. "No spark. I may as well have been kissing your brother."

Eden sputtered on her wine. "My brother? You kissed Logan, too?"

Simone's blue eyes brightened. "Hey, I had to have someone to compare Cole to, didn't I? We weren't exactly social butterflies, and the guys were, well, nice. Really, really nice."

"Cole never told me," Eden muttered. Then again, why would he? It wasn't as if they had been anything other than friends. Or had they?

"I doubt he even remembers." Simone settled back on the sofa and, for an instant, reminded Eden of when they were in high school, asking for Simone's advice on… well, everything. "When it comes to our good buddy Cole, he's only ever had eyes for you, Eden. Even back then."

"Okay, now I know you're kidding." A bit of pizza clogged her esophagus.

"She's not," Allie said and sent Eden's heart racing. "Please tell me you kept your hands off my foster brothers, Simone."

"A girl doesn't always kiss and tell," Simone teased. "Speaking of your sibling brood, I ran into your mom yesterday at the K-Street Market. How come you didn't tell us Nicole and Patrick were moving back to town?"

Allie shrugged. "Because you talk to my mom more than I do."

"So you haven't seen them?" Eden asked.

"My foster siblings? Not yet, no." Allie's strained

smile was all too familiar. "According to Ma, they've bought a restaurant in midtown. She's glad to have some of her kids back around her."

"She has you." Simone blinked with the same shock Eden felt.

"Yeah, well." Allie gave herself a shake and shot them one of her trademark plucky smiles. "I'll make it a point to see them. And Ma. Soon."

"Make reservations at their place and we'll all go," Simone said before shooting Eden a knowing look.

Allie, her parents' only natural child, often had a difficult time in a household overrun by her parents' do-gooder desire to save the children of the world. If they weren't traveling to third-world countries, they were bringing in troubled kids, often leaving Allie lost in the shuffle. Eden would never forget the look on Allie's face when, on the first day of kindergarten, she, Simone and Chloe had asked Allie to play with them. It was as if Allie didn't realize people could see her. From then on, Allie had spent most of her time in one of their homes, preferring to stay far away from her own as much as possible.

Was it any wonder she'd become a shrink?

"Let's get back to this Cole situation." Allie shifted topics with practiced ease. "What is it that's bothering you?"

Now it was Eden's turn to shrug. "I just think whatever this is with Cole is more about the promise he made to Logan."

"What promise?" Simone asked. Allie set her pizza down again and pinned Eden with that look that normally had her patients spilling their deepest secrets.

Why should she be any different? "He promised

Logan to always look out for me. In case Logan wasn't around."

"Ah." Allie nodded. "Hence the confusion. You're afraid this new kind of attention is merely him fulfilling an obligation."

"Thank you for spelling it out, Dr. Freud." Simone rolled her eyes. "I seriously doubt Logan included kissing you as part of Cole's duties. In fact, I'd bet heavily against it."

"Cole's my friend. My best friend. Aside from you guys," she added in case they took offense.

"Please." Simone sighed and nibbled the edges of her pizza, as if she could defer calories. "We're beyond best friends. Always have been. But you're right. Cole is your go-to guy. What's wrong with it being more than that?"

"Because if we try to be more, I'm going to mess it up and then where will I be?" She'd be minus one of the few people who made her life worth living.

"Aside from potentially sexually satisfied, stuck with your two spinster best friends," Allie said.

"Again, speak for yourself." Simone pointed a knowing finger at Eden. "Honey, for being as brave as you are with these maniacs you go after, you've always been a bit of a shy rabbit in the relationship department. Admit it—the idea of falling in love with anyone, especially Cole, scares you. It's the only reason for all these walls you've built around yourself."

"I thought Allie was the therapist. And who said anything about falling in love?" Eden questioned. When had they taken that detour? "I said he kissed me, not that he declared his undying devotion for me."

"You're right." Allie waved a warning finger at Simone, discouraging her from speaking. "You didn't say that. But it's what you're afraid you're thinking, Eden.

It's why you brought it up in the first place. If Cole kissing you can confuse you this much—"

"Imagine what tumbling in the sheets with him would do," Simone interjected.

"Yeah." Eden gnawed on her bottom lip. "Imagine."

"The great thing about pizza?" Allie crumpled the paper plates and smashed them into the garbage under the sink. "No dishes."

"All the more reason to continue to finish the wine," Simone said and toasted them over the counter. "No bottles to save."

"Are you drunk?" Eden couldn't remember the last time always-in-control Simone Armstrong was tipsy.

"I'm happily sedated." Simone hoisted herself onto a bar stool. "Speaking of sedated, Eden, you seem to be taking this whole abduction thing pretty well."

"I thought we weren't talking about that." Not that she minded a return to the topic. Personally, she'd much rather discuss the Iceman and her bloodletting than delve any more deeply into the topic of Cole Delaney.

"Anesthetics like Propofol can definitely affect some people's memories," Allie said in that no-nonsense medically trained way of hers. "Do you remember anything about when you were taken?"

Eden sighed. "I've tried. I get flashes, like disjointed pictures, but nothing I can make sense of."

"So there is something in there." Allie tapped a fingernail against her teeth, her short-cropped dark hair catching in the fluorescent light of the ceiling bulbs. "I've had success using a hypnotherapy technique with some of my patients who have suffered certain types of trauma. Mostly to help them when it comes to testifying in court, but I wonder—"

"Heads up, Eden," Simone announced. "You're about to be her next guinea pig."

Eden chuckled as Simone leaned heavily on the counter. "What do you wonder?"

"If we go back to the parking lot, re-create the same circumstances as the night you were kidnapped, you might remember something important."

"Nothing says an uneventful evening out with your friends than reliving your worst nightmare," Simone said. "You think that's safe?"

"I think it might be worth a shot," Allie replied. "I'll walk you through it, Eden. I'll be there every step of the way. You'll never be fully under. It's like a dream state."

"I'll be backup," Simone offered. "Whatever help I might be."

"I'd ask you to take notes but I'm not convinced you could operate a pen," Eden said. She wanted to remember...didn't she? If she could recall even one detail, an image, a smell, a feeling, something that could help them make a connection to the Iceman, what was there to lose? She glanced out the window. "So let's go."

"Tonight?" Allie's spine straightened and she frowned. "Eden, I meant we should plan for it, maybe tomorrow or the next night or even the weekend—"

"No, now. I want to do this tonight." Before she lost her nerve. Before Cole returned and talked her out of it. Before the Iceman caught someone else in his hooks. "Cole will probably be late tonight. We can be back before then. It's...what? Six thirty? That's about the same time I got there the other night."

"Okay," Allie agreed. But Eden saw a flash of doubt on her friend's face. "But only if you leave him a note. Just in case. I don't want to get into trouble for this."

"Believe me, the only person who would catch trouble

is me." And that, Eden realized, would shift their relationship into an arena she could handle.

"Let's go!" Simone's arm shot up in the air as she nearly toppled off her stool.

Eden dived forward to catch her. "Allie, you're driving."

"No kidding."

"It doesn't matter how many notifications you make." McTavish strolled into the conference room as Cole hung up the phone. "This part of the job never gets any easier."

"I couldn't agree more," Cole said.

Mr. and Mrs. DeFornio had been both horrified and relieved to learn their twenty-seven-year-old son's body had been found along with Eden. After sixteen months of wondering, they finally had their answers. But Cole had more questions. Eric DeFornio had had his share of troubles, from drug addiction to petty theft. As far as his parents knew, he was living in a run-down motel in downtown Sacramento, but he'd always call on Sunday afternoons, when he knew his parents were home from church. Until he hadn't.

"That was the last one." Cole sagged in his chair and glanced at the clock. Almost seven thirty. His eyes ached, feeling gritty and heavy from the long, tiring day.

"I'd offer to buy you a drink, but I'm not sure you could manage to stay awake." Jack sat on the edge of the table and pushed the files aside. "Oh, hey. Bowie and I checked out 221BB like you wanted. Eden was right. There's nothing there."

"You sure?"

"221BB is actually Enid Snappman. Sixteen years old with serious acne and terabytes running through her blood. We might have to worry about her hacking into the Pentagon in another few years, but as far as the Iceman is concerned?" Jack shook his head. "It's just her spouting off her thoughts and ideas, hoping for attention. Which we gave her. She seemed excited to talk to us. I'm betting we get star status on her next blog."

"Awesome." *Blog* was fast becoming a four-letter word to Cole. "Do me a favor and don't let on to Eden about this just yet. I'm not up to another round of 'I was right' with her." Especially not after selling his soul—and a series of interviews about the Iceman case—to two TV stations and three papers. He kept telling himself it would be worth it if they'd leave Eden alone.

Time would tell.

Jack's smile was one of understanding. "Speaking of Eden, we're making copies of the latest victims' details, so you can share them with her. Should be ready by tomorrow afternoon."

Cole sighed. Yeah, he couldn't wait to add more victims' pictures to her wall. He couldn't remember wanting to close a case this badly. "Simone and Allie were planning to keep her occupied this evening. And honestly, I'm beat. Can you lock things down tonight? Make sure everyone's back here at nine tomorrow morning. We need a plan of execution." So to speak. "Rain check on the drink?"

"You got it. See you tomorrow, partner."

It wasn't until he was in his car driving to Eden's that Cole realized that for the first time he was heading home to something, to someone other than an empty space. He loved the solitude his boat provided, and his social life had been active enough over the years. Half drought, half flood, sure, but no woman managed to spark his interest the way Eden did. Part of him had hoped that by kissing her he'd finally scratched that particular itch.

Instead the need to be with her had only burrowed deeper.

An odd apprehension built inside of him as he considered what would happen once the Iceman was caught. Was this *thing* with Eden merely adrenaline-induced attraction? Was he grabbing hold so hard because he'd come so close to losing her?

He scrubbed a tired hand down the side of his face. He must be getting punch drunk to be thinking along these lines. What he needed was a hot shower and preferably eight hours of gnome-free sleep.

He parked behind Simone's perky little white sports car with top-down tendencies, noting briefly that Allie's cute red mini SUV was gone. That didn't surprise him. Knowing Allie's practical leanings, she was probably already home and in bed, having left the babysitting duties to Simone.

He got out his spare key, but found he didn't need it. Shaking his head, he wondered, not for the first time, if Eden had left whatever common sense she possessed in that freezer. "Eden! You left the door unlocked!"

Every lamp in the living room was on, as were the lights in the kitchen. He could smell the pizza they'd had for dinner—or maybe it was his overanxious stomach anticipating Allie's promised provisions. Empty wine bottles and glasses were falling over themselves in the sink. The town house was oddly silent. He shrugged out of his jacket, heading for the fridge to retrieve one of the beers he'd been thinking about for the last hour.

"Eden! Simone!" His voice echoed at him. The padlock to the basement sat unlatched on the counter, the door wide-open. He picked up the lock, hefted it in his hand for a moment as the barest prickle of unease worked its way up his spine. Setting his bottle on the counter, he did a quick check upstairs. Nobody here. "Probably dragged her into that dungeon of hers."

He could only imagine Simone's and Allie's reactions to Eden's level of obsession when it came to her office. Then again, it could be the wake-up call she needed. She might not pay much attention to him, but she'd never be able to ignore her two best friends. "Hey, you guys, didn't you hear me—" He stopped halfway down the stairs and ducked down.

The basement was empty.

"What the…?" He scanned the room, noted the paperwork, boxes and the lit candle in front of Chloe's memorial photo at the end of the sofa.

Cole pulled out his phone as he returned to the kitchen, dialing Eden first, but it went straight to voice mail. Same with Allie's phone. He unlocked the patio door and checked the parking space behind the town house.

Eden's car was gone.

Familiar knots of frustration wound tightly with a new form of panic that had lodged itself in his gut. They were up to something.

The yellow sticky note on the counter confirmed it.

Testing a theory with Allie at Monroe's. Hope to be back before you see this. —E

All thoughts of sleep vanished as he grabbed his jacket and keys and stormed out the door.

Chapter 10

"I haven't seen Simone this blotto since Vince served her with divorce papers," Eden murmured to Allie as they stood beside Eden's car in the half-filled parking lot of Monroe's. Despite the late-spring air that carried the promise of summer warmth, Eden shivered. Regret—along with nerves—settled. No doubt this was the kind of thing she did that made Cole nuts. Suddenly, venturing back to the scene of the crime didn't seem like such a smart idea. She glanced around the dimly lit lot. At least she hadn't come alone. "Any idea what's going on with her?"

"Only what I've heard around the DA's office." Allie glanced over her shoulder to the open SUV. Simone, blond hair cascading, restless bare feet swinging, sagged sleepily against the passenger seat, humming in her usual tone-deaf key. "Her main witness in the Denton case is getting wiggy. You know Simone. She only lets loose like this when she's second-guessing herself. Or when things aren't going her way."

"At least she didn't drag us off to Vegas to cope this time. So. Are we going to do this or what?" Eden pushed away from her car and took a deep breath, slapped restless hands on her jean-clad thighs and tugged her jacket closed. "What do I do?"

"Exactly what you did that night. Get in your car." Allie opened the door and waved her inside. "Don't overthink anything, don't force it. Just sit there for a moment and try to clear your mind. I'll guide you through."

"I can't remember the last time my mind was clear." Eden slid in behind the wheel and, because she needed to hold on to something, gripped the steering wheel until her knuckles went white.

"That's why I said 'try.'" Allie squatted beside her, keeping herself between Eden and the open door, a reassuring hand on her arm. "Now close your eyes. Relax. And focus on the sound of my voice, Eden. There you go."

Eden felt herself slipping, letting go of that control that kept her upright most days, and put her trust in her friend. She could hear Allie's voice as if from a distance, leading her, encouraging her as time slipped away. "Tell me, when is it where you are."

"Friday night." Her voice sounded strange; remote. Detached. "It's late. I'm late. I hate being late."

"Why are you late?"

"I stalled. Because I'm tired of arguing all the time. Tired of defending myself."

"Against Cole?"

"He thinks I'm reckless. Careless. He thinks I don't care if I live or die."

"We both know he's wrong," Allie said. "How do you feel?"

"Angry. Frustrated. Distracted." She wanted to focus, but her mind wouldn't lock on to anything. "I've missed something. The case is at a standstill. Not even writing my last blog post broke anything free. I don't want to hear 'I told you so' from him. I'm thinking maybe it's time to stop looking for the Iceman. But I can't. I don't quit."

"So you're defensive from the go. Let's accept that and move forward. You've parked your car. You turn off the engine. Look around, Eden. What do you see? Anything odd or unfamiliar? Something that shouldn't be here? Open your eyes and look."

"I don't—" Eden shook her head as she blinked open, a slight haze coating the cars in the parking lot, the barely there overhead lights that offered none of the protection promised. "I can hear music from Monroe's. Jimmy Buffett. And…cars." Eden could hear paper rustling from beside her. "Not many. Slow night."

"Can you see the makes and models? Plate numbers? Take your time. You're safe here."

"Um, yeah." Eden's pulse picked up speed as she recited the car information. She looked into the rearview mirror. "Wait. There's something shiny and white against the wall. Back there." She leaned out of the car and squinted at the gray brick building a good forty feet away. "It looks cold." Eden shivered. What was it?

"Is it a vehicle, Eden? A truck or a van?"

"No. No, it's…" A delivery vehicle they could trace. Her heart skipped a beat. "In between. There's a logo on the side, big letters and a picture, but it's dark. I can't see what it is." She glanced upward. "The streetlight above it is broken."

"So let's see if we can get closer. What did you do after you got out of the car, Eden?" Allie backed away as Eden shifted her feet free.

"Got my purse out of the backseat." She pulled her seat forward and reached for the bag that wasn't there.

"Do you see anyone around you? Hear anyone?"

"No. It's quiet except for the music." She sniffed the air. "I smell something. Alcohol. Strong." Her eyes burned with the memory.

"Beer? Wine? Can you identify it?"

"No, not drinking alcohol." She pressed her fingers under her nose. "It's medicinal. Like peroxide." She choked as the smell reached into her throat. "Now there are heavy sounds. Getting closer. I'm locking the door and I hear it behind me."

"Footsteps? It's a person?"

"Yes." Eden started to shake. She closed the door. The light in her car went out. Something solid locked around her throat, stopping the air in her chest. Eden reached into her purse, searching for the strap of the Taser she carried. She tried to bend forward, to dislodge her attacker, to bring her arm up so she could elbow whoever it was behind her. "Can't breathe," she gasped. Her purse dropped, her belongings scattering on the ground, under the car.

Tires screeched; a car door slammed. Angry voices. Cole's voice. No. That wasn't right. That hadn't happened. Cole had been waiting for her in the restaurant. She felt herself pulling free of the hold, her mind clearing as the fog of memory lifted.

"No, Eden. Stay where you are. I'm right here. Nothing's going to hurt you. Cole, shut up," Allie said in a tone Eden had rarely heard her friend use. "Eden, you're safe. We're right here." Eden felt the arm tighten, a stabbing sensation striking her in the side of her neck. Her legs went numb. She dropped to the ground, felt the cement break her fall as she stared blankly into the coming darkness. Gasping, she clawed her fingers into the ground, tried to lift her head.

The streetlamp blinded her. She wanted to blink but she couldn't. She ducked and shook her head to focus. Dark fabric over shiny shoes. Weird shoes. What were they? Not boots. Not loafers. Thick. Squeaky. She reached out, or attempted to, but her arms were frozen.

"Can you see him, Eden? Can you see anything?"

The light dimmed as she felt herself pulling free of the past. There. She gasped. For a moment, she saw the white vehicle she'd seen here the night she was kidnapped. Slick white, coated in red.

She pressed her lips together, a sob catching in her chest.

"Okay, Eden." Allie's voice again, soft, commanding. In control. That was right. Allie was here. "I want you to come back to me now. Focus on my voice, on what I'm saying to you. I want you to remember where you are, that you're safe and that you're with friends."

The darkness abated, shifting her back to reality, to the parking lot as it was now, onto the ground next to her car. Eden dragged in a harsh breath, as if surfacing from a mile-deep dive. Had Allie brought her a pillow? She shifted her cheek against soft, worn fabric.

Strong hands stroked her hair. She saw Allie crouched on the ground beside her, concern shining in her dark eyes.

"Hey." Eden managed a weak smile. "Wow. You know how to work the hypno-voodoo. Talk about sensory overload. I need to sort through all—" But Allie was too far away to be touching her hair. She shot up, head spinning, and found Cole had been sitting beside her. "Um." For the life of her she couldn't decipher his expression except to suspect she wasn't going to like what came next. "I guess you got our note."

"Yeah. I got your *note*." He shoved to his feet, barely giving either her or Allie a second look as he brushed off his pants.

"Cole, we had it all under—" Allie took a step back as Cole shook his head. "Okay, I see you're upset. I can respect that."

"I don't care about your respect. When are the three of you going to clue in? There is no control where this case is concerned. Her, I get." Cole jerked a finger at Eden, who shuffled her feet even as a fragment of the fear she'd been struggling with the last couple of days faded. "But you, Allie? I expected at least some coherent thought from you."

"There was plenty of coherent thought." Allie planted her hands on her hips and tilted her chin up to meet his gaze. "There are three of us, remember? Simone was here if we needed—"

The three of them turned toward Allie's car. Simone lay on her back, passed out, legs hanging out of the car.

"Well, shoot." Allie kicked out a hip. "That's so inconvenient."

Eden couldn't help it. She laughed. Then she slapped a hand over her mouth as Cole spun on her, eyes blazing.

"Can you drive?" he asked.

"Better than you," she countered, even as her hands continued to tremble. "You want to help us get Simone—"

"Figure it out yourselves." Cole stalked over to his car and wrenched the door open. "It seems to be what you're best at."

* * *

"You didn't have to follow me home." Eden jingled her keys in her hand as she climbed out of her car while Cole slammed out of his. She'd forgone her assigned parking space, something she was sure her homeowners' association would send her a notice about. "And stop glaring at me like that. It wasn't like I was alone out there." She could practically hear his teeth grinding as the motion lights snapped on. "You're just mad because your pizza's cold." She gasped as he locked his hand around her upper arm. "Cole—"

Whatever else she was going to say got caught by his mouth as he kissed her. She could taste his anger, feel his frustration as he took charge, his lips demanding of her, a moment she slipped into more easily than she would have liked. She clung to him, her fists gripping the front of his shirt as she matched him stroke for stroke, breath for breath until he broke off. But he didn't release her. If anything, he brought her closer and pressed his forehead against hers, holding her tighter still.

"How do you think I felt," he whispered in the glow from the living room light streaming from inside her place, "when I got here and you were gone?"

"I thought we'd be back—" she tried to explain, except there wasn't an explanation. Not really. She knew she would upset him, but she hadn't cared. Or had she? She knew how to deal with a Cole who was angry with her. It was a familiar dance. She licked her lips. Until he'd changed the music.

"You didn't think at all," Cole muttered. "How can you, of all people, not think of the consequences, Eden? You know what can happen. That you'd just walk out of the house, leave all the lights on, doors unlocked—"

"Wait—what?" Eden planted a hand against his chest

and pushed back. "What do you mean I left the lights on?" She dived for her door and squealed when Cole dragged her back. "You didn't do this?" she asked and pointed through the window.

"The lights were on when I got here. The front door was practically standing open."

"I locked up, Cole. I swear I did. Call Allie and ask her if you don't believe me. I was complaining because the new key stuck in the lock."

Cole pulled out his gun, released the safety and lowered it to his side.

"You want me to call for backup?" Eden dug into her purse for her phone.

"Maybe." He gestured for her to unlock the door. "You do exactly as I say."

"As long as your orders don't require me to hide in my car while you check *my* house." She jutted her chin out for good measure.

"Stay behind me, understand?"

Eden mimicked his footfalls, scanning her living room as they ventured to the stairs. It didn't take long to search the bedrooms and bathroom; one of the advantages to having a small home. Downstairs didn't reveal anything except...

Her entire body went cold as she picked up the padlock. "Did you do this?"

"That's where I found it. I assumed you'd taken Allie and Simone downstairs."

"No. Simone made me lock this before dinner. Someone's definitely been here." Forgetting the promise she'd made, Eden darted out of his grasp and raced downstairs, heart pounding, eyes blinking against the harshness of the lights she clearly recalled turning off. She scanned the space.

"Anything missing or moved?" asked Cole as he joined her.

"Not that I can tell." Eden hugged her arms around her torso. The photos on her board were how she'd arranged them; Cole's stacks of papers still clung to the edge of her desk. The blankets lay huddled on the sofa right beside the—

Eden swallowed the rush of nausea that had her knees going weak. "The candle."

"What about it?" Cole followed her stare to Chloe's illuminated picture.

"I watched Allie turn it off before dinner." That someone she didn't know would have touched her memorial made her so angry she could barely stand. "Unless you—"

"It's not my place."

That he understood the sanctity of that photograph loosened something fragile inside her. "Cole?"

This didn't make any sense. Why would the Iceman have broken into her house and turned on the candle only to leave all her notes undisturbed? But who else could it have been? No one else knew the significance of that picture. No one except…

Eden lifted a hand to her throat, clenching her fingers to stop herself from trembling. It couldn't be… It wasn't possible… After all these years, it couldn't possibly be Chloe's killer. Could it?

"Pack a bag, Eden." Cole reengaged the safety on his gun before he locked his hands around her waist and pushed her toward the stairs. "You're coming home with me."

"Can't you just check me into a motel or something?" Eden sighed as Cole parked in his assigned space at the

Crest View Marina just off the Garden Highway. "Or anyplace that doesn't wobble?"

Cranky Eden had reemerged in the time it took for him to collect her files from the basement, stashing whatever he could fit, along with the boxes Jack had brought them, into the back of his SUV.

There were many facets to Eden he'd gotten used to over the years, most of which flipped every switch he possessed. He'd lost count of her idiosyncrasies. But there wasn't anyone else who could make him question the oath he'd taken, the rules he'd vowed to obey. He couldn't, wouldn't, let this maniac come near her again.

As relieved as Cole was to witness another flash of vulnerability—albeit less heart-wrenching than seeing her in the emergency room—he almost preferred Eden in fight mode. He knew from experience fighting him was the best way to make that happen. "You'll have your sea legs in no time." He pushed out of the car, the dim light battling against the even dimmer bulbs of the overhead streetlamps.

"That's not the sea. It's the Sacramento River." She clutched her zip-up sweatshirt closed as she joined him and grabbed her bag out of the back. "I need a place to work. How can I spread out on a dinghy?"

Dinghy? Wow, this woman could try the patience of a saint. "I guess we'll find out, won't we?" He stacked two boxes and hefted them from the trunk. "I'll come back for the rest while you're…acclimating."

"I was out of Dramamine," she called out as she walked behind him, dropping heavy feet against the narrow planks toward the edge of the dock. "I'll probably puke first thing."

"Just aim over the port side."

"You see the irony in this, don't you?" Eden hurried

to catch up as he headed for his boat. "Do you know how many serial killers use boats to stash their victims? You could just be making it easier for him."

"I'm certainly not making it easier on me." He took a deep breath and reminded himself this was Eden's pattern when it came to fear. She struck out at whoever was closest. It was easier than surrendering to it. Sometimes, though, he wished she'd try letting the fear win. Just once. For variety's sake, if nothing else. "Come on, Eden. I know this isn't ideal, but you'll be off the grid here when you're not with me or at the station."

"How about you strap an anklet to my leg and track me like a poodle?"

"Don't think the idea hasn't crossed my mind." The empty slips surrounding his boat reminded him how isolated they were out here. Drought aside, this particular marina had never been one of the more popular ones. And while his boat exceeded the length limit for most of the skiffs, he'd worked out a deal with the owners, who liked being able to claim a member of local law enforcement as a tenant.

As far as he knew, he was the only owner who lived on his craft, and not many boaters even ventured this far down the river for longer periods of time than a weekend. Cole, on the other hand, loved it. He knew every sound possible in this place—the lapping of minuscule waves, the lack of electrical buzz, aside from the generator, which hummed to life thanks to his solar panel system. For him, there was nothing more comforting than the creaking of the beams, the gentle rocking motion, the promise of solitude and peace.

Eden had her basement.

He set the boxes down on the deck bench and took a cleansing breath. Cole had the *Cop Out.*

"What's this?" Eden stopped short of stepping over the railing, spinning around, frowning as she searched their surroundings. "Where's your boat?"

"Oh, this is something new we do at the marina. We just take the first one we like." He held out his hand to help her over the side. "What do you think I've been doing the last five years, Eden? I told you I was restoring her."

"But..." Awe shone in her eyes and lightened his mood. "But this is beautiful. Classy. You let me believe all this time—"

"You could have come here anytime, Eden. You weren't interested." Not that it bothered him. Much.

"Yeah, well, clearly I'm an idiot." She grabbed hold of his hand and leaped onto the deck. "Or you've been holding out on me."

"We'll call it even. Let's go." He pulled open the hatch, flipped the switch on the underside and motioned her inside. "I'll show you to your cell."

He couldn't remember the last time he'd stunned her into silence. For a few moments, the specter of fear and worry that had plagued him the last few days vanished as he watched Eden set foot inside his home.

Cole wasn't an arrogant man. There was, however, one thing he took an inordinate amount of pride in: the *Cop Out*. He'd stripped it bare and refinished the gentleman's cruiser from bow to stern with the best he could afford. From the polished wood cabinetry that matched the wooden trim and deck, to the marble countertops and higher-end appliances, to the large-stall shower in the bathroom he'd purposely expanded. The boat wasn't merely a place to live. It was his passion, his hobby and, given the amount of money he'd sunk into the '60s cruiser, his retirement.

One day he'd pull up anchor and just…sail off. House, home and sanctuary all in one.

Seeing Eden standing in the spacious living area, which included a small pullout sofa across from the easy-access kitchen, confirmed his decision to make the space as modern and as un-boatlike as possible. Shifting the galley table to the other side of the sink provided more space for guests. He could still smell the trace hint of varnish and sweat, but he chalked that up to the countless hours of sanding and painting that had been his life for what seemed like endless months. Now that the boat was finished, he scarcely knew what to do with himself on the weekends.

"Cole, I have no words." Eden dropped her bag on the floor and planted her hands on her hips. Her gaze softened as she spotted the collection of framed pictures he'd displayed on one wall, including one of her parents from the first summer family vacation they'd taken him on. "This is so…real. And look!" She held out her arms and braced her feet apart, not coming close to covering the fourteen-foot expanse. "I'm not wobbling. Neither is my stomach."

"It's not like the river is known for its tidal waves." He grinned as he passed her, heading to the kitchen, and popped open the fridge to stash the beer and sodas he'd picked up earlier today. "Take a look around while I grab the rest of your stuff. And my dinner. Good thing I like cold pizza. Oh, your room's under here." He leaned over on his way up the ladder and pointed to the open door to his left. He'd planned to make it an office, but the last thing he wanted to do in this space was work. A guest room had seemed a viable second option, especially given how many times Jack had crashed at his place on their weekends off. "It's not huge, but it should suffice."

He welcomed the night air as he stepped outside, jogging to his car and organizing what was left into trips. He could go back to her place anytime, he'd told her, but that hadn't stopped him from taking as much as he could. He'd talk to the lieutenant in the morning, see about getting a few lab techs out to her house to check for any evidence, but he already knew they wouldn't find anything.

The Iceman had shifted to playing head games, which, as far as Cole was concerned, made him even more dangerous than before. It would also upset Eden even more, which would make Cole's job to keep her out of harm's way that more difficult.

Her giant boards would have to go, but he'd found a few smaller magnetic ones stashed between her filing cabinets that she could use. He needed her happy here, or, as that probably wasn't possible, content. A content Eden was one who was less likely to take risks.

If this didn't work, he'd take that tracker idea under advisement.

For now, Eden was safe. Under his roof. His protection. If anything happened to her now…

It would be on him.

Chapter 11

Eden gripped the edge of the door frame and reached around to flip the light switch to the triangular guest room. A double bed in the corner, a dresser-desk built in right next to it. Cabinets along the other side of the room. A long, narrow window stretched the length of the mattress. Two small recessed lights shone above the pillows. Neat, organized, streamlined. Everything she knew Cole to be.

Never in her wildest dreams had she imagined such a stately boat. His attention to detail, right down to the cubbyhole and peekaboo drawers in the narrow shelf under that window, was meticulous. She sank down on the bed, staring wide-eyed first at the narrow closet next to the sliding door, then at the recessed small-screen TV across from her. She caught sight of a wireless modem in a cubby just above. Internet. And Wi-Fi. She smirked. Something else she'd been wrong about.

Every unkind word she'd ever said about his home reverberated in her mind. She tried not to live with regrets. Who had time for them? But given the comments she'd made, she realized how lucky she was that Cole still considered her a friend. She really didn't make things easy on him, did she?

She didn't make things easy on anyone.

A heavy thud hit above her. She darted back out and up the stairs as he set another stack of boxes onto the deck. Before she could say anything, he was off again. Eden inhaled, slowly, deliberately. And tried to relax.

There was something oddly comforting about the absence of sound. Certainly no squeaky gnome yard ornament to keep them awake.

If she could even sleep.

That was twice the Iceman had come after her. Or was it? What if she'd been home? What if she'd come face-to-face with whomever had invaded her home? Eden frowned as she sat on the edge of the polished bench and slipped her hands under her thighs to keep them warm even as she basked in the cool night breeze. Why sneak into her home when she clearly wasn't there? What purpose did that serve? Had he left something? Taken something she hadn't noticed or didn't think was important?

He hadn't disturbed any of her notes or files on the case. She couldn't shake the idea that the focus on Chloe meant the Iceman didn't have anything to do with the break-in at her home. She was overthinking things. Reading too much into this. Clearly she thought the photo was important; it had been set aside as a focal point. But the timing…

Chloe. Twenty years almost to the day and the briefest thought of her childhood friend could send her dropping into the past like Dorothy's tornado to Oz. It was wishful thinking she could have a shot at finding Chloe's killer after all this time.

Wishful thinking. That was all it was.

With decades' worth of practice, she pushed the pain and memories aside and concentrated on the present killer. The one still in her sights.

The one she had a hope of catching.

"It doesn't make any sense," she whispered into the darkness as she tried to puzzle together the information she had. What was she missing? What did he want?

Why had he left her alive?

"I figure tomorrow you can organize everything," Cole grunted as he returned to the boat with what she hoped was the last load.

"Tell me all this won't make the boat sink," Eden attempted to tease.

"She's got a pretty strong frame," Cole said with a sharp nod. "She'll survive."

Eden shifted on her seat. Were they still talking about the boat?

"Why don't you head downstairs and I'll hand these off to you."

Eden nodded, uncertain about so many things. She refrained from speaking. She stood on the second-to-last step and held up her arms.

"Ah!" Cole pulled the first box out of reach. "Only if you promise to leave these be until tomorrow. We both need some sleep."

Eden nodded, too exhausted to argue. "Agreed. I have enough to think about." Like what that image on the shiny white surface had been when she'd done her Allie-guided flashback. Maybe when she stopped thinking, maybe if she started doodling, it would come to her.

They loaded all of Eden's stuff into the cabin, stacking

the boxes and such aside. Eden curled up in the corner of the sofa, while Cole grabbed a couple of sodas, one of which he handed to her, and got busy with his pizza. She watched him sitting beside her, her eyes unable to focus. She rubbed a finger against her temple and tried to put the fragments of memories Allie had helped her retrieve into some kind of coherence.

"Might help to talk it out," Cole said.

"Talk what out?"

"You're thinking more loudly than most people talk."

"What does he want?" Eden asked, grateful for the verbal open door. "Everything he's done over the years, taking me, leaving me in the locker, calling you, then breaking into my home? It's not right. It doesn't fit."

"Serial killers aren't out to fit anyone's mold, Eden. They do what they want, when they want. For whatever reason they want."

She inhaled the spicy scent of pepperoni despite the lack of heat as she sipped her soda, enjoying the moment. "But why the change? I mean, yeah, I got to him with what I said on my blog, and yes, I know it was stupid," she added before Cole could. "But it got us a result. He panicked and he struck out." At her, unfortunately, but at least someone innocent hadn't had to pay for her arrogance.

"He was angry," Cole added. "You humiliated him."

"Why would he care?" Eden stared.

"The ego, even the ego of a psychotic, is still fragile, you know. You made fun of him. As if what he's doing isn't important."

"Is what he's doing important?" Eden asked as the wheels in her head began to turn again.

Cole shrugged. "It is to him. What is it you writers say? The villain is the hero of his own story?"

Eden's ears tingled in that familiar sensation that struck whenever she was onto something. "Could it be that simple?"

"Depends what your definition of *simple* is."

"What is he doing with these people he chooses?"

"He kills them."

"Then why keep them for weeks, months even? If killing them was his goal, then why does he still need them?" She shifted on the sofa and grabbed Cole's arm. "Do you think Mona would let me see the bodies?"

Cole winced. "Are you sure you want to?"

"I want her take, a *medical* take on what she thinks was done to them. He wanted them for a reason. He *needs* them for a reason. What if their similarities have nothing to do with who they are or where they are but *what* they are?" She jumped up and raced to the boxes and ripped off the first lid, dragged it over to the polished table on the other side of the kitchen sink.

Nothing was in any kind of order, something she muttered about while she started sorting again. She was wrist deep in the box when she felt the air around her chill. When she looked over at Cole, she found him watching her, jaw locked, eyes sharp.

"What?"

"Nothing."

She pulled her hands free. "That's not a nothing look, Cole. What?"

He shrugged and took a long drink of his soda. "I just shouldn't be surprised you couldn't let it go tonight. Despite what you said."

"I know what I said." She waved off his reminder. "But this can't—"

"Wait. Yes, I know. Nothing ever can, can it? And nothing else matters except what you want. What you have your laser focus pinned on. Not even your promises."

She crossed her arms over her chest, not liking the accusation. "You're saying I don't keep my word? Because I opened a box?"

"Exhibit A." He got up and stashed his remaining pizza in the fridge. "You couldn't even make it a half hour."

"It's a box, Cole."

"It's proof you don't think about anything other than what you want."

"That's not true." Except…was it? "Cole, it's papers and notes. It's not like I'm—"

"You know what? Forget it." He downed the rest of his soda and wiped his mouth, the harsh shake of his head snapping her to attention. "You don't want to get into this with me, so why do I bother."

"Maybe I do." What else did she have to lose? She was trapped here, with him, at least until it was safe for her to go home. They might as well get all their issues out, right? Otherwise whatever this was between them was only going to get in the way of their investigation.

Eden hopped up on the counter beside him, forcing her attention onto him and away from the box that could hold the answers to the case. "Go on. You have more evidence you want to throw in my face? Have at it."

That he only hesitated a moment told her he'd been thinking about what to say to her for a while. Unease bubbled in her belly.

"You agreed to stay home tonight," he said. "With your friends. Where I knew you'd be safe."

Eden pressed her lips together. "Allie had an idea and I needed to jump on it." She tapped a finger against her temple. "I needed whatever was in here to get out."

"You couldn't have waited until I got back, or at the very least called me so I could be there."

"We didn't need you, Cole. Besides, I hoped—" She broke off when he moved in and planted his hands on either side of her hips. She wanted to squirm. She almost did. Especially when he pressed forward so he was almost nose to nose with her. All the nerve endings she thought had been dormant tingled to life. "Okay, no, it didn't matter. I didn't let it." She couldn't let it matter. This was her life. She wasn't about to let anyone dictate how she should live it. Not even Cole.

Particularly not Cole.

"I've pleaded with you for months, almost years, to ease off the Iceman," Cole said. "Or at the very least, to be careful. And what did you do after assuring me you would? You practically skywrote he's a pervert and dared him to call your bluff."

"Impulse. I was mad," Eden mumbled and caught her lower lip between her teeth. Okay, so he had a pretty good case against her. But she got results! How could he not see that? "I was afraid I'd run out of clues." Or that the Iceman would disappear again. She was close this time. So close.

"And again, what Eden wanted was all that mattered. You don't take anyone else into consideration, do you? Have you ever once wondered how the rest of us would feel if something happened to you?"

She hated the disappointment she saw on his face, heard in his voice, felt in his touch as he stroked a finger down her cheek, a sliver of warmth in the cold reality of her life. "Something did happen and I'm just fine, remember?" A bit weirded out now, maybe a tad more uneasy, but she was alive. And that was all that mattered. "Cole—"

"Just once I'd like you to keep your word to me, Eden. Just once I'd like to know that what I want, what I think, matters to you."

"You do matter." Eden caught his hand when he pulled away, tugged him closer as she hitched to the edge of the counter. She hooked her foot around the back of his thigh to hold him there, realizing too quickly just what she was opening herself up to. "Cole, I swear you're important to me. Just like Allie and Simone—"

"I'm not Allie or Simone," he said, that expression in his eyes shifting to one of cool determination. He moved in that last inch and held her hips, pulling her into him in a way that set her desire humming. "I'm here, Eden. I always have been." His hand let go of her but only long enough to bury itself in her hair and cup the back of her neck. "You scare me. Not only because of the chances you take, but because I'm terrified you believe your life isn't worth living."

Eden's breath hitched as he leaned in and brushed his lips against hers. Featherlight, a promise of sorts. A promise she wasn't sure she could live up to.

She closed her eyes against the heat coursing through her, told herself she couldn't afford the complication of a relationship. "I thought we decided—"

"We didn't decide anything." He kissed her forehead, and if she could see him, she suspected she'd find him flinching against the reality of their situation. "I've told you how I feel, Eden. I want to see where this could go. But—" he released her and stepped back "—I'm not entirely sure I can trust you."

"You can." She really didn't like the sound of that. "Cole, you have to know there's no one else I trust more in this world than you." Except Allie and Simone.

"Prove it."

"How?" Now she was the one who narrowed her eyes. Even with everything that was between them, she couldn't refuse a challenge.

"Let those boxes alone for tonight. Just put the case away for a few hours. Do that, and then maybe I can begin to." He let her go and took a step away. As he moved, the muscles in his arms flexed, capturing her attention the same way they had when he'd been ready to shoot her garden gnome. "Now, I'm going to lock up and take a shower before I go to bed. Bathroom is down there, first door on the left. My bedroom's at the far back."

"Why do I need to know where your bedroom is?" She was going for haughty, but sounded kind of sad even to her own ears.

"You know why, Eden. And now you know what it'll take for me to let you in. I'll see you in the morning."

It was too quiet.

Eden flopped onto her back, stuffed the second pillow under her head and stared up at the too-close ceiling.

Cole Delaney and his sanctimonious rationality! Every time she tried to concentrate on her memories from the parking lot and find a clue as to who the Iceman might be, she got pummeled with erotic images of tangled sheets, entwined limbs and a very naked potentially former best friend.

She couldn't remember the last time she'd ached to be touched, but since Cole had kissed her in the kitchen the other day, that heavy, pulsing need hadn't diminished. Instead it clung and wrapped her up in a haze of confusion, longing and sexual frustration.

Eden swung her legs over the side of the bed and sat

up, tempted to let the growl building in her throat free. She needed to get this out of her system.

She needed to get *him* out of her system.

Going to bed with Cole was practical. It would satisfy her curiosity, so she could get on with what really mattered.

She grabbed her phone, stared at the time.

Two thirty. Yeah. She could do this. It was just sex, right? How much damage could it do?

Even as the debate raged in her head, the sound of rustling on the other side of the door had her getting out of bed.

"Well, that's a sign if I ever heard one." She pulled open the door, poked her head out and blinked against the lights. "Cole?"

"Go back to bed," he said from around the corner.

"What are you doing going through my boxes?" The heaviness eased as her brain kicked into gear. Not completely, though. The sight of Cole clad only in low-riding blue pajama bottoms, exposing a solid six-pack—not to mention those estrogen-boosting chiseled hip bones—had her considering the quickest way to divest him of the fabric. Oh, yeah. She'd spent far too much time thinking about this. "I thought we were leaving those until tomorrow." It had taken every ounce of control she'd had to slip the lid back on and set the box on the pile after he'd gone to bed. A new kind of challenge. One she'd won and been proud of.

If only she hadn't been stewing over it ever since.

"It is tomorrow and that was up to you, not me." He shifted the top box aside and hauled the second one over to the table. "Something you said during your little hypnotherapy session with Allie reminded me of something."

"Reminded you of what?" She joined him, making

fists to keep herself from digging through the box with him. "What's that?" Eden stepped closer and brushed her fingers over his bare arm.

"Chloe." He handed her the carefully wrapped frame from her basement. "I didn't think you'd want to leave her behind."

Tears prickled her eyes. Most times looking at her childhood friend reignited her anger. Tonight, Chloe's face was a reminder of just how short life could be.

"Put the papers down, Cole." She set the frame aside and put herself between him and the table.

"Eden, this is important." He couldn't have sounded more frustrated if he tried.

"*This* is important." She reached up and grabbed hold of him, then pressed her mouth to his. Now she knew what startled tasted like. Intoxicating, arousing, with a hint of spice and more than a touch of heat. She rose up on her bare toes, stretching herself against him even as she felt that slight twitch in his lips, the same twitch Simone had teased her about earlier this evening. A surge of possessiveness made Eden's head spin. The heat of his bare chest soaked through her thin tank and tightened her nipples. She wanted him, wanted his hands on her skin, wanted to feel his mouth everywhere his fingers touched. Eden stroked her tongue over his—long, deep strokes that he mimicked in return.

He reached around her, shoved the box aside and hauled her onto the table. He slipped between her legs. His searching, determined hands skimmed down her sides and inched up under her shirt to caress her bare skin. Firm fingers explored and trailed up her spine as she felt him fighting for control.

When he dragged his mouth from hers, she felt a burst of feminine pride at the dazed look in his beautiful forest green eyes. The almost feral glimmer intensified as she inched closer and felt him harden against her. "Clearly you've done some thinking," he murmured as he drew his lips down the side of her throat.

"Ironic how I wasn't the one who couldn't leave the boxes alone." She moaned as his teeth nipped at the pulse in her throat. Her entire body tingled, screaming out for his attention as she locked her legs around him. "Hearing you out here gave me the excuse I was looking for."

"You needed an excuse?"

"I needed this. I needed to clear my head. To stop thinking— Cole?" She caught her breath as he pulled away, his entire body tensing…and not in that good way.

"Couldn't stop thinking about me? Or about the case?"

"Oh, man, what does it matter? We need this. We both want this." To prove her point, she nudged a hand under the waistband of his pants. Before she could make contact, he jumped away, the passion she'd seen in his eyes only moments before vanishing under accusation.

"I'm not some pressure valve you push for release, Eden."

"That's not what this is," she argued.

"Isn't it? You weren't in your room trying to think about the case? Trying to clear your head for what really matters? Such as the Iceman?"

"What do you care why I'm doing this? I thought you wanted it, too," she demanded before realizing her mistake. "Cole, wait! That isn't what I—"

"That you have to ask that question proves how different we see things. I got you started, honey," he said, grabbing the nearest box and slinging it to the side of the room. "Now you can enjoy the rest of your evening."

He slammed the door so hard the brass lamp above the dining table swung back and forth.

Eden let out a breath, the heat of humiliation burning her cheeks. She pushed to her feet, her knees wobbling. "Dumb, dumb, dumb."

And why did she feel as if she'd just lost something she never knew she wanted?

"Thanks, Mona." Cole glanced over his shoulder as Eden emerged from her room, heavy eyed and somewhat pale. Something akin to satisfaction slithered through him. At least he hadn't been the only one who'd had a rotten night. "Yeah, ten sounds good. We'll see you then."

"What was that about?" Eden asked.

"A hunch." He brewed himself a second cup of coffee and tried to ignore the longing she'd ignited in him hours before. He'd always imagined she'd bring that meticulous attention to detail she possessed into the bedroom. She'd all but branded him with those kisses of hers. Sometimes being right just stank. "Coffee?"

"Thanks. What hunch?" Confusion fogged her eyes as he pulled his cup free, set a mug under the maker and added a new pod. The coffee machine hummed.

"You said something about blood when you were with Allie in the parking lot last night."

"Out loud?" She frowned. "I remember seeing it. Or an image of it against that shiny white surface. I didn't realize I'd said anything. Think it means something?"

"I think you're right." He reached across the counter and set her mug on the table. "The victims themselves aren't the common denominator. It's something they have."

"If you're thinking blood, news flash. Everyone has it."

"Something *in* their blood." Dealing with sarcasm after a sleepless night was justification for ending a friendship, right? "It's what I'm hoping Mona will confirm, anyway." It would be a big break in the case if he was correct. It would be something to go on, instead of cursing himself for not taking Eden up on her carnal offer.

"Okay. Great." She cringed as she took a seat at the far end of the kitchen table. The opposite side from where they'd nearly feasted on each other. "Look, Cole," she said with more trepidation than he'd ever heard before. "About last night—"

"Drop it, Eden." The last thing he wanted to do was talk about it.

"But how can we? Whatever's going on between us—"

"I know you see me as one of the girls, but I'm not particularly interested in discussing my feelings." He dumped a spoonful of sugar into his mug before he remembered he'd given it up six months ago. Gah. He nearly gagged when he sipped. He dumped it down the sink and started over.

"I'm well aware you're not one of the girls." She arched a brow and lifted her mug to her lips, but not before he caught the gleam in her eye. "I just want to know where we go from here. Clearly we're physically compatible."

"Clearly," he muttered. Why did he feel as if they were suffering a terminal case of role reversal in this relationship? The heck with it. "Maybe I'm looking to be something more than a substitute for your nighttime fantasies."

She slammed her mug down. "That's not fair."

"True. So we should set all this aside until after the Iceman is taken care of. Like I said, let's forget what happened last night or what either of us might want."

"What do you want?" Eden's question caught him off guard, but it didn't occur to him to lie.

"I want it all."

"With me?" She seemed stunned. "You mean this isn't about getting each other out of our systems so we can move on?"

Disappointment crashed through him as he grabbed his coffee. It had never occurred to him it would be a one-and-done thing. All these months, all this time he'd wondered what it would feel like to have her in his arms, to know what it was like to kiss her, to touch her, to make love to her. It had taken seconds for him to know he could very well never get his fill of her. Because…

He stared at her, cold realization washing over him like a tidal wave.

Heaven help him. He was in love with Eden St. Claire.

"This might come as a shock to you," Eden said when he couldn't find the words to respond. "But I'm not a romantic like you, Cole. Sex is sex. It's practical and sometimes it's flat-out needed. There's a reason I've never had a long-term relationship. I'm not good at it. Mainly because I honestly haven't cared. I'm not a nice person, Cole. I'm selfish and I'm rude and I make things way too difficult on anyone who even thinks about caring about me."

"Do you think that comes as a surprise to me?" Where was she going with this?

She lifted her face, and for the first time he saw genuine confusion shining in her eyes. "It scares me how well you understand me." The small smile she gave him felt like a victory. "This…us? This would be different. This time…"

"This time, what?" He could very well need the jaws of life to pry the truth out of her.

"This time I have something to lose."

"Eden—"

"You got to say what you wanted. Now it's my turn. I meant what I said the other day. I don't want to lose you as a friend."

"And what if we could have something even better?" So much for not talking about his feelings. Thankfully there wasn't anyone other than Eden around to witness the beating his male ego was taking.

"You don't know for sure that's what would happen."

"Think back a couple of hours, Eden." Cole arched a brow at her and earned another smile. "Then try that again."

"You're making fun of me."

"No. At least not on purpose." He did not need this distraction. Not when she was distracting enough. "Look, we're both running on an abundance of adrenaline. That could be all this is." And now he was lying to himself. Great start to the morning. "Let's take this an hour at a time and see where things lead, okay?"

"Okay." She shrugged as if they'd just agreed who was going to do the dishes. "If you think that's best."

"I think what's best is if we're honest with each other. So I'll get this out now. Don't use me because I'm convenient or because you're afraid."

"Got it." She drank her coffee and her eyes cleared. "You're not a tool, by the way. Good thing we don't have any other plans for the day outside of stalking a serial killer and figuring out his motives. Speaking of which..." She shifted her gaze to the stack of boxes.

"We're meeting Mona at the hospital at ten."

The healthy pink glow in Eden's cheeks faded. "The hospital?"

"Afraid so. She's taking over the pathology class for one of the doctors."

"Maybe you should have added some whiskey to my coffee." She headed for the bathroom. "But at least I'll have you by my side, right?"

"Always," he said, then realized he was talking to a closed door.

Chapter 12

"Mom! Dad!" Fifteen-year-old Eden threw her hands out, reaching for her parents as the gurney she was on sped down the overlit hallway of the emergency room. The light hurt her eyes as the sobs piled up in her throat. Every breath ripped through her chest. The hissing and odd wheezing sound buzzing in her ears was making her dizzy. "Where are they taking them?" Eden tried to scream, tried to call, but she was whipped around a corner and slid into a curtainless room. Beeping monitors filled the air along with the putrid stench of blood and terror.

Someone poked at her, her arms, her ribs, her stomach, before she pried open her eyes and another light flooded them. Eden whimpered, kicking her legs. Tried to kick her legs. Her left one wouldn't move. She grunted, thrashing her upper body to one side and then the other, needing to find her parents. "Mom!"

A flash of movement caught the corner of her eye as the people around her murmured. Eden blinked, tried not to think about the needles piercing her skin or the sound of fabric ripping as someone sliced her jeans off her body. "Mom. Mommy?"

From mere feet away, locked into her own gurney, Juliette St. Claire turned her head, glassy gray eyes focusing on Eden, a small, peaceful smile settling over her lips as she stretched out her hand to her daughter. "It'll be okay," Juliette whispered, tears spilling from the corners of her eyes. "You'll be okay, baby. I love you."

The horrific flatlining screeched in Eden's ears as her mother's hand fell limp.

"Mommy, no!" Eden strained to see more. She could barely keep her eyes open as she searched for her father's familiar solid and comforting presence. "Daddy." Her broken whisper ripped from her throat like a scream as the bloodstained sheet was pulled up over Christopher St. Claire's gaunt face. "Don't leave me! Logan?" Eden arched her back off the bed as she threw every bit of energy she had into her brother's name.

"I'm here, Eden!"

And then he was. Tall, steady, reliable Logan, whose own grief spilled free as he stood at the foot of her gurney, hands reaching out to grab hold of her legs as she struggled beneath the combined weight of fear and shock.

Relief surged through her. Her brother hadn't been in the car. He hadn't been hit by that drunk driver. He'd driven separately. Had been right behind them... He'd seen... "I'm right here, Eden. I'm not going anywhere. We aren't."

"They're dead." She couldn't breathe. Not out of grief. Because she couldn't find any air. She could hear her-

self choking, feel herself slipping into the swirling gray as another figure moved into sight.

Cole. He'd been there. Even then.

"Do something!" Cole yelled at the doctors. "Don't you dare let her die! Eden, you fight, you hear me! Don't you dare give up on us. We need you..."

The past faded as she closed her eyes.

"Eden?" Cole's voice again, deeper this time, less frantic. "Hey." She felt his hand on her arm. The merest touch of his fingers brought her out of the nightmare of her past. The night her entire life had changed.

"Hmm?" Standing in front of the plate-glass window on the second floor of Mother of Mercy Hospital, she caught her faint reflection in the glass, felt the dampness on her face from the tears she hadn't realized she'd shed. "Did you say something?"

"I only asked if you were okay."

She shook her head, tried to dismiss his concern. She didn't want to be needy, or to need him. And yet… "Fifteen years." She rolled her eyes in an attempt to shove away the barrage of emotions that set upon her every time she entered a hospital. "How can it still hurt this much after all this time?"

It was a question she'd never asked anyone else. Why would she? No one had any answers for her. No one could ever explain to Eden—not fifteen-year-old Eden or almost-thirty-year-old Eden—how a man with four drunk-driving convictions had been behind the wheel of a car. A man who'd walked away without a scratch while Eden and her eighteen-year-old brother had been left to bury their parents.

"I think about them a lot." Cole stroked a hand down her arm. She could feel the uncertainty coursing through him, the hesitation in his voice.

"They loved you." Eden swiped her fingers under her eyes and forced out a laugh. "From the minute you got busted with Logan for smoking behind the gym in fourth grade." She'd been, what? Almost eight then? She could still remember the smell of her father's hobby shop—sawdust and hot metal—as she'd sat perched on a stool listening to him lecture Logan and Cole on the dangers of cigarettes. Her father had been a horrible woodworker and putterer, but he'd loved trying.

"It wasn't as if my parents could be bothered." Cole shrugged. "Where do you think we got the cigarettes from? My old man kept a huge stash of them in the basement."

It had always amazed her how Cole held no animosity toward his mother and father, who, the second Cole turned eighteen, had sold the house he'd grown up in, packed up and moved to Florida, their parental obligation seemingly done. Then again, Cole Delaney didn't have a bitter bone in his body.

He did, however, have a very long memory. "Juliette and Christopher never let me down." Cole moved closer as he gazed out the window at nothing more than air-conditioning units with silver coils that looked like they'd been discarded from NASA. "You know it was your father's idea for me to join the police force. He told me he thought I had an aptitude for criminal justice."

"He would have known." Her father had been a criminal psychologist and one of Allie's early inspirations. That her parents had welcomed their children's friends into the house as if they were their own was a gift Eden would never be able to repay. Or thank them for.

"He thought I'd make a good cop," Cole continued. "He and your mom were killed before I could tell him I'd decided to follow his advice."

"Daddy knew a good bet when he saw one." Because she needed to, because she wanted to, she moved in and wrapped her arms around Cole's, settling her head against him. "I'm sure Mom had some choice words about his advice."

"I recall her trying to change my mind. Something about me trying to get myself shot. So far I've proven her wrong." He reached his hand over and stroked her cheek. "I know it's hard for you, being here. If there was another way—"

"We all have to face our fears sometime." Eden shivered despite the odd sensation of having a weight lifted off her chest. The stark terror she'd kept at bay for almost half her life hadn't overtaken her, not with the same ferocity as it normally did. Maybe it had been her emergency room visit the other night, or the subsequent hours she'd spent being pricked and prodded for more blood. Or maybe…

Maybe it was knowing Cole was beside her.

Maybe it was knowing just like that night fifteen years ago, he wasn't going to let her stop fighting.

"Not that I'm up for a jaunt through the emergency room," she added with a strained laugh. "Let's not get carried away."

The door at the end of the hallway swung open and Mona Hendrix strode down the hall, a stack of files clutched against her chest. "I'm sorry I'm late." She pushed her thin-framed glasses higher up on her nose before tucking her silver bob-length hair behind her ear. "Apparently I'm more captivating than I realized. Dr. Landry's students had more questions than I anticipated."

"I'm afraid to ask about what," Cole said as Eden scrubbed her hands over her face again. If Mona noticed Eden had been crying, she didn't let on.

"You should be. Nothing like a room of inquisitive pathologists. Be still, my heart, the future looks bright." She grimaced, but there was that telltale touch of humor Eden always found intriguing. She supposed being a medical examiner meant you had to have a sense of humor—if not an odd one. Talk about survival techniques. "I should be back in my office in the next couple of days if you want to stop by to view the bodies before we release them to their families."

"Thanks." Eden hefted her bag higher on her shoulder and followed Mona into Dr. Landry's office. She really hoped that wouldn't be necessary. She'd gotten a pretty close-up look during their time together in the freezer. "Cole said he asked you to run—" The words dropped out of Eden's brain as she gaped around the room. "What is this place?"

"Insane, isn't it?" Mona chuckled, paying no mind to the umpteen specimen jars filled with every type of preserved body type—from multiple species—lining the shelves of an otherwise elegantly decorated room. The bookcases were high-end, with recessed lighting and stuffed with books and medical instruments from throughout history. "I like to think if Sherlock Holmes and Dr. Frankenstein shared an office it would look like this."

"Whereas Mona's office downtown is filled with daisies and gumdrops." Cole took a seat across from Mona as she settled behind the desk and started tapping away on the computer.

"Now, now, Cole. Be nice, otherwise I won't admit your hunch was spot-on." Mona dipped her chin and peered over her glasses much like a judgmental Sunday-school teacher. Eden made her way to the chair beside Cole.

"About the blood?" Eden asked. "How so?"

"It was the only thing all of them had in common," Mona said. "It's the only thing our killer took from each of them."

"What about the missing organs from the first three?" Eden asked. "Any guesses as to why he'd have taken from those victims and not the others?"

"A learning curve? The spleen, liver and kidneys are all vital to the way blood traverses through the human body. Maybe he got what he needed from those." Her arched brow was pointedly aimed at Eden. "Answering the why is going to be up to you, but I can confirm the what. They were all missing the same thing you were." She folded her hands on the top of the desk and looked at Eden.

"Blood." The image she recalled in the parking lot burst into her mind. "So, what? You're saying he's some kind of wannabe vampire draining his victims?"

"I'm not saying anything, although that would have been a clever way to hide what he was doing. Clearly your guy isn't after headlines. But there's only one puncture wound in each neck." Mona tapped her finger against the side of her throat. "Right at the jugular. Neat and precise."

Eden rubbed her own neck when she felt a twinge of pain.

"Here's what's interesting," Mona continued. "Your jugular wasn't tapped for blood, Eden. They found residual traces of that sedative around that injection mark. What blood he did siphon from you—a fraction of what was missing from the other victims—was from your arm. And that made me ask why. So I ran more tests and compared all the victims' blood to yours."

"And you found something," Cole said.

"Would I have dragged you down here this morning if I hadn't?" She hefted a soft-sided leather briefcase onto the desk and pulled out a stack of files, then pushed them toward Cole. "Copies of my findings along with each of your victims' medical records. I requested them after all eleven blood samples revealed unusually high iron levels."

"Iron?" Eden asked. "I thought we were supposed to have iron?"

"Some, yes, and while women are more prone to lower levels naturally, every one of the Iceman's victims were definitely at the top of the scale. Some were even being treated for various health issues as a result."

"How common is that?" Cole asked.

"High levels are more rare than low. A good percentage of the population is anemic, but that's easily treatable with iron supplements and a healthy diet. DIOS, on the other hand—"

"DIOS?" Eden asked.

"Dysmetabolic iron overload syndrome."

"DIOS it is," Cole said.

"DIOS has a wide range of symptoms and related health issues. From osteoporosis to hair loss. It's even been known to accelerate neurodegenerative diseases like early-onset Parkinson's, MS and epilepsy."

Cole shifted in his seat. "One little mineral can do all that? What causes it?"

"Environment in some cases. Recent studies have found a connection between lead levels and an increase in iron-related blood illnesses. Sometimes it's as simple as losing the genetic jackpot. Certain ethnicities are more prone to the disorder than others. In any case, I believe you've found your common denominator where your victims are concerned."

"Why would someone be interested in iron in the blood?" Eden asked.

"That would involve guessing and I deal in facts," Mona said. "Cole just asked me to prove his theory. If no other commonalities could be found for these victims, and I couldn't find any medically, this is what you're left with."

"Maybe he's some kind of lunatic who thinks other people's blood gives him something?" Eden glanced at Cole. Not that it answered the whole freezing-the-bodies issue.

"The vampire angle again?"

"He's pretty meticulous for someone that mentally disturbed." Mona booted up her laptop. "First three victims aside, I'm finding very little trauma to the bodies. That's not to say all those urban legends and myths about the supposed benefits of various minerals in human blood, iron included, aren't coming into play, but to me, they read like test results. Or..."

"Experiments." Eden felt a piece of the puzzle click into place. "Could he be experimenting on these people? On their blood? Some of them had been dead for a while. If he was using them as test subjects that could account for this, right?"

"It's as good a guess as any. I also found evidence of long-term tissue damage. As if he kept them in varying temperatures over longer periods of time."

"Like a meat locker?" Cole glanced uneasily at Eden. "Is that how he finally killed them? He let them freeze to death?"

"They died of massive blood loss, not hypothermia. Besides, that particular locker has backup temperature controls. Unless you're inside one of those things for, say, thirty-six to forty-eight hours, you wouldn't die from it.

No." Mona shook her head. "He was done with them before he stored them."

"He must have cold storage wherever he's keeping the corpses. Another factor to look for." Cole got out his phone and started making notes. "Okay, this will take us down a whole other avenue of investigation. Thanks, Mona."

"Wait." Eden put a hand on Cole's arm when he started to stand. "This still doesn't explain how he finds and targets them. It's not like we list our iron levels on our drivers' licenses. Would anyone other than a medical professional have access to that information?"

"In this day and age, who knows?" Mona shrugged. "People share every aspect of their lives online. Might be you're looking for a needle in a needle stack. But, given the lack of damage done to the bodies and the care that was taken, I wouldn't exclude your killer having some medical training."

"At least now we have a needle to look for," Cole said. "You wanted to start over with the victims, Eden. Now we have a real lead. I've also asked a friend in the missing persons department to give me an updated list every couple of days. I'm betting the Iceman's not done."

"Unless he's found what he was looking for." Eden followed Cole and stood up.

"Something tells me we won't be that lucky," Cole said. "Thanks, Mona."

"You bet. Keep me in the loop. And I'll get the last of my reports to you as soon as I can."

"Out of curiosity…" Eden turned back at the door. "How were my test results?"

"Peachy keen." Mona grinned. "Nothing to worry about with you. Iron-wise, anyway. Be glad." She picked up her folders again. "It probably saved your life."

* * *

"You know if I have to stay here with nothing to do for hours on end, neither one of us is going to be happy." Eden perched on the edge of Cole's desk at the station and flicked her finger against the fuzzy yellow-haired troll in front of his computer screen. "You still have this guy?"

"Some little brat gave that to me for Christmas one year." He smacked her hand away. "Leave it alone."

"I wasn't a brat. Very often," she added. "Come on, Cole. You've got other cases you have to catch up on and I am bored out of my mind. I don't even have my laptop with me. If you aren't going to give me access to a computer—"

"Bite your tongue."

"—then at least let me go down to the lab and see if Tammy—"

"Why do you owe her a bottle of tequila?" Cole leaned back in his chair and looked at her.

"Um, for Cinco de Mayo?" She fluttered her lashes. She wasn't sure their fragile truce could withstand the revelation she'd convinced Tammy to provide her with a list of stalled-out cases for the past five years so she'd have fodder for her blog. Cases, Eden had to admit, that had fallen by the wayside thanks to her focus on the Iceman.

"Leave my techs alone, Eden. Just because you have an in with me doesn't give you unfettered access."

"Then give me something to do. Or I'm going to start dancing on top of tables. Oh, hey, there's an idea." She jumped to her feet and made to climb onto his desk. "Remember when that actress flashed—"

"Don't you dare!" He was out of his chair so fast she almost didn't see him. He grabbed her around the waist and spun her away from his desk, earning an enthusiastic response from his fellow cops. The whistles and catcalls had Eden thinking they should try out for that dancing reality show. "You're going to make a spectacle of yourself if I don't give in, aren't you?"

Eden squirmed against him, taking inordinate pleasure in watching his pupils contract. It would be interesting to see if their delayed interaction could withstand their attraction. Whatever they were trying to preserve friendship-wise seemed to have developed a serious crack in its foundation.

"As much as I love all this togetherness—" she paused and pressed her hands flat against his chest and would have purred if she didn't have another agenda "—if we don't extend this tether I'm going to smother you in your sleep." She moved in and stood eye to eye with him. Or make that nose to chin. "And remember, I know where your bedroom is."

His mouth twisted even as his eyes glinted with laughter. She loved finding new ways to play with him.

"Let me go see if Simone's free for lunch," she pleaded. "She's five blocks away, Cole. I'll keep my phone on and even call in with hourly reports of my status." The idea of actually experiencing sunshine for even a few minutes had her champing at the bit.

"Don't make promises you can't keep, Eden." The reminder came in that deep, dangerous tone that sent chills racing down her spine.

"I'll be back here by three. That I will promise." She held up her Girl Scout salute as if she'd been one.

"What about that throng of reporters out front?" As if Cole needed to remind her she was still fodder for headlines and lead stories. She'd listened to at least a dozen voice mails asking her for televised interviews, most local but a few national. The idea had her swallowing hard. She just wanted to report the stories, not be the story.

She dug into her bag for her sunglasses and tied her hair up. "Better?"

"Yeah, you've completely disappeared." Cole rolled his eyes. "Go out the side alley, okay? Plenty of cops around to keep an eye on you."

"You really believe he'd try something around here in broad daylight?"

"Neither one of us knows what to believe about him, so I'm not ruling anything out. If you don't like it, they loaded up new tuna sandwiches in the vending machines this morning."

"Ick. I'll see you later." Before he could change his mind, she hurried off. She spotted at least half a dozen uniformed officers milling about in the alley. She hadn't realized how cooped up she'd felt, but the second that fresh-diesel-tinged air hit her lungs, something inside her broke free. Her normally brisk pace slowed. She savored every step. Though that didn't stop her mind from racing circles around the Iceman.

She stopped briefly at the newsstand on the corner, one of the last in the city, to pick up a copy of today's *Sacramento Tribune*. Enjoying the sun's beating rays, she flipped through the pages, even more convinced she'd made the right decision to let her paper run copies of her blog posts. Not to bring more attention to her abilities as a reporter and writer, but because there were still a few holdouts when it came to embracing technology. She knew of plenty of people who still got their news delivered to their front porch every morning, despite the fear that print was dying.

Something her editor was struggling to overcome with his dedication to sensationalizing the smallest stories around town. Eden skimmed the articles on the struggling local basketball team she continued to root for; the prospects of an end to the construction moratorium in surrounding districts; the expansion plans for the rail yards; and the grand opening of a string of small businesses hoping to cash in on the recently built sports arena. And it was time for the firefighters' annual blood drive. With more than a bit of relief, Eden noted her personal ordeal with the Iceman had been relegated to page three, replaced front and center with Benedict Russell's surprisingly articulate write-up on a string of assaults and robberies in the Pocket area.

"Huh. I guess miracles do happen." She tucked the paper into her bag, turned and plowed right into another pedestrian. "Oh, sorry!"

Her eyes watered as the smell of cotton candy assaulted her. She coughed, head spinning as she reached out and grabbed hold of the lamppost nearby, the ghostly sounds of childhood laughter echoing in her ears. "Chloe." Her friend's freckled face exploded in her mind, her face-stretching smile, the lilt of her voice. And the smell of the perfume Eden had bought Chloe for her birthday a few months before her death.

Eden spun around, looking for whomever she'd collided with, but the afternoon lunch crowd had begun to emerge from buildings, hurrying this way and that.

She closed her eyes, shaking her head to dislodge the scent and the memories. Coincidence, she told herself. Plenty of people wore sickly sweet perfumes, not that she'd ever had the scent of one slam her that far into the past before. The hair on her neck prickled. Lifting her sunglasses, she studied the other side of the street. Tightening her hold on her purse, she joined the crowd, scanning faces, glancing over her shoulder, unable to shake the sensation that someone—while maybe not following her—was watching her.

Eden had kept a low—a very low—profile ever since her abduction. Now she was beginning to scare herself. She'd been reacting these last few days; not acting as she normally did. No wonder she was out of sorts and imagining things. She chewed on her bottom lip, still unable to get the smell of hot sugar candy out of her mind.

Maybe it was time to change the game again. Write a new blog, make another deal with her editor to run it with her old ones and maybe give serious consideration to returning some of those interview-request calls. At the very least she could chime in on those comments Cole thought were so fascinating. If she could get Cole to agree. She could just imagine—

Eden stopped at the corner, letting the noonday sun bathe her in its warmth. Was she really going to consult Cole on her plan of action?

Two days ago—heck, twenty-four hours ago—it wouldn't have crossed her mind. She'd have dived in. But now…

Going full bore wouldn't only anger him. It could ruin the potential for…whatever it was they might have started.

This was ridiculous. Since when did she let her emotions get in the way of what needed to be done? She didn't take other people's thoughts, other people's *feelings*, into consideration.

Eden dropped her head back and blinked into the sun, pushing the unease away with an even more unsettling thought. *I'm sounding like a girlfriend.* She clomped her way down the rest of the block, trudged through the glass doors to the criminal justice building, determined to get her thoughts—and unease—under control before she ventured into the all-seeing realm of Simone Armstrong.

She signed in at the desk and gave the familiar security guard a weak wave as she headed for the stairs to the third floor, glancing one last time at the lobby before letting the door shut.

Maybe burning off some excess energy would help her figure things out. Instead all the climb managed to do was remind her she needed to get her butt back to the gym.

She pushed through the door into the DA's department, where Simone's office was located. As it was lunchtime, the place was fairly quiet. Hiking her glasses on top of her head, she wound through the maze of cubbies and came to a stop at Simone's assistant's desk.

"Hey, Kyla."

"Look who's out and about." Kyla smiled up at her. "You doing okay? All thawed out?"

"Peachy keen, according to one doctor," Eden said, appreciating Kyla's joke while hopefully bypassing any subsequent conversation about her ordeal. "I hear you're going to take the bar exam next month. How goes the studying?"

"Torturous," Kyla groaned and tightened the colorful scarf that kept her springy ebony curls off her face. Warm, sepia skin glowed under the office lights, and those dark eyes of hers didn't miss a trick. She might look young and innocent, but Kyla had become a ferocious guardian of the gate when it came to Simone. "And your friend in there isn't helping." She jerked a thumb toward Simone's open door.

"I heard that!" Simone called from inside the glass room.

"She keeps dropping tests on my desk," Kyla leaned

forward and whispered. "Over the weekend she had me write a five-thousand-word essay on MacClaren versus Taurus Construction."

"Oh, hey, I covered that case." Eden snapped her fingers. "The plaintiffs sued over the fact the sewer lines in the housing complex were never hooked up properly. Caused constant backups. Sexy stuff." Gag-worthy stuff.

"As were the plethora of subsequent health issues. Did I mention I had to write this *over the weekend*?" Kyla sighed.

"I'm surprised Simone's working so hard to help you pass," Eden said. "She won't be able to survive without you."

"I'm not going anywhere," Kyla insisted. "Not as long as I have student loans to pay. Besides, who better to learn the ropes from?"

"More like you're going to push me out of a job," Simone said from the doorway. "Not bad, kiddo. I made some notes, but I think you're going to do just fine."

"Does that mean you'll stop with the homework assignments?"

"Not a chance." Simone clicked her tongue and turned her bright-eyed attention to Eden. "This is a surprise. I hear you've recently had a change in address and picked up a roommate. You'd better come in and spill."

"How do you not have a hangover?" Eden closed the door behind her as Simone returned to her desk. Her friend perched daintily on the edge of her chair as she scribbled on a legal pad. "Allie told me it took her over a half hour to get you into bed last night."

"It wouldn't have taken her half that time if she'd been naked and male." Simone flipped the page over. Typical Simone. Old-school dedication to the job.

Eden reached across the desk and poked her friend in the forehead. "Seriously? No headache?"

Simone swatted her hand away without batting a perfectly outlined eye. "I hydrate. And I worked out this morning. Got rid of the toxins. Give me a second." She carried her notepad out to Kyla. Eden glanced around Simone's office, thinking how if ever a place evoked someone's personality, this managed it. No dark woods or color in here. Pale yellow coated the walls, and an interspersing of brass and glass shelves kept her books, awards and certificates neatly displayed.

Eden's furniture had at least an inch of dust covering it, while the very idea of dust probably hadn't even crossed this office's mind. Simone wasn't a sentimentalist. At least, not here. Here was where her friend displayed her accomplishments, which had multiplied exponentially over the years.

The few personal photographs she did display were of herself, Eden and Allie from various adventures during their lives, including one from Simone's wedding day in Napa four years ago. That Simone and Vince separated almost before the ink was dry on their license was evident by the lack of husband-like mementos. Or images.

"I thought Cole had you under house arrest at his place," Simone said as she returned to her desk.

"He had some work to do and I got to tag along." Like a pet puppy. Eden pointed to the photo of Simone and her parents. "You hear from them lately?"

"Mother is enjoying a cruise on the French Riviera for the next six weeks," Simone said in that perfect "whatever makes her happy" tone. "Dad's working on some kind of deal in Hong Kong. Probably has to do with wife number four."

"The deal or the trip?"

"Hmm." Simone simply smiled. "I'm sure I'll be reading about it in his company's press release. Why are you asking about them?"

For once Eden didn't hedge. This was, partially anyway, why she'd come. "I was at the hospital earlier. With Cole. Brought things back." That heaviness had returned, but not with its familiar intensity. "About Mom and Dad." No wonder she was out of sorts.

"Oh, Eden." Simone held out her hands and, as Eden always did when Simone made the infrequent gesture, she took them. "Are you okay?"

"Yeah." Eden squeezed her fingers around Simone's. "For the first time, I think I am. It's still there. The panic. The fear. But something was different."

"That something being Cole, I'm betting." There was that sly look Eden had been waiting for. "Is that what's brought you to my office? Need a little of that advice you avoided last night?"

"He's…confusing." Eden wished she had Simone's talent for speaking. "Everything's getting so jumbled up. I need to pick your brain. Not that I don't love Allie to bits…" But what she didn't need was a therapy session. She also didn't need Allie telling her why she had commitment issues.

"Understood." Simone nodded. "She's testifying in that custody case today anyway. How about Giraldi's for lunch?"

"Really?" Eden whined and sounded like the eight-year-old brat Cole sometimes accused her of being. "They practically have a dress code and they look at me weird when I slurp my soup. How about Marvin's Burgers?"

"Not on a bet." Simone retrieved her purse—white and gold, of course—from her desk. "Let's make it Cavanaugh's. I can get a salad and you can scarf down one of those double-decker sandwiches you're so fond of."

"And wine?" Eden asked hopefully as Simone linked her arm through Eden's.

"Always wine. Kyla, we're headed out. I'll be back in time for that meeting with Jason at two thirty." Simone skidded to a halt in front of her assistant's desk. "What's that?"

"Oh, this was just delivered for you." Kyla picked up the basket of flowers and twirled it around. "Aren't they pretty?"

Eden felt the color drain from her face as she stared at the clusters of wild violets.

"Something wrong?" Kyla's brow furrowed.

"What does the card say?" Simone trembled as she gripped Eden's arm. "Who are they from?"

"I didn't read it." Kyla plucked at the envelope and pulled out a folded piece of petal-pink stationery. "It doesn't say. It just says 'happy anniversary.' Why would your ex-husband send you flowers now that you're divorced?"

"Vince never sent me flowers, anniversary or not. They're from someone else. Eden?" It took a lot to shake Simone, and right now, as she looked at the note card, it was as if she'd been cracked to her core. "Tell me not to think what I'm thinking, please."

"Maybe it's been delivered to the wrong person." Eden's fingers felt like they were burning as she touched the basket handle. "Kyla, would you call Woodnymph Florist to confirm and let us know? If that's the case, I'll drop them off after lunch." But that wouldn't be the case. Not with that note. Not with that message.

And not with those flowers.

And not with the lit candle in her basement.

She tucked the letter into the envelope and slipped it into the plastic holder in the basket.

"Yeah, sure." Kyla picked up the receiver. "Are you going to tell me—"

"Later." They hurried off, not saying a word until they were securely in the elevator. "That has to be a coincidence, right? We're overthinking this?" Simone breathed heavily as she braced a hand on the wall and looked at Eden, who swung the basket behind her. "A wrong delivery, or just—something else?"

"Maybe," Eden lied. An hour ago, even a half hour ago, she might have believed it. But now? "It could be one of those mistakes—"

"So close to…?" The grief Eden had seen in the mirror so frequently was reflected back at her in the face of her friend. "And that note card looks like… Oh, no." Simone sagged against the elevator wall. "It's been twenty years."

"Next month." Eden had to remember to breathe. First the candle, then the perfume, now the flowers. "Twenty years since Chloe's murder."

"I don't know how you say that so casually," Simone snapped, then blinked back a sudden rush of tears. "I'm sorry. Sometimes your ability to disconnect really infuriates me."

"Don't apologize, Simone. I'm me, remember? I compartmentalize and lock things up. I don't feel anything." Except Eden did feel. She felt everything. She remembered everything.

From the last time she heard Chloe laugh during their campout that night, to how Eden had whined when Chloe had asked Eden to go with her to the bathroom.

Eden had pouted, said no and gone back to sleep. Two days later they found Chloe's body.

In a field of violets.

Chapter 13

"Boy, you just don't realize how dreary a day is until you see something like that." Jack McTavish's chair squeaked as he let out a huff of approval. "Like an angel from heaven, I tell you. Brightens my day every time I lay eyes on her."

"Who?" Cole busily arranged the additional files Mona had sent over, the techno-medical jargon boggling his brain. The buzz of activity from his fellow officers and detectives was the white noise he needed to focus. He'd compile a list of doctors and see what, if any, commonalities the victims' blood had. Then, maybe, he'd bring Agent Simmons up to date. And throw him a bone by having him do a quick check on all those who'd commented on Eden's blog.

When Jack let out a low whistle, Cole glanced up. Eden and Simone were headed his way, Simone in one of her attention-grabbing white outfits, wearing a tasteful thin gold chain and heels sharp enough to pierce a man's heart. "Trust me, my friend. She's way out of your league. Did you two decide to take me to lunch?" Cole's teasing grin faltered when he noticed Simone's pallor rivaled her clothes, and still she had more color in her cheeks than Eden.

"What's wrong?" He looked down at the wicker basket of flowers Eden dropped on his desk. "What," he finally asked, "are those?"

"Those are flowers, man. Get with it." Jack joined them and reached for the card. "Secret admirer, Ms. Assistant DA?"

"I hope not," Simone muttered.

"Leave it be, Jack." Eden smacked his hand away. "It's evidence."

"Whoa, easy, Eden."

"Evidence of what?" Cole asked. What was she up to now? "What do you want me to do, send them down to the lab for fingerprint and DNA analysis? What's the deal, Simone?"

"Those were delivered to Simone's office a little while ago." Eden's voice sounded overly controlled, as if she couldn't trust herself to speak. "They're violets, Cole."

"Violets." Silence rang in his ears. He scrubbed his fingers across his forehead as if he could scrub away the past.

"And before you ask," Eden plowed on, "Kyla just texted us to let us know they didn't come from the florist listed on the envelope."

It took a long moment for the information to sink in. When it did, he looked at the basket, at the flowers. He shook his head, not wanting to think, not wanting to believe… "That could just be a—"

"Coincidence?" Eden interrupted. "We've been down

that road and we aren't buying it. Not when it's almost twenty years to the day. And not when the card—on stationery that looks like the type Simone used as a kid—says 'happy anniversary.'"

Eden crossed her arms over her chest, jaw set in that stubborn "no one is going to convince me I'm wrong" stance of hers. "It's him."

"Right now, it's a basket of flowers," Cole said even as a cold, sick feeling washed over him. He'd finally gotten through to her where the Iceman was concerned, or as much as he was going to. Adding *this* to the mix would only stir up an entirely new tempest. "And flowers don't prove anything other than someone has either a sick sense of humor or a bad sense of direction."

"We just told you they weren't delivered by mistake. What are you going to do about it?" Eden demanded.

"Someone want to fill me in?" Jack shifted from one foot to the other, the pretense and humor fading from his face. "Who's this Chloe you're talking about?"

"Chloe Evans." Cole kept his eyes on Eden as he answered his partner. "Nine-year-old girl found strangled in a field..."

"In a field of wild violets," Eden finished in a voice so tight he thought she might shatter. "Nice summary of the crime, Cole. Simple and succinct."

"Eden, don't." Simone placed that motherly hand of hers on Eden's arm.

"Yeah, Eden, don't." Cole's temper snapped. "You don't get the monopoly on grief where Chloe's concerned. She was my friend, too." To prove it, he yanked open his bottom desk drawer and pulled out the dog-eared file to hand to Jack. "Feel free to catch up." He rounded on Eden. "You really want to bring all this up again? With everything else going on? You're going to use a basket of flowers and a pink note card to push that pain to the surface?"

"You have to ask?" Eden shot back with something akin to hurt in her eyes. "There's no beneath the surface for us, Cole. The pain is always there. That man…that *murderer*, is why I do what I do. He made me."

"Why would you give Chloe's killer that much credit?" Cole demanded. "*You* made you and you did a good job of it, but just to remind you, we're already buried in one of your cases. You're good, Eden, but I don't think even you can juggle two killers at the same time."

"You asked me to stop going off on my own. You asked me to trust you," Eden said, her expression full of confusion. "I could have gone to Tammy, asked her to do it or to put me in contact with someone else who could. But I didn't. I came to you, Cole. I'm trying here, I really am. So are you going to help us or not?"

Wow—he'd lost this argument before it had even started.

"Simone?" Cole looked to his usual voice of reason. "Help me out. You want to dive into the deep end with her?"

"It's the absolute last thing I want to do." Simone fingered the tiny heart pendant she always wore. The pendant that once upon a time had belonged to Chloe. "But if we don't, I'll always wonder. If it'll help, I can have an official request from the DA within the hour."

He didn't need any paperwork. He needed a level head. He was weak enough when it came to Eden. No way could he withstand both of them coming at him. "You're that sure about this?"

"No, I'm not," Simone said. "That's the point."

"We should call Allie." Eden touched her hand to Simone's shoulder.

"And tell her what, exactly?" Cole could feel exhaustion creeping over him. "You don't know anything for certain at the moment except that your imagination is working overtime. The chance these flowers are connected to Chloe's murder is remote at best. Don't let your paranoia get ahead of you."

"It's not paranoia—it's logic. It's him, Cole."

He should just start naming his headaches Eden. "Why do you always jump to the absolute worst conclusion possible?"

"Because in my experience it's usually the right one."

"Fine." Cole snatched up the basket and headed toward the elevator. "It's not like we have anything else going on around here."

"I'm coming with you." Eden raced up behind him.

"I'll just stay here, then," Simone called. Cole glanced over his shoulder as he pushed the elevator button. Jack pulled a chair over to his desk for Simone and said something to her, earning a thin smile. Good. Jack was good with people; he could always put them at ease. Simone looked as if she could use a distraction right about now.

"I didn't mean to imply you don't care about Chloe," Eden said in that too-tight voice of hers.

"Could have fooled me." The elevator doors opened and they got in. "You know as well as I do this is probably some crackpot who's spent too much time reading your blog."

"I don't blog about Chloe. And who would have known about the stationery?"

Good to know there were some lines she didn't cross. "Pink isn't exactly a unique color, Eden. Maybe it's someone who's getting off taunting you and Simone about the anniversary. You've been in the headlines these last few days. Your past is bound to be mentioned, as is your friendship with Simone, and she's certainly made her share of enemies. It isn't out of the realm of possibility someone's jabbing at her by using this case."

She folded her arms across her chest and glared up at him. "Those flowers are from him. I know it."

"And Eden St. Claire is never wrong, is she?"

"Not about this." She jutted out her chin in that way that forced him to choose between arguing with her and kissing her. "Never about Chloe."

"Why can't you get panic attacks or a crisis of faith like normal people?" He stepped out of the elevator, Eden right on his heels. "This case, these cases, they're going to be the end of you, Eden." Why couldn't she see how obsessed she'd become? How much damage this did? He turned to face her before he pleaded, "Why can't you let it go?"

She didn't waver, didn't blink. If anything, her face turned to stone as her eyes hardened. "Are you going to reopen the case or not?"

"Reopen the—" Now he was the one who stared. "Eden, I can't reopen a case because Simone got a basket of violets." But he could inch closer to starting a new investigation if the lab found anything useful. Cole prided himself on knowing Eden better than she knew herself, but at this moment, she'd dropped a curtain around herself he couldn't pull open. He couldn't see, couldn't identify, but he knew, without a doubt, something was twisting inside of her that even she couldn't stop. "There's more to this than you're letting on. What aren't you telling me?"

She pursed her lips, as if keeping the words locked inside her. He could almost hear the words, hear her begging him to let the subject drop.

"Eden—" He pushed a little harder but she backed up a step.

"Run the tests, Cole. Or don't. I'll see you back at the boat."

He didn't know what struck him harder. The defeat in her voice or watching her walk away.

"LT." Cole knocked on the door frame of his boss's office after the final shift change of the day. "You wanted to see me?"

"Come on in." Santos waved him forward. "I swear if I'd known this much paperwork was involved with being head of a department, I'd have stayed in uniform. If Selena ever leaves me, she'll be able to claim the department as a respondent in the divorce papers." He slapped a file folder shut. His brows knit as Cole closed the door behind him. "How goes our vampire hunt?"

Cole smirked. "We're making progress. I've made copies of all of Eden's notes, and they're ready to go up on our boards in the conference room. Eden's working her way through the list of doctors Mona provided and I came across a number of support groups for patients with blood disorders."

"Speaking of Eden." Santos cleared his throat and leaned in. "Heard you had a bit of a row this afternoon." The lieutenant looked wary. "Everything okay with you two?"

"Honestly, I don't know." He settled into his seat. He knew he could trust his boss. "I can't decide if I want to debate her or..." How had he let her get this far under his skin?

"The *or* might be a more productive use of your time." Santos stretched and rolled his head against the back of his chair. "Test results came back, by the way," he said before Cole could think of a diplomatic response. "The ones you had Tammy run on that basket of flowers. Want to fill me in?"

So much for keeping this quiet. "Depends. Did she find anything?"

"Enough to make me worry." The lieutenant nudged a thin file toward him. "About you, anyway. We're both aware of how the Chloe Evans case has affected you in the past. Now isn't the time for you to go to the dark side, Cole." Santos's penetrating gaze was more effective than any lie detector on the market. "I need you on top of your game. You know that, which tells me you had a very good reason for requesting the tests. I also know how persuasive Eden can be. Especially when she wants something."

"It wasn't Eden," Cole said, hearing the defensiveness in his own voice. "It wasn't only Eden," he added at Santos's dismissive snort. "Simone did, too, and made it official. Yes, Eden was angry and forceful and demanding—"

"What else is new?"

"But Simone." Cole shook his head. "I remember that look from when she was a kid, Lieutenant. She was lost. And scared. Simone does not scare easily. And she doesn't cry wolf."

"And you? What did you think when you saw those flowers?"

That he'd been hurtled into a past that continued to haunt all of them. "Truthfully? I wanted those tests to prove them wrong. Someone's messing with them. Someone who knows their history." A stalker, an obsessive, they could manage. A child killer?

As far as Cole was concerned, there wasn't a more vile or evil creature roaming the earth.

"Well, whoever it is, they know the case," Santos said. "Your hunch about the soil samples was dead-on. They're a match to the field where Chloe was found."

Whatever reassurance the lieutenant's company had provided evaporated. Instead of rushing off, he pushed to his feet, walking the few steps to the window in an attempt to lose himself in the growing darkness of the city. "What now?"

"I've scheduled a meeting with Captain Montague in the morning." Santos's reference to his superior in the Office of Investigations offered both hope and dread for the coming weeks. "I'll fill him in on what's going on. Maybe give Simone a heads-up in case he wants to talk this over with her in her capacity as assistant DA before any decisions are made. But I want you to listen to me, Cole. However this shakes out, whatever happens down the road, I will back you up. I understand how you feel."

Cole clenched his jaw. Impossible. His lieutenant hadn't helped Chloe pound the heck out of a donkey piñata when she was six years old or hoisted her onto the ladder leading to the tree house in Allie's backyard. Or wondered every day if there was something he could have done to prevent the little girl's disappearance and murder.

"I was three weeks out of the academy when Chloe was killed." Lieutenant Santos continued, "I helped work the crime scene. I went with the lead detective to notify her parents and brothers. I remember what that case did to this city. While I'd love to lock up the creep who killed her, I'm not in any hurry to reopen those wounds."

"I want in," Cole said before he could think too long on it. "If it's reopened."

"Get in line," Santos said. "But for now you've got enough on your hands with the Iceman, Cole. Let me run with this for the moment. Let me shoulder it, and when and if something develops, I will let you know. But for now, put it as far out of your mind as you can."

"Yeah." Sure. No problem.

"Agent Simmons has been patient, but he's getting antsy again. He wants an update."

Right. "I'll give him a call first thing in the morning." He faced his boss. The lieutenant was right. He couldn't afford any distractions, not with Eden's life at stake. He needed to focus on the case.

And on her.

"Go home, Cole. Relax, talk to your girlfriend—"

"She's not my—"

"And you call *her* stubborn? I couldn't do this job without Selena." He knocked a knuckle against the photograph on his desk. "Knowing she understands this job, that she understands me, that she's waiting for me, even at—" he glanced at the clock above the door "—ten at night, ready to listen to me, or let me sulk, it's why I'm sane. Eden might be one of the most infuriating, demanding and aggravating people I've ever met in my life, but she gets you, Cole. And when the chips are down, I'm not the only one who will have your back. She will, too."

The sound of footsteps on the deck above woke Eden out of a fitful doze. She shot up on the sofa, sending the files on her lap sliding to the floor, eyes narrowed against the table lamp beside her.

"Cole?" She rubbed her eyes as his feet appeared on the ladder. "Is that you?"

"Sorry I'm late." He ducked inside and pulled the hatch closed. Instant warmth enveloped the cabin. "I wanted to get my desk cleared and I had a meeting with the lieutenant. Plus—" he held out a shiny new manila folder "—I was waiting for this."

Eden bit her lip and accepted the results. He'd run the tests.

If he cared about the mess she'd made of his boat—dozens upon dozens of notes, photographs and reports taped to the walls, stacks of miscellaneous bits of information all over the table and floor—he didn't say. Instead he headed for the fridge and grabbed a beer.

Eden looked down at the file, the thank-you stuck in her throat. "Did Tammy find anything?"

"No prints, not even a partial. No DNA or prints on the note or envelope, either." He took a long drink and leaned his arms on the kitchen counter.

"So you were right." She'd been so sure. Especially with what had happened at the newsstand.

Or she'd been paranoid. Just as Cole had suggested.

"She also ran the dirt samples from the flowers themselves." He cringed, as if the beer had slit his tongue. "The soil content is identical to the readings from the field where Chloe was found."

"How would she—"

"Because I drove out there and collected a sample this afternoon."

Eden closed her eyes so tight she saw stars. She should have known he wouldn't let her flounder out there on the edge alone. "So what now?"

"It's not conclusive enough to reopen the case. But it's got the lieutenant's and the DA's attention. The latter probably due to Simone."

"You told her about the results?" So if they weren't reopening the case, what were they doing?

"She waited for a while, but I called her when I was driving home. Nice of you to leave her behind, Eden. How did you get back, by the way?"

"Bowie drove me. He was coming off shift." Nausea rolled in her stomach. "And I told you I'm a rotten friend." A friend who wasn't sure Simone or Cole would believe her about the perfume. She'd sounded crazy enough for one day, hadn't she?

"You're lucky Simone isn't."

Luck had nothing to do with it. "So what happens now?"

"Now we leave it in my lieutenant's hands and focus on the Iceman." He took a deep breath and stood up straight, as if he expected her to argue. "I know how important this is, Eden. I'm not going to let it go. I need you to believe me."

Anyone else, she might not have. "The Iceman first," she said softly with a nod. As determined as she was to track down her friend's killer, Chloe didn't deserve any less than Eden's best. And that would only come once they closed the book once and for all on the Iceman.

"Figured out who the Iceman is yet?" Cole asked with what she could tell was forced humor. "Tell me my boat hasn't been sacrificed in vain."

Was that a tease or a taunt? Or a distraction? "Before we get into all that, there's something I'd like your opinion on." She retrieved her laptop from the kitchen table and passed it to him. "It's my blog post for tomorrow. I'm not asking your permission, but I wanted you to be aware of what I was doing before I did it."

"And you're going to do it whether I approve or not. Never mind." He held up his hand in surrender. "Let me read it and we'll go from there."

"Why don't I fix you something to eat while you read."

He eyed her with suspicion. "You don't cook."

"I can make a sandwich and open a bag of chips." More than one, as evidenced by empty bags in the trash.

Her iron levels might be normal, but she'd bet her sodium was sky-high. "Besides, it's after ten and I'm betting you haven't eaten anything."

"I had a candy bar from the vending machine."

She didn't care for this new way they had of interacting, as if both of them were walking on eggshells.

She missed her friend. She missed the Cole she could tease or goad without wondering if her words were destroying their relationship, whatever relationship they had. But she also couldn't stop thinking about the possibilities he'd talked about this morning. Or how he'd made her feel last night. What if she was missing out on something that could be...what she never thought she could have?

"Ham and cheese okay?" She moved around him as he settled down at the table.

"Sounds great, thanks." He was already reading, his eyes flying side to side as if he were gobbling up her words.

"I'm not walking away from the case," she said as if what she'd written weren't clear enough. "I'm not letting him scare me off. I can't. Not if I want to be an effective voice for victims and their families who think they've been forgotten."

Cole held up a finger. "Reading, here."

"He needs to know I'm still onto him. That I'm going to use whatever and whoever I have to in order to stop him. I didn't put anything in there about the blood or Mona's tests—"

"This will go faster if you stop talking."

She almost ripped the plastic zip-top bag apart. Would he pick up on the fact that she agreed with what he'd said? Or what she'd been doing since she'd left his office?

Hence the wallpaper job she'd done on Cole's boat. She had a plan of action now, beginning with what would probably amount to a tour of every medical facility in the city. Good thing her hospital paranoia had ebbed in the last couple of days.

She set his sandwich on a plate, added a handful of his favorite multigrain chips and placed it on the counter beside him on top of her files.

He looked at her, that unfamiliar expression on his face making her stomach do a combination somersault. "Well?"

"It's good." He nodded, a slow approving smile stretching across his lips. "It's colder than your regular posts. More determined, detached even. Focused. It's like you're speaking directly to him."

"I am." And here she thought he was going to blow his last gasket over this. "You're not mad?"

"Mad? No. Concerned? Always. What you allude to will only make him guess and question what you plan for him, which should keep him off his game. He already messed up once coming after you. There's a chance he might again."

"Something I'm ready for." It was a risk, but she'd rather he come after her than another innocent victim. "And it'll be good timing since the *Tribune* is going to run the first feature of my blog in the morning."

"Something *we're* ready for. I had a feeling you were going to do something like this, especially after what happened today with those flowers. Which is why starting tomorrow, you're going to have police protection around the clock."

"I have police protection. I have you."

"Let's just say I think my judgment where you're concerned might be a bit cloudy these days. I need some more objective eyes on you. For my own peace of mind."

"Even if it drives me out of mine?" She didn't like the idea of being followed. By anyone.

"You won't even know they're there," Cole said. "This is nonnegotiable, Eden. You post this tomorrow, that's the price you pay. You're putting an even bigger target on your back, not only for the Iceman, but for whoever is playing with you and Simone."

"Are you giving her an armed escort, too? What about Allie?"

"We can talk to her tomorrow, see if she's noticed anything strange."

"Like weird flower deliveries? She'd have told us."

"She's also been testifying in court all day. Simone rarely leaves her office, but there will be a couple of officers assigned to watch her apartment, as well. We'll also talk to the security team in the building. Not that she's any happier about it than you are. We want to keep things under wraps for now. Until we see what else develops."

"Yeah." She swallowed hard. "Yeah, I understand."

"You do?"

"You ran the tests, Cole." And her heart tipped slightly. "You're willing to pursue whatever this is. I'll follow your lead." Unless he stopped leading. But that was a decision for another day.

"I appreciate that. Whether I'm happy about what's going on or not, the truth is, if you hadn't taunted the Iceman the way you did, we wouldn't have these new leads to follow." He grimaced as he scanned his once-beautiful wood room. "And the sooner we get this case solved, the sooner we can focus on other things."

Other things. "If you're trying to keep me confused

and off guard, you're succeeding." Why wasn't she fighting him? Why wasn't she angry? Why...?

Why wasn't she running like a scared jackrabbit the second he stood up and walked over to her?

She backed up until she'd wedged herself into the corner, nowhere to go, nowhere to direct her gaze other than at Cole as he looked her straight in the eye.

"What you do has value, Eden. I realized today I've never made it a point to tell you that. The truth is, you're good at what you do despite the recklessness. It also makes me furious that you don't give yourself the credit you deserve."

"Ah." She nodded and tried to duck her head, but he caught her chin with his finger. "This is because of what I said about Chloe's killer, isn't it?"

"That depends. Are you still clinging to the ridiculous idea he's responsible for what you've made of your life? Does that mean he made me a cop or Allie a psychologist?"

"No. Yes." She frowned. "I don't—"

"What he did do was change our lives." Cole continued, "He changed all our lives in a brutal, inhuman, cruel way. None of us has been the same since Chloe died, but don't give him credit he doesn't deserve. Don't give away what and who you are because of someone else's actions. You've been fighting for Chloe and every other victim you've come across ever since. That was all you. Not him."

"There's a *but* in here, I know it."

"There's going to be a price to pay, Eden. None of us is going to come out of this clean. Please, please don't take any more chances than necessary. You trusted me today, you came to me first with those flowers, and I can't tell you what a relief that is. It's like you've finally heard what I've been telling you all these years."

"Yeah, well, a girl can only take so much before she has to admit she's wrong." She nibbled on the corner of her lip, her eyes widening as his gaze fell to her mouth. Finally, she understood what he'd been saying this morning, about him wanting more than just fun-time sex. And yeah, okay, that was what she'd called it for the better part of the day, but at this moment, she knew what he was asking for. He didn't just want her body. He wanted all of her. Her mind, her emotions. Her soul.

How did she know? Because she wanted the same from him.

She lifted her hands and captured his face in her palms, a battle between reason and desire waging inside of her. "Please don't push this anymore today." She pressed her forehead to his and closed her eyes. "I need to think—"

"Instead of just feel?" He moved in and up, breaking contact with her hands even as his lower body shifted hot and hard against her. "Imagine what will happen when the two of us are on the same page." He wrapped his arms around her and held her close, the sound of his heart pounding against her ear soothing her frayed nerves. "How about I eat my dinner before it gets cold and you can fill me in on what you've found."

"Sandwiches don't get cold." But she smiled anyway.

"Not around me they won't." He brushed a kiss across her cheek and released her. "Now let's catch this guy before he finds his next target."

"Detective Delaney? Ms. St. Claire? I'm sorry to keep you waiting. I'm Dr. Avery Tanner."

Eden stuffed the brochure for the Sanguinem Clinic

into her bag as Cole returned the curvy brunette's enthusiastic greeting. For a medical facility, the abundance of color was a nice change, as were the overstuffed chairs and cubby spaces designed exclusively for children's entertainment. Eden never would have imagined so many people being affected by blood disorders, yet apparently there were enough to keep a steady stream of employees, not to mention patients, milling about the first-floor waiting area.

"Thank you for being willing to answer our questions, Doctor," Cole said. "Yours is the fourth facility we've visited today, so we hope not to take up too much of your time."

"Not at all. I was just finishing up in the lab." Dr. Tanner stuffed chubby fingers into the pockets of her lab coat and smiled at Eden. "My apologies for the less-than-formal attire. Sometimes I live in scrubs. How may I be of help?"

"We're looking into the deaths of a couple of your former patients," Eden said. "Callie Woodrow and Nathaniel Hoffstead."

"Oh, yes, of course. I should have realized." She motioned for them to follow her up the curving staircase, her thick plastic shoes squeaking slightly against the metal.

"Those look comfortable." Something niggled along the edges of her mind.

"They're called Gators," Dr. Tanner said over her shoulder. "And they're a godsend for anyone who spends a lot of time on their feet. Not very attractive, I know." She kicked her foot up as if to confirm their bulky detour from fashion acceptability. "But at least they make them in more neutral colors. I had a heck of a time matching my neon pink or green ones to anything in my closet."

Eden slipped her phone out of her bag. Once Dr. Tanner resumed leading them down the hall, she snapped a picture of the doctor's shoes.

Cole arched a brow at her.

"Tell you later," she mouthed.

"Obviously Dr. Hendrix got the copies of the files we sent to the coroner's office," Dr. Tanner said. "We were all in shock to hear, of course. I can't believe one let alone two of our patients were killed by this Iceman person."

Neither could Cole and Eden, which was why they'd included the clinic located in the suburb of Rancho Cordova on their inquiry list. "What disorders do you treat here, exactly?" Their footfalls were muted by the multicolored carpeting, which also lessened the dulcet tones of medical monitors beeping in the distance.

"We deal with a variety of illnesses and conditions, actually. Please." She pushed open a thick glass door and ushered them into a spacious, sterile office overlooking a landscaped water-and-rock garden toward the far end of the property. She sat behind her desk and tapped on her computer. "I assume since you're here you've already been through Callie's file and Nathaniel's. Ah, here we go." She skimmed the screen. "Okay, yes, all caught up now. We last saw Callie— Oh, my. Less than a week before she was reported missing. And Nathaniel." She clicked open another window. "A bit longer than that. We'd actually managed to stabilize his iron levels, so we pushed his appointments to every other month."

"And what did those appointments consist of, exactly?" Cole asked.

Dr. Tanner frowned. "I'm not sure I'm at liberty—"

"We aren't asking for test results, Doctor." Cole kept his voice friendly as Eden struggled to let him take the lead. "We're hoping to figure out how your two patients were targeted by their killer."

"Yes, of course. I'm sorry. We would have run a battery of tests, of course, beginning with a ferritin test, which evaluates the amount of iron stored in the patient's systems. We'd also run a transferrin test—a protein which is formed in the liver and carries the iron through the bloodstream. We'd then follow with a TIBC to test for the protein that transports iron in the system, and then we examine the saturation levels, which helps us determine whether there's been organ damage."

"These are the tests you perform on all your patients with elevated iron levels?" Eden asked. "And they helped determine the treatment needed?"

"Yes. We found frequent blood donation for Callie helped lower her numbers significantly, so we monitored that and helped her find a place close to her home to make it easier to fit into her work schedule."

Eden's ears prickled. Dr. Tanner was the third person they'd spoken to today to mention blood donation.

"Does blood type figure in to the frequency of an occurrence of DIOS?" Eden asked.

"Not that we know of, no." Dr. Tanner shook her head and folded her hands together on her überorganized desk. Eden would bet she used a ruler to keep that collection of pens in line. "Did Dr. Hendrix find any commonality in that regard?"

"According to her notes, all of the victims were all negative blood types with excessive iron levels," Cole said. "We're trying to ascertain who would have access to that type of patient information. Ms. Woodrow or Mr. Hoffstead, for example. Did they see the same medical professionals every time?"

"They each had their own doctor." She glanced at her computer. "But I see a number of the same nurse practitioners and lab techs listed on their records."

"And all of them would have had access to their lab results?" Cole asked.

"As would anyone with access to our computer systems. I can get you a list of employees if that would help, but I can't imagine anyone on our staff being connected to these killings. We save lives here, try to make their lives and health better. No one has any interest in harming people."

"You'd be surprised what people can hide," Eden said.

Dr. Tanner's frown increased. Cole knocked his foot against Eden's in his silent way of telling her to ease up.

"I certainly hope you leveled these accusations at the other facilities on your list." The open friendliness dimmed in Dr. Tanner's dark eyes.

"Absolutely," Cole assured her. "They've been quite cooperative in getting us what we've asked for. Finding out who killed these people is important, but not as important as finding him before he kills again. We also plan on visiting a number of support groups that meet in the area. I understand you sponsor a number of those, as well."

"Yes, we do." Dr. Tanner's fingers clenched as her lips thinned. "Blood diseases can affect every aspect of a patient's life, and coming to terms with a chronic illness isn't easy. Learning how to cope with those symptoms can go a long way to making day-to-day living less stressful."

"But there are cases where that's not possible, isn't that correct?" Eden said. "Where managing these illnesses becomes more difficult."

"That's correct. Not all the illnesses we deal with are treatable. But most can be managed if not made more tolerable with recent advances. Medications, treatments, procedures—nothing's off the table. There have been rumors about experimental treatments attempting to prove the theory that removing a patient's spleen might help reset a patient's blood enzyme levels."

"Organ removal?" Cole shifted forward in his chair as Eden's breath caught. "That seems a bit extreme. Is that something that's common practice?"

"We never made it to the trial stages, I'm afraid. There are some experiments that are too radical to implement without putting a clinic at risk of violating medical ethics, which could result in closure."

"Would you be able to put us in touch with any of the doctors who worked on that theory?" Cole asked.

"Ah, yes, I suppose I could. May I get that information to you later? I just want to run this by our legal department."

"Absolutely," Cole said. "And the employee records, as well?"

"Certainly." Dr. Tanner stood. "Was there anything else I can help you with?"

"I'm sorry—I do have another question," Eden said. "What kind of training would someone have to have in order to determine someone's blood type?"

"Most first-year medical or laboratory tech students would have the training as well as access to the equipment needed. The antibodies would probably be the most difficult to come by if the person isn't in the medical profession. Other than that, a microscope and blood technician supplies would be plenty."

Yet another needle in the haystack, Eden thought. "Thank you, Doctor. We'll leave you to your patients."

"I do hope you catch him, this Iceman. The *Tribune* this morning implied whoever is responsible might be stealing his victims' blood. If that's true, even if he thinks he's doing it for some noble purpose, he's causing more damage than he realizes." Dr. Tanner walked them to the door. "It's difficult enough getting people to donate and help fund research. We certainly don't need someone driving potential contributors away."

"I can't comment on what the papers are saying," Cole said, angling an irritated look in Eden's direction. As if she could control what her fellow reporters did. "That information we requested will go a long way, Dr. Tanner. Thank you again." Cole placed his hand on the base of Eden's spine and guided her downstairs.

"I don't know about you, but I'm about ready to take my MCAT," Eden told him.

"Give me a second." He headed over to the reception desk and turned on that million-watt smile of his, which had the expected effect on the very young, very blonde, very busty woman behind the counter. A few murmured phrases later, Cole winked—actually *winked*—and tapped his knuckles on the countertop before he rejoined Eden. "Misty over there—"

"Misty?" Eden rolled her eyes. "You have got to be kidding me."

Cole grinned. "I never noticed how lovely that particular shade of green looks on you." He surprised her by slipping an arm around her waist and steering her out the front door to the parking lot. "Misty is going to provide me with a list of their volunteers and lab students who are getting their hours in for medical school."

"More names to add to our growing list." Eden foresaw a long night ahead. "This was the last clinic on our list for today. Back to the boat?"

"To the station," Cole corrected her as they reached his car. "Time to report in to the FBI. Hopefully we've made enough progress to keep them off our butts for another few days."

"From your lips," Eden said. "Agent Simmons is all yours. I've got some shopping to do."

Chapter 14

"I thought being abducted by a serial killer would make you more attuned to your surroundings," Allie's voice whispered in her ear.

Eden yelped and spun in her desk chair, the pencil she'd been chewing on dropping out of her mouth. She pressed a hand against her racing heart and smacked her friend's arm with the other. "What are you trying to do, scare whatever lives I have left out of me?"

Allie chuckled and set her purse down on Eden's—or rather Bowie's—desk. "Sorry. Couldn't resist. Ugh." She braced her hands on the desk and peered into the screen. "Sweetie, I know you're fashion challenged, but even you can't be this out of touch. Those shoes are hideous. If you're planning on buying a pair, we need a serious intervention."

"Says the woman who dresses like an Easter egg," Eden teased.

"Bright colors help me deal with the darkness of the human condition," Allie said, reciting her usual platitude. "What's up with the Gators?"

"The number one choice for footwear of medical personnel, according to their website." Eden clicked through the surprising array of colors and glanced at her friend. "They might also be a favorite of our number one vampire. That regression thing you did on me the other night… I remember lying on the ground and staring at his shoes. Weird, clunky shoes." She clicked on the navy blue option. "These beauties."

"You're thinking he's in the medical profession." Allie pushed Eden aside and clicked through the website.

"It's looking that way." Eden leaned over to catch a glimpse of Cole in the lieutenant's office along with Agent Simmons, who was looking more haggard than the last time she'd seen him. "Cole and I spent all day talking to doctors and administrators about our victims. Between the blood references, the supplies needed and the knowledge necessary, he's had training. I'm convinced of it."

"How about instead of bouncing in your chair like an overexcited five-year-old, you get your butt in there and help Cole keep the case?" Allie jerked her head toward the office.

"What are you talking about?" Eden frowned, her gaze moving from Lieutenant Santos standing with his hands on his hips, to Agent Simmons, to Cole just as he slapped a file onto his boss's desk. "You think that's what's going on?"

"Body language, raised voices—and I believe that's Agent Anthony Simmons, isn't it?" Allie pulled out her phone. "That's interesting."

"Is it? I don't hear anything." But the second the words were out of her mouth she heard Cole let loose a string of expletives that never should belong together. "How do you do that?" She shooed Allie away from the computer and returned to her screen, hit Print and waited for the pages to emerge from the printer across the room. "You must have supersonic hearing. What are you doing here, anyway?"

"I read your blog this morning. Doesn't make me worry about you at all," Allie said, as she made a call.

The blog. How could she forget? "It was Cole approved, in case you were wondering."

"I was, actually. Given the responses I've read on the page, might I suggest you take a look. It seems your fan base is salivating. Hang on." She held up a finger. "Hey there, Fitz. It's Allie Hollister... Yeah." She grinned and a hint of pink tinged her cheeks. "I've got something to ask you. Just a minute." Allie pressed her phone to her chest and blinked at Eden. "What?"

"You usually call me when you have observations to share." Or text, which Eden vastly preferred. Texts were so much quicker to delete and forget.

"I don't like finding out thirdhand my friends are being stalked." Allie lowered herself into Eden's abandoned chair and crossed her legs, the rainbow yellow skirt tightening around her knees. "But we can talk about flower deliveries later. Go on." Now she was the one who did the shooing. "Go rescue your man before he gets himself arrested for assaulting a federal officer."

"He's not my man." Had she really said that through gritted teeth?

"Don't lie to a shrink. It only makes us think you're hiding something. Oh, great. Your case notes." Allie flipped open the top folder on the notes Eden had brought with her from the boat before rejoining her call. "I'm back, Fitz. Uh-huh, it's good to hear your voice, too. I'm hoping you can help me with something." She stuck a manicured finger into her mouth and settled into Eden's research and her conversation.

Eden's muttering to herself almost blocked out the sound of Agent Simmons's anger blasting through the door. "...about time you had some concrete evidence proving you're making progress—"

Eden knew that tone. The FBI was about to drop the hammer on Cole and his fellow cops.

She knocked on the glass window twice before pushing the door open. "I'd apologize for interrupting, but seeing as you're sharing your conversation with the rest of us anyway..." She pointed over her shoulder to where she knew the other detectives and officers in the squad weren't even attempting to hide their eavesdropping. She looked at Cole. "You were right. He's in the medical profession."

He'd never come out and said it, certainly not in the various doctors' offices or even to her, but she was beginning to understand how his mind worked. He wasn't going to utter the words until they—until he—had proof.

She wasn't sure what she saw flash in his eyes: gratitude? Surprise? Relief. She gladly accepted all three as she held out the printout.

"You're sure?" Cole asked.

"It's the only thing that makes sense." Without addressing Agent Simmons directly, she made her case. "Mona's report alludes to a killer who is precise in what he does. The first three victims' organs were removed, but the cuts and wounds weren't sloppy or erratic. Steady hand despite the carnage. All of the victims had similar blood types as well as similar blood conditions, meaning our guy knows how to test for both or at the very least has access to their patient information. We've speculated he's experimenting on his victims, something that Dr. Tanner mentioned when we spoke to her. And now this."

"And now what?" Agent Simmons held out his hand for the paper in Cole's hand.

"The other night I went back to the parking lot and did a regression exercise to try to remember what happened when I was abducted."

"You did what?" Lieutenant Santos turned weary eyes on Cole. "She did what?"

"Don't even ask," Cole murmured. His entire body seemed to relax as he backed up and sat on the edge of the windowsill, crossed his arms over his chest and gave her the floor. "Go on, Eden."

"I saw his shoes. I didn't remember exactly what bothered me about them until we saw dozens of lab techs and doctors wearing the same ones in the facilities we visited today."

"So because he was wearing a certain kind of shoe, you assume he's in the medical field."

Eden's nerves caught fire. Could he sound any more condescending?

"Looking at the files, I'd draw the same conclusion." Allie spoke from the doorway, open file in her hand as she flipped through the pages. "Agent Simmons, correct?" She extended her hand and slipped on that mask of professional detachment that always astonished Eden. "Dr. Allie Hollister. I'm a consulting psychologist with the Sacramento Police Department. I had the pleasure of working with Agent Fitzroy last year on the Corwin murder case."

Agent Simmons shifted on his feet.

"The killings of yacht owners up and down the Eastern Seaboard?" Eden frowned. That case had garnered national attention. "I didn't know you consulted on that."

"I offered a profile of the killer." Allie shrugged as if she'd passed along her grandmother's Bolognese recipe. "He had a thing about water and small spaces."

"See?" Eden looked over at Cole. "I told you. Boats and killers. Classic combination."

"Eden." Cole shook his head, quickly deflating her humor given the sullen feeling in the room.

"I'm going to concur with Eden and Cole's evaluation on our killer," Allie told the lieutenant and Agent Simmons. "Though I've only had a few minutes with the information—"

"Try five," Eden mumbled.

"Eidetic memory and speed-reader, remember?" Allie turned on that oh-so-charming smile she was known for. "I agree the evidence is pointing to someone involved, either currently or at least recently, in the medical profession. Shoes aside, it's clear he has some skill when it comes to medical procedures. The sedatives administered were the right dosages—not one overdose of medication, not even on the first three victims, which in theory would have been his learning curve. The wounds inflicted were clean and precise. He took care with them. Like a doctor would with his patient."

"You're saying he cares about them?" Agent Simmons scoffed.

"I'm saying he cares about something. Probably about someone. Whether that person is alive or dead, I can't say. He's a caretaker. He's…protective. What he's doing has a purpose, a purpose he's deemed more important than these people's lives. And Eden, when she called him out in the reckless and careless way she did on her blog—"

"All I did was call him a—"

"It doesn't bear repeating." Allie leaned her shoulder

against the filing cabinet beside her as she pinned her attention on Agent Simmons. "What he's doing is important to him. For what reason we don't know. Yet. But she made fun of him, made light of his cause. Reduced him to nothing more than a stereotypical killer, when that is quite far from the truth. He punished you, Eden, because you devalued what he's doing. And he left you with the evidence of his work. But by doing so, he's inadvertently given you everything you need to catch him."

"We still don't know what he's doing," Agent Simmons countered.

"Cole and his team have the information they need to figure that out. They've got an abundance of data to cross-reference now. I'd bet in another couple of days they'll have a list of suspects that will be more than manageable. He won't be a loner," Allie continued. "He'll have or will have had family. He's sociable because it takes an open personality to be able to approach his victims. Friendly. Unassuming. He won't be overly attractive—he won't stand out. He'll be quite average looking. Enough to blend in with a crowd."

"I think we've found another consultant for the case," Cole said. "Unless, Agent Simmons, you'd like to move forward with your formal request to take over things officially."

"I doubt Agent Simmons will be doing that." Allie stunned the room into silence. "I thought your name sounded familiar, so I did some checking." She pulled the second file folder free and handed it to Eden. "Denise Pageant. The Iceman's third victim. Under 'known family.'"

Eden scanned down the information. Parents, deceased. Husband, Raymond. Siblings… Her head shot up. "Denise Pageant was your sister."

"What?" Cole was by her side in an instant as Agent Simmons shifted into military attention. "You've been playing us?"

Eden placed her hand on his arm, trying to see past Simmons's obvious grief.

"I never meant to interfere in the case." Agent Simmons took a deep breath and dropped his head back. "And I'm not going to apologize. I asked to be assigned to the Northern California office last year, so I could be close by in case Denise's killer reemerged. I hadn't planned to do anything but keep tabs on the investigation, but when I saw a reporter had become involved, had become the center of the entire case, I couldn't help but think you were going to damage whatever progress there had been."

"So your superiors are unaware of your involvement?" Lieutenant Santos asked.

"I told them you'd requested my advice." Agent Simmons flinched. "I— You need to understand. Denise's death devastated my parents. They were gone within months of her murder. And Denise's husband..." He shook his head. "I can't even talk to him about what happened. They'd only been married a couple of years. Had started talking about having a baby, something she'd always been cautious about because of her medical condition."

"The elevated iron levels," Eden said. "One of the effects is infertility."

"Her doctor recommended donating blood on a regular basis, to try to get those numbers under control along with medication. The last time I talked to her, it was working."

And then all of Denise's dreams for the future were dead. Along with her.

"Donations again."

Eden nodded at Cole's under-the-breath comment.

"So what was this just now?" Lieutenant Santos demanded. "This threat that we turn this investigation over to you."

"It was just that," Agent Simmons said. "A threat. I don't have any jurisdiction. I just want to find the monster who killed my sister." He twisted his wedding band on his finger. "I want him to pay for everything he took from my family, from all the other victims. I just haven't been able to get a foothold strong enough to try for the case."

"This is what destroyed your marriage, isn't it?" Eden asked. "The other day when we spoke, this is what you were talking about."

"Letting go isn't my strong suit."

"Then I suggest you put it to good use." Allie slapped her hands together and made everyone jump. "Cole, Eden, you two need all the help you can get at this point. Agent Simmons needs to do something proactive. Plus, he's got resources that might make your cross-analysis go even faster. So, work together. The sooner you close this case, the sooner all of you—" she paused and aimed a knowing gaze at Eden "—can get on with your lives. Problem solved?"

"Uh—" Lieutenant Santos cleared his throat.

"You know if you'd told us the truth from the start, we'd have let you in," Cole said. "We all would have understood."

"I couldn't take the chance," Agent Simmons said. "I had hope, though. The other day, Eden, when I realized you weren't doing this for a headline or a byline."

"At least now we know where we all stand." There was still hesitancy in Cole's voice, however.

"Great." Allie snapped out of professional mode. "Eden, I'd like a word, please. Gentlemen, let me know if I can be of further assistance. And don't worry, I won't bill you for the time."

Eden handed the file over to Cole and followed her friend back into the bull pen. "I so owe you," she said as Allie retrieved her purse.

"You bet you do. And I'm cashing in tonight. You and Cole need a break, so dinner is on me at Casa Brunetta. You're both wound so tight your corks are going to pop."

"We can't," Eden argued. "We've got way too much information to compile—"

"And I just found you your backup. Agent Simmons in there is going to want to make up for his deception, so trust me, he'll be working double overtime to help you out. Which gives you and Cole and Simone free rein to remember you're still human, not to mention alive. Doctor's orders." Allie took a long, deep breath. "And you know not to argue with your doctor."

Why did Eden suddenly have the feeling she and Cole weren't the only ones who needed some decompression time? "Okay. Cole and I would be happy to go."

"Go where?" Cole asked as he joined them at the desk.

"Dinner. Tonight. Eden will fill you in. Thanks." She gave Eden a hug, squeezed her hand on Cole's arm before she left.

"You're like a college senior during finals." Cole stopped at a red light and reached over to flip the folder in Eden's lap closed. "You have to give the information time to sink in."

"I can't help thinking the answer is right in front of us."

"Which answer?" Cole went one step further and took the stack of folders from her, then set it behind him on the floor of the SUV. The light changed and he turned left onto Folsom Boulevard. She'd snagged copies of photographs they'd taken in the first victims' homes. Something they were working on acquiring from the most recent group of bodies found, since some had been missing upwards of three months and some, like Eric DeFornio, had been essentially homeless.

"The how of it all." She tapped a finger against her temple. "I feel like it's in here. If I can just puzzle that piece out, the why might present itself."

"We may never know that. How about we talk about something else?" As if getting her off her favorite topic was going to be so easy. "What about a weekend in San Francisco when all this is over?" He had to try.

"No one sees him take these people. It's like he waves a magic wand and they disappear into his lair." She rested her elbow on the door and chewed on her thumbnail before she snapped to attention. "What did you say?"

"You heard me. You, me, a long weekend. Human contact. Connection." He grinned. "Room service."

"You want to talk about this now?"

"I'd like to talk about anything for five minutes that doesn't include blood, serial killers or organ removal."

"I haven't been that bad." She tilted her head. "Have I?"

Giving her any answer would only lead to an argument he didn't want to have. "Does that mean San Francisco looks good to you?"

"San Francisco always looks good to me." She cringed before she glanced out the window. "Do you think that's a good idea?"

He knew what she was really asking. Was that taking things too far, too fast? Did he honestly want to move ahead with what passed for a relationship for both of them? It was probably a bad idea, but one he hadn't been able to get out of his head for longer than he cared to remember. After all these years, after all his gentle nudging, prodding and hinting, maybe it was time to finally go for it. And take her with him. "I think it's a great idea."

"After the case is closed, though. After we get him." The accusation in her eyes told him she needed verbal confirmation that he understood where her priorities were.

Sadly, he did. "After we get him."

"Fine. It's a date."

"Be still, my heart." At least it was progress. Kind of. "There's nothing more we can do, you know? We're making headway on cross-checking the information from the blood centers, but those shoes might end up causing more problems than we anticipated. If they only did internet sales it would be one thing—"

Eden huffed and, now that they were back to talking about the case, she smiled at him. "Thankfully they offer wholesale items to only two uniform chains in California."

"And in three other states," Cole reminded her. "It was a good lead, Eden. It's just going to take a while."

"But if we could figure out what triggers him to which people, we'd have a time frame to work with."

"Yeah, nothing cops love more than dealing with a ticking bomb."

"They call them 'deadlines' for a reason." She leaned over and checked the clock on the dashboard. "We're going to be late."

"Ten minutes, max. I've texted Allie to let her know. They already commandeered a table in the back. It'll be fine, Eden. Agent Simmons said he'll bring the night shift up to date. They'll pick up where my other officers and Jack left off. We should have some solid ideas by the morning, and if we don't, then we've got that list of support groups to start vetting."

"In the meantime, he's probably circling his next victim."

"Or not. We can't know for sure, and worrying about something you can't change one way or the other isn't going to do anyone any good." Least of all her.

"They were all taken in the evening, after dark, near as we've been able to tell, right?"

"Correct," he replied.

"And people's guards are up even more in the evening, so he'd have to approach them in such a way as to not alarm them."

"True."

"What kind of medical professionals are out at night, Cole? EMTs, firefighters, police—"

"He's not a cop," Cole snapped.

"Brainstorming here, not accusing," Eden said, waving his comment aside. She should have known he'd take exception to that idea. "Doctors, nurses, who work in clinics, in neighborhoods as well as hospitals. We probably need to expand our searches beyond blood clinics."

"You get to be the one to tell Simmons, then."

"Already on it." Eden reached over and grabbed her purse off the floorboard. She slammed her hand on the dashboard and gasped. "Cole, stop!"

His foot hit the brake before his mind caught up. Tires and brakes squealed behind him, horns blared and cars darted out of the lane to avoid crashing. "What's happened?" Cole scanned the street. "Did I almost hit someone?"

"No, no. Turn at the corner." She waved him over as if directing traffic, bouncing in her seat. The second he pulled into a shortened space, she was out of the car like a shot, her phone in her hand as she raced to the corner.

As part of him wished he'd left her back at the station, Cole turned off the engine and hurried after her.

"I know that look." He came up beside her as she aimed her camera phone at the billboard overhead. "You're having one of your eureka moments, aren't you?"

She pointed up. "We need to go over all the victims' schedules again for the months before their deaths. When we do, I bet we'll find they did have something in common after all."

Cole looked up at the billboard advertising the city's upcoming fund-raiser and…

"A blood drive." He blinked, dropped an arm around Eden's shoulders and squeezed. "Uh-huh, we know—"

"A lot of blood drives these days are run out of mobile units. Those vehicles come to you." She nodded at him. "And they're everywhere."

"The drinks are on me tonight," Eden said as she slid into one of the chairs across from Allie and Simone. "Well, hey there, Jack." She knocked her shoulder against his and grinned. "I didn't know you were joining us."

He toasted her with his drink. "Simone thought I needed a night out."

"Did she?" Eden's grin widened.

"We all needed a night out, according to Allie," Simone said, sending Jack a sly-enough look that Eden's relationship radar began to blip.

"Sorry we're late," she said to Allie. "I never get tired of this place." Owned by a local celebrity chef, the Italian-inspired restaurant was both sophisticated and welcoming. She wondered how long she could resist the call of fresh-baked focaccia and the little crock of garlic-infused butter.

Sparkling white architectural accents offset the muted yellow of the walls. Brass sconces and a collection of large potted palms in the center of the dining room added a fresh and softened atmosphere. Between the friendly service, exceptional menu selection and the promise of wine and friends, Eden couldn't dream of a better way to spend the evening.

"Where's your partner in crime?" Allie asked.

"He had to call Lieutenant Santos." She was so excited she was almost vibrating in her seat. "We figured out how the Iceman is finding his victims."

Jack swore and finished his drink. "The one day I leave a half hour early. Well?" He shifted in the seat so he faced Eden. "Spill already."

She clicked open her phone and pulled up the website for the charity event. "Mobile blood drives." She set her phone on the table and angled it toward him. "These days anyone can donate just about anywhere. Doctors' offices, hospitals, charity events..."

"Motor homes that look like buses," Cole added as he claimed the other chair next to her. "It would finally explain how he transported the victims without rousing suspicion. Who's going to question or even pay much notice to medical personnel? They blend in."

"Another point of reference for our suspect search." Jack toasted them. "Well done, you two. I'd appreciate it if you didn't put me out of a job, Eden."

"No chance of that." Eden surprised herself by shifting closer to Cole. His surprising offer of a weekend away had caught her off guard, but not for the reason he probably thought. When was the last time she'd had something to look forward to? When had she thought of anything other than the next crazy, the next story?

Cole's romantic attention had done more than throw

her off kilter; he'd made her start thinking about the future. Her future. She nibbled on her thumb for less than a second before Cole reached up and pushed her hand down, slipping his fingers through hers. *Their future.*

She cleared her throat, wishing she could do the same to her mind. "You cops still have too many rules for me. Allie?" Unaccustomed to her friend's silence, she transferred her attention between her and Simone. "Everything okay?"

"She's upset we didn't tell her about the flowers." Simone winced and leaned back in her striped upholstered seat.

Eden's excitement over a possible break in the Iceman case fizzled. "We didn't—"

"That was my call." Cole cut her off. "We didn't have anything to tell you, Allie. We still don't. But we are looking into it."

"You're reopening Chloe's case, then?" Allie sounded caught between hope and suspicion.

"Not officially, no." Cole signaled to a passing server so they could order drinks. When the waitress left, he continued, "But we're not ruling it out. It depends what other evidence develops."

Allie looked at Eden, then Simone, her stoic silence shifting Eden into alert mode. "Then I guess that answers my next question." She reached into her purse and pulled out a pink envelope in a plastic baggie.

Eden sucked in a breath so hard her teeth froze.

"I found this slipped under my office door this afternoon when I got back from the station." She slid it across the table as Simone sat forward. "I didn't realize what it was until I opened it. I'm sorry. I didn't think about prints."

"That's my stationery," Simone whispered as she

stretched out tentative fingers. "From when we were kids."

"It's the invitation you and Chloe sent us for the camp-out," Allie said, tucking her arms around herself. Her skin looked even paler beneath the cap of dark hair, her bright eyes suddenly glassy. "It still smells like—"

"Cotton candy." Eden covered her mouth as Cole picked up the baggie and pulled out the invitation. "Chloe's perfume."

"Two of us getting vivid reminders of Chloe's death is two too many," Simone said. "Especially in one day. What is going on?"

"Three," Eden whispered. "Three reminders."

"Three?" Cole pulled the familiar crooked, folded paper free and exposed the lettering in purple marker with the when and where of their camping excursion. The kitty stickers in the corner, the smiley faces with hearts for noses, Chloe's trademark signature, staring at them.

Eden steadied herself. "On my way to Simone's office I bumped into someone, or someone bumped into me." She couldn't be certain now. "All I could smell was cotton candy." She could smell it now, wafting off the paper. Cole sealed the invitation back up in the bag and passed it to Jack, who pocketed it. "I didn't think much of it, not even after the flowers..."

"You thought enough to ask me to run the flowers through the lab," Cole reminded her with more tension in his voice than she would have liked.

"You already didn't believe us, Cole. And I didn't feel like trying to justify something even I was uncertain about." Clearly whoever said confession was good for the soul had never had to confess to Cole Delaney.

"It wasn't as if you could go around downtown sniffing people," Simone said in a strained attempt at humor that cut through Eden's familiar wave of guilt. "I'll have another discussion with my boss in the morning."

"As will I," Cole agreed as the waitress brought them their drinks. "In the meantime—"

"In the meantime—" Eden wrapped her fingers around the stem of her wineglass and swallowed the admission she should have made years ago "—why didn't you ever tell me you kissed Simone?"

"What?" Cole couldn't have looked more surprised. He frowned at Simone. "I did? When did I do that?"

"Yes, when did you do that?" Jack leaned forward to glare at his partner.

"And with those words—" Simone pressed a hand against her heart "—I'm proven right. I told you he wouldn't remember."

"You really don't?" Eden's heart swelled.

"Uh, no." Cole shook his head. "I swear I— Oh, wait!" He snapped his fingers. "Freshman-junior picnic at the river. Yeah, I remember now. You had on Daisy Dukes and a pink-and-white-checkered shirt."

"Daisy Dukes?" Simone laughed as their waitress approached again. "Perish the thought. You're not even close, lover boy. But that's okay. My guess is you've just saved your own life. Eden doesn't have a reason to strangle you now. Can we please order? I'm starved."

Chapter 15

"I can't believe you cut me off after two drinks," Eden grumbled as they climbed out of Cole's car at the marina. "And what's all this about having to get to bed?" She waited for him to come around the front of the car before poking him in the chest with an irritated finger. "I was hoping we'd go back to the station and see how Agent Simmons was coming with the—"

Cole moved so quick the last of her statement was lost in his mouth as he kissed her. He tasted of beer with a hint of spicy red sauce and more than a hint of promise. She moaned low in the back of her throat, pushing aside any rational thought as his hands moved to her back, up her spine, holding her against him as she curved her arms around his neck.

"Are you trying to catch me off guard?" she murmured. She drew her fingers across his lips as she looked into his eyes.

"Depends." He kissed the tip of her nose. "Are we finally on the same page?"

"Well, we're definitely reading the same book." To prove it, she kissed him this time, pushing herself forward so he stumbled against the hood of his car. She'd never gambled with her heart before, not with such high stakes, but Simone's words of wisdom struck deep. The risk to her and Cole's friendship didn't matter. Not when compared to the regret she'd have if she didn't take what she wanted. And right now, what she wanted was Cole Delaney. All of Cole Delaney. "How alone are we out here?"

"You'd be more comfortable in my bed," he breathed.

"Have I mentioned how much I've enjoyed working with you?" she teased. He shifted his hold, and the two of them stumbled down the path and onto the dock. "And these fringe benefits you're offering are simply stellar." She nipped at the underside of his chin as he lifted her onto the boat.

"How about we refrain from discussing work for the next few hours?" He unlocked the hatch and flicked on the light.

"Hours, huh?" She stepped down and turned to find herself staring at his belt buckle. "Sounds pretty optimistic if you ask me." She grinned up at him, a surge of feminine power washing over her at the primal sound he made. She flexed her fingers in anticipation.

"Hey, stop teasing or we're both going to get hurt." He gripped the railing tighter.

"I've never done it on a ladder before." She leaned into him. "How sturdy is this thing?"

He reached for her hand. "Don't start something you don't plan to finish, Eden."

She didn't flinch. She didn't blink. She didn't hesitate.

"I expect you to finish it," she whispered and wove her fingers through his even as a tiny prickle of fear wove its way up her spine.

What if she was wrong about this? What if all this between them was nothing more than a brief flash of desire?

Her breath caught in her throat as she watched him.

When was she going to accept that thinking got her into trouble? There was no going back, not once this happened. But where it would go from there…

He closed the hatch behind him and she moved farther inside the cabin. She dropped her purse, shucked off her jacket, pushing aside the last of the doubts. He dropped his coat and untucked his shirt. Shoes came next, then socks, hers flying one way, his the other. Only when his hands began to unbutton his shirt did she say, "Stop!"

Before he misconstrued her meaning, she quickly replaced his hands with hers and drew his shirt up and over his head, stretching up on tiptoe as he let her toss the garment aside. She paused. Until this moment, she didn't realize how much she'd wanted this, wanted him. Eden drew his arms down and around her. She laid her hand on his chest, felt the ripple of control beneath his skin, the slight dusting of hair against her fingertips awakening every synapse in her body. Her fingers knocked against his belt buckle, hesitating briefly as if she'd discovered the last threshold to cross.

His breathing quickened. His fingers tightened around her hips as he whispered, "One of us is seriously overdressed." With barely any effort, he sent her shirt to the floor, landing on top of his.

"I'm not a fancy girl," she murmured. His hands cupped her full, straining breasts through the plain white cotton bra. "I've never really cared for—"

"You won't have it on long enough for me to, either." He bent down, kissing her right above her navel, trailing his lips up between the valley of her breasts.

She shuddered and gripped the back of his head. "So what about this bedroom you've been bragging about? Unless you want to finish what we've started on the kitchen—"

He shot up and captured her mouth. His hands slipped down to her butt and lifted her so she could curl her legs around his hips. Every step he took had her gasping as she felt him, hard, ready and pulsing against her. She couldn't remember ever hating clothing before, the only barrier between them, as he walked them down the hall and into the surprisingly spacious confines of his bedroom.

He clicked on the light, maybe with the power of his mind because she didn't realize he'd stopped touching her. The enormous bed took up most of the space and she couldn't wait to explore how much they could cover together. He leaned over and set her on her back, braced his arms on either side of her as she refused to relinquish her hold on him.

"Hang on, Cole," she murmured, finally having to let her legs fall away so she could reach into her back pocket. "Just in case—"

He stood up, reaching into his back pocket. Their foil packets glinted in the light.

Eden grinned. "Simone wanted to make sure I was prepared."

"I sure love that woman. But I've been preparing for this longer than you know." He plucked the packet from her fingers, set both condoms on the nightstand. "Wait!" he blurted. His arms at his side, his hair mussed by her anxious fingers, he stared down at her, his stomach muscles rippling as he breathed. "I want to look at you."

He didn't just look. He devoured. She could feel the heat of his gaze over every inch of her body.

He was proving her wrong, on so many things, but especially on this. There was more to sex than just sweat and bodies. But this wasn't sex. This was...more. This was what she'd been convinced hadn't been for her.

This was Cole.

Eden bit her lip. She tried not to think about how her bra didn't fit properly or the fact that she ate way too many carbs and hadn't been to the—

None of that mattered. All that did was that she was here, with Cole, a man who made her feel safe, protected. Wanted.

"Okay, that's enough." He unbuttoned her jeans, lowered the zipper and, with a quick and efficient tug, pulled them and her panties off in one fluid motion. Cool air bathed her bare skin. She arched her back and sat up. Had she any inclination to remove her bra herself, she was thwarted yet again. He knelt on the floor and, using only the tips of his fingers, unhooked the bra and drew the straps down her arms.

Riding a wave of confidence she'd never felt before, she got rid of the plain cotton and leaned back, exposing herself—throat, breasts, stomach and lower—to him completely. "Now who's overdressed?" she asked. In the blink of an eye he was naked, and the flush in her cheeks was part anticipation, part pride when she saw the effect she had on him.

Never in her life had she trusted enough to dare. Now she couldn't have turned away from him if her life depended on it.

She hadn't any particular interest in how men covered themselves, but watching him slide the condom on had her anxious to have him put his hands—and other parts of him—to good use.

"Cole," she whispered. And he placed his knee on the mattress between her legs, nudged them apart so he could settle himself. She held his face, wanting to see him, wanting to look at him as they surrendered to each other. She kissed him, luxuriating in the sensation of him drinking her in as if he couldn't get his fill.

"I wanted to make this last," he said, as his fingers wandered.

She smiled, the pressure building.

"Next time," he said, and he pressed inside her, slowly, as if to draw out every moment of pleasure.

She groaned as his searching mouth found her breasts. Eden traced her fingers along his spine, lower, grasping him and drawing him in.

"Next time," she breathed as he began to move, "but not this time."

She enveloped him, sheathed him. Every cell in her body alive as she matched him, thrust for thrust. She stared into his eyes, deeply, losing herself in the barely veiled determination she found there. They were moving together, no longer two beings but one, becoming something more.

Her body burned where he touched her; felt cold where he didn't. She shivered and moaned in equal measure, wanting nothing more than to stay like this, with him, for as long as possible. Where nothing other than Cole could ever touch her again. For now, for these moments with him, she let herself believe.

"Eden," he whispered, and his body tightened under her hold. The tiny explosions he set off inside her erupted to life as she locked her legs around him, kissed him and closed her eyes as they soared together. Longer and harder than she ever dreamed possible.

"And to think we could have been doing this for years." Eden stretched against him, threw her leg over his hips and nestled into his side. Cole drew the bedspread up, still unable to relinquish his hold on her. He sank his hand into her hair, pressed his lips against her sweat-damp forehead and reveled in the bliss he'd been waiting years for.

"We might never have gotten anything else done." He tilted her chin up with his finger and kissed her, the sated passion he'd surrendered to reawakening as her hands slowly skimmed over him. "You were, however—" another kiss, this one almost erasing all thoughts from his head "—definitely worth the wait."

She'd inhabited his dreams for years, but nothing prepared him for the reality of Eden St. Claire in his arms. In his bed. If he'd thought tonight would purge her from his system, he'd never been more wrong. If anything, he'd only become even more addicted to her.

She grinned against his lips. "We're definitely onto something with this whole friends-first thing." Eden's fingers tangled in his hair as she rolled onto her back and pulled him on top of her. "Mmm. That's perfect." She linked her arms around his shoulders and closed her eyes. "I was getting chilly."

"I'm too heavy for you."

"No." She looked at him, eyes heavy lidded, passion sparked, and drew the tip of her tongue across his mouth. "Never. We have a lot of lost time to make up for."

"Not lost." He trailed kisses down her nose, landing on her mouth. "Postponed. Only one thing has ever terrified me, Eden." Cole stroked her soft skin as he uttered the admission he'd kept secret for so long. "That this would never happen."

Her laugh was throaty and rich, thrilling him from head to toe. He filled his hand with her breast, teasing her nipple to a tight peak as desire soared through every inch of his body.

"How long has this been on your mind, Detective?"

"October fifteenth, your sophomore year of high school. You, Simone and Allie snuck into the junior-senior prom thinking no one would notice."

Another laugh, this one tinged with surprise. "And all these years we thought we'd gotten away with it. You saw us?" She moved against him and had him biting back another groan. "Prove it," she said.

"You were wearing a red dress, thin straps." He traced a path over her shoulders down to the swell of her breasts. "Draped neckline and a solitary diamond pendant." He pressed his lips to the place he remembered so vividly. "Your hair looked like spun gold with hints of fire. All I wanted to do was sink my hands into it. Like this." His nearly eighteen-year-old self awakened as he dived deep, the feel of her silky hair in his fingers fulfilling a long-suppressed dream. "And kiss you. Like this."

She kissed him back, proving that it was she, and never him, who held all the power.

"My brother would have tackled you on the spot," she teased. But he saw tenderness in her eyes.

His prom had ended the second he'd spotted Eden laughing and dancing with her friends. Cole stopped his machinations, recognizing the opportunity he'd been waiting for. "I think Logan knew."

"He—what?" Eden gasped, her legs falling away from him. She gripped his shoulders. "He knew what?"

Cole took a deep breath. He'd gone this far. "That I

was in love with you." He couldn't stop staring at her, naked, in his arms, in his bed. "He knew before I did. I think him asking me to watch out for you was his way of giving me the okay."

"You're—in love with me?" Eden's brows knit.

"Why do you look as if I just told you the worst thing possible?"

Her entire body seemed to have gone stiff. "I don't know what to do with this."

"You could have fooled me," Cole joked even as his heart fractured. He knew she viewed sex as little more than an urge that needed satisfying every so often. Had he been fooling himself to think this could be more than a roll in the sheets? He wanted her. All of her. And not just for tonight or tomorrow. "There's no obligation here, Eden," he lied. "And I don't mean to confuse you. But I thought you had a right to know."

"I—" She shifted under him, as if seeking escape, but she held fast, some of the tension faded from her body. "Cole, why—"

He kissed her, kept kissing her until he told her, "At some point you have to accept you're worthy of being loved, Eden. That you don't have to spend your life alone."

"This wasn't about a life. It was about tonight." A solitary tear escaped her control and slipped down her cheek. "It was about a moment and not—" She broke off.

"Not what?"

"Not having regrets."

"Are you saying you would have regretted not sleeping with me?" He smoothed a hand down her spine and paused in the curve above her butt. "Because I think that means you're closer to being in love with me than you realize."

"I don't want to hurt you," she said, her tears drying as she skimmed her fingers over his lips. "Please don't let me hurt you."

"Then how about this." He settled her over him. He slipped his hands up toward her breasts, hoping to distract her from whatever inner demons were coming between them. "For now, this is enough."

She arched her back and then began to move, setting a scorching pace.

For now, it would have to be.

Chapter 16

Eden awoke with a start. "Oh my God." She bolted up, shoved her hair out of her face. Bare threads of sunlight filtered in through the collection of small circular windows above the bed. "It was a van."

"No. It's a boat. In fact, it's a Craftsman 280," Cole groaned and rolled over onto his side. "Eden, some things you'll just have to accept."

"Funny. But no, I meant in the parking lot. That shiny white image I couldn't make out the night he took me." She slapped at Cole's roaming hands before climbing over him and out of bed. "It *was* one of those big blood donor vans that travel around. And there was this enormous blood drop on the back end." She searched the floor for something to wear, grabbed his T-shirt because it was closest and tugged it on. "White and red. Glossy, almost wet looking. I need to find that logo."

"Eden, it's..." He picked up his phone. "It's not even six yet."

"Think about that next time you go for round three." She planted her hands on the mattress and looked down at him. She'd never seen a sexier sight in her life than Cole Delaney the morning after. She kissed him quickly, avoiding his hands as they reached for her again. "If we catch the Iceman, we'll have more time for play."

"There's a bit of motivation I hadn't considered." He dragged himself up. "Can I at least have a shower and some coffee first?"

"You shower. I'll get your coffee."

She darted out of the room and went straight to the kitchen.

While his coffee brewed, she booted up her computer, doing everything she could to stop herself from dwelling on Cole's admission last night. He loved her. Loved. Her.

The idea shouldn't paralyze her, shouldn't make her shiver as if the grim reaper himself had draped her in his chilly cloak. Eden pressed her fingers into her temples. Love wasn't supposed to be a part of this. It *couldn't* be.

Eden had spent most of her life avoiding the word, not to mention the feeling. She didn't say it; she'd spent years learning not to even think it.

Love was important for Cole. The word, the emotion, the expression, were vital to his life. And while part of her thrilled at the idea of being loved by him, how could she take the chance? Everyone she'd ever loved was dead. First Chloe, then her parents, then Logan.

In her experience love was never the beginning; it was always the end. The second she thought it, the second she felt it, she'd lose. They'd lose. But how could she say no to Cole?

How could she deny to herself what she was feeling?

"You're thinking overtime again, I see."

Eden glanced over her shoulder as he joined her in the

galley. Stark naked. She couldn't help it. She grinned. "Nice outfit."

"Thought you might appreciate it." He pulled his mug free. "Besides, I couldn't find my pants." He sipped and reached out for her with his free hand. "Come here." He tugged her close and kissed her to the point she'd forgotten what she'd been worrying over. "Join me in the shower?"

"It's not very big." She pressed her hand flat over his heart.

"Neither is the water heater." He nibbled his way down the side of her neck. "I've always wanted to test just how long it would take to run out."

"Cole—" Wow, when had she become so…wanton?

"I bet some steam would help you remember more about that van you saw." He stepped back, set his mug down and wrapped his arms around her, pressed his mouth to hers. "Let's get that mind of yours all nice and scrubbed, shall we?"

"It's not my mind you're interested in at the moment." She laughed and set the mounting doubts and fear aside. And then they were in the bathroom and he was pulling her shirt off. "Okay, you win." She stepped into the shower with him as he turned on the water. "Scrub away."

Half-dressed, Eden dug through her suitcase and searched for her zip-front sweatshirt. One of the valley's unpredictable temperature drops meant they were in for a cooler-than-usual spring day. Shirts were tossed aside, jeans, errant socks, underwear scattered over the guest room floor.

A gentle metal clink, followed by the tinny notes of *Swan Lake*, echoed from her bag.

Eden's throat tightened, and the memory of her friend's

face when she'd opened that birthday gift flashed behind her tightly closed eyes. Steeling herself, she lifted the music box out of the bag, watched the tines pluck against the wheel. Twenty years. It seemed like just yesterday they were mere kids. Logan, Allie… Cole. When the tune wore down, she clicked the box shut.

Only then did she see the small folded card that had fallen out.

She stopped in her tracks. It was then the smell caught her nose. Sweet. Sickly sweet. Cotton candy.

Cole arrived with another cup of coffee. "Here. Thought you could use—"

"It wasn't the Iceman." Eden struggled to make every syllable count. The last few days shifted in her mind as she struggled to comprehend.

"It wasn't the Iceman what? Come on, Eden, you're white as a sheet." He set the mug down and walked over to her, but she pointed to her bag.

"In there. The note card." The same stationery as the one that had been delivered with the flowers.

The same one Allie had received at her office.

Cole unfolded the paper. She watched his jaw clench as he read the contents. "'Happy Anniversary.'"

"It wasn't him. The Iceman didn't break into my home the other night," Eden breathed even as she fought for oxygen. "The candle in the basement, the way nothing else seemed to have been touched. He wanted me to know he'd been there. This wasn't about the Iceman murders. This was about Chloe."

"You don't know—"

"I keep that box next to my bed, Cole." She gripped his arm and willed him to understand. "Wherever I've lived since she was killed, it goes by my bed. I play it when I can't sleep. When I need to remind myself why I do what

I do. But the other day, after I got home from the hospital, it was on my dresser. I thought maybe Allie had moved it or even you had." She held her breath, waiting for the familiar argument to begin, but it never happened. "You believe me, don't you?"

"I do." He held the card by the edges and used his free hand to touch her cheek. "I do, Eden. I'm going to get this to evidence. Have them compare it to the one Allie was sent. And Simone."

"It'll match."

He wrapped his arm around her, drew her in, and for a second she let herself lean on him, draw strength from him. Need him.

She clung to him, surrendered again, because she was safe. Because he had been and always would be her one constant. She squeezed her eyes shut, ordering herself not to be greedy; not to take too much, too soon.

Needing anyone—needing him—would only mean pain for both of them in the long run. Being with him last night and again this morning, waking up in his bed, looking into his eyes first thing showed her what was possible.

And just how much more she had to lose.

"We'll get him, Eden." He brushed a kiss against her temple. "He won't hurt you or Simone or Allie. I promise."

But for the first time, Eden wasn't sure she believed him.

"You okay?" Cole asked as he parked the car and plugged his phone into the charger.

"I'm fine." What else could she say? Besides, it wasn't as if Eden St. Claire ever admitted fear. Or defeat. "Hopefully we'll have better luck with this group."

"We should," Cole agreed. "This support group was at the top of Dr. Tanner's list. Largest number of members, and it's been around for almost a decade."

Eden walked beside him, down the narrow hallway of the community center just off Q and Twenty-Third. "Jack's investigating the other two?"

"Supposedly. I'd hoped to check in with him earlier, but *someone* distracted me."

Just as he was trying to do for her now.

"You're the one who wanted to buddy up to save water." Humor, she told herself, would see her through despite whatever doubts crept in. Back on the case now, where she didn't have to think about Chloe's killer or Cole and her feelings...well, Cole.

Since seeing Mr. Sexy Cop mussed and tousled in bed wasn't enough, she'd watched him shave clad in nothing but a low-riding towel. And it wasn't even her birthday. Her brain wasn't large enough to compartmentalize all this. "On the bright side, we can now confirm it takes well over a half hour to drain the hot water tank dry."

Cole chuckled. "Meeting room's up here. I'll call when we get back to the car." He poked his head in the open doorway and knocked on the frame. "Jenna Batsakis?"

"Yes?" The whir of a mechanized wheelchair buzzed as a young woman spun to face them. Slight, frail even, with a spring-yellow dress, matching sweater and tumbling dark curls, she smiled wide and looked doll-like. "May I help you?"

Eden glanced around the outdated yet neat and clean room. Two young men arranged cushioned folding chairs into a large circle in the center, while another set up coffee cups and a coffeemaker on a table by the window.

"Detective Cole Delaney." He showed Jenna his badge.

"This is Eden St. Claire. We'd like to ask you some questions about the support group you run here at the center?"

"Oh?" She glanced at Eden as if she was trying to remember her from somewhere. "Professionally or has one of you been diagnosed with a blood disorder?"

"No, I'm afraid this is in reference to a case we're working on."

"A case? Eden on Ice?" Jenna flipped the toggle on her chair and she shot forward. "I thought I recognized your name." She extended her hand. "I'm a bit of a crime junkie. Spending as much time as I do in and out of the hospital, I'm always looking for interesting reading. It's a pleasure to meet you."

"Likewise. Are we interrupting?"

"No, no. Our next meeting isn't until this afternoon. I've been cooped up for the last couple of weeks, so when I'm set free, I don't let grass grow under my wheels. Please, have a seat. Thanks, guys!" she called out to her helpers as they headed out. "I can't imagine I'll be of any assistance to you, but I'm happy to try." She folded her thin hands in her lap.

"Dr. Tanner at the Sanguinem Clinic suggested we speak with you. She said you've dealt with a number of patients and their family members over the years."

"Avery, of course. Yes. I was a patient of theirs once upon a time."

"You aren't any longer?" Eden asked.

"No." Her smile never even dipped. "They'd exhausted all treatment options for my condition. I'm afraid the only hope for me now is a bone marrow transplant, and despite having a donor, that isn't looking promising. My current doctors agree I seem to be past the point of being able to tolerate such a severe procedure."

"Forgive me, but you don't seem too upset by that,"

Cole said. Eden marveled. He had such a way with people; he put them at ease almost immediately. How she envied that.

"Why would I be?" Jenna looked truly baffled at the notion. "I'm twenty-six years old, Detective. I was diagnosed with paroxysmal nocturnal hemoglobinuria shortly after I was born. Truth be told, I wasn't supposed to see my fifth birthday, so I'm not about to complain now that I've had twenty-plus more of them."

Eden shifted uncomfortably. And she was whining about *her* problems? What right did she have to be afraid of a little four-letter word compared with what this young woman was going through?

"When did you form Aima? That's Greek for *blood*, isn't it?" Cole asked.

"Yes, it is. My mother's idea, actually." She gestured to three framed photographs hanging about a small desk in the corner. "After years of volunteering at St. Augustus, she understood how a group like this could work. I took it over after she died. She called Aima her silver lining."

"Do any of these names look familiar to you?" Cole pulled out the list he'd written and handed it to her.

Jenna scanned the names. "One or two. But I can't be certain if it's from the group or from one of the other facilities I've been treated at. I meet a lot of people."

"That's kind of what we're counting on," Eden said. "What type of people come to your meetings?"

"Anyone who's dealing with their own health issues or those of a loved one. Having a support system when dealing with any chronic illness is vital, especially if that patient is a child. It's not pretty." She tugged the sleeves of her sweater down over her hands. "Do you mind me asking which case you're working on?"

"The Iceman," Eden said before Cole could decide.

"We're exploring the theory the killings are somehow connected to his victims' blood."

Jenna blinked, her already pale face going gray. "I don't understand. How could they be?"

"That's what we're trying to find out," Cole said, brushing his fingers lightly against Eden's knee as if to tell her to ease off. "Have you had any newcomers to the group lately? Or someone drop out all of a sudden?"

"Ah." Jenna clutched the collar of her sweater at her throat. "I'm afraid I couldn't tell you. As I said, I've been in the hospital for almost a month. Blood clots." She stretched her frail legs out. "Completely unpredictable. I was reading up on your blog, actually, Ms. St. Claire. Did…?" Jenna drew in a shuddering breath. "Did he take your blood, as well?"

"Some of it," Eden said. "My doctors seem to think I didn't have what he's looking for."

"And what would that be?" A blind person would have been able to tell Jenna was shaking. Eden's heart began to pound.

"Iron." Now it was Cole's turn to surprise Eden. "Are you all right, Jenna? You seem a little nervous all of a sudden."

"Fine. I'm fine. Iron, you say?" Her voice trembled.

"Yes. All the victims had been treated for varying degrees of DIOS."

"I see." Jenna swallowed and nodded. "I assume many of them also donated blood frequently. That's one of the recommended treatments normally."

"According to their medical records, yes." Cole angled a glance at Eden.

"Is there someone who oversees the Aima meetings when you aren't able to, Jenna?" Eden reached out and touched the young woman's shoulder. "A friend or family member?"

"Um, no." She tucked her hair behind her ear. "No. We haven't been having them while I've been ill. I'm afraid it's just me."

Eden didn't buy it. It was obvious how much this group meant to Jenna. She wouldn't take a chance and let it flounder without her. She'd have a contingency in place.

"And how do you let your members know a meeting's been canceled?" Cole asked.

"We post it on the community center's website and the staff puts a notice on the board. Most of my regulars know to double-check before making the drive downtown. I'm sorry—is there anything else? I'm suddenly not feeling very well."

"That'll be all for now. Would you like us to call someone for you?" Cole asked as she pushed her chair forward and around.

"I'm just going to lie down in the spare room for a while." She was almost to the door when she spun back around. "D-do you know why he's taking their blood, Detective?"

"We'd only be speculating, Jenna. We think he could be experimenting with it. Looking for a cure for himself."

"Or for someone he loves," Eden added.

Jenna's gaze flew to hers. "That would still make what he's doing wrong," she whispered, and in that instant, Eden knew.

"Yes," Eden said. "It would."

Jenna nodded and zoomed away.

Eden tugged Cole from the room and they exited the building. Fast.

"Um, Cole? Did we just hit the jackpot?"

"So much so our next stop should be Vegas. Give me your phone." He held out his hand as they hurried to the car. He dialed. "Yeah, Jack, it's me," he said into the cell and skidded to a stop. He signaled to Eden. "Wait—what?" Now it was his turn to grab hold of her. He listened, and as Eden watched him, she saw the pulse in his neck throb heavily. "No, yeah, my phone died. We're heading in now. I want you to get everything you can on a Jenna Batsakis. She runs a blood disease support group downtown called Aima. Dig deep, Jack. We're getting close." He hung up and tossed Eden her phone. "Get in."

"What's happened?" Eden cried over the hood of the car.

"Missing person's report just came in. Jeff Cottswold. Medical student. His girlfriend came home early from a girls' trip to Mexico. She talked to him yesterday morning, so he hasn't been gone long."

"We're sure it's the Iceman?" Eden hopped into the car as Cole flipped his visor down and hit the siren.

"He was headed home from a doctor's appointment when he called her. At the Sanguinem Clinic."

Eden whooped.

"Yeah," Cole said. "We wanted a break in the case. Looks like we've got one."

"Somebody tell me where we are!" Cole yelled as he and Eden hurried through the double glass doors. He dodged uniformed officers scrambling for phones and computers, the din of determination echoing in his ears. "Jack?"

His partner jumped to his feet from behind his desk, phone tucked under his ear. "Give me five!"

"I'll be in the conference room." Eden brushed a hand over his arm and raced off.

"Lieutenant?" Cole caught up with his boss, who had his nose buried in a file.

"I recruited Missing Persons," Lieutenant Santos told him. "They're on board with whatever we want to do until we get a result on this."

Cole heard the silent *or don't get one* loud and clear.

"Who's this Jenna Batsakis you told McTavish about?" Santos asked. "Bowie! Where's that updated license registry on medical vehicles?"

"Coming through now, Lieutenant."

"Batsakis runs a support group for patients with blood disorders out of a community center downtown." Cole caught sight of a haggard-looking Agent Simmons waving Eden over to him through the glass window of the conference room. "Progress?"

"We'll see. Simmons has a contact with the state medical board. He's gotten us a list of all approved medical transports operating in Northern California. We're looking into Nevada and Oregon, as well, just in case the guy got clever and tried to stay off the radar." Lieutenant Santos finally glanced up at Cole. "This Batsakis woman? She a viable suspect?"

"She's not physically capable. Not on her own, anyway."

"But you're not ruling her out as far as being involved."

"Anything's possible." An award-winning actress couldn't have been more convincing. "Nobody gets that nervous that quick if they don't have something to hide. She knows more than she's saying. I'd bet my pension on it."

"I doubt you'll have to." Jack hung up and flipped

through his antiquated notebook. "Jenna Batsakis, born February 20, 1989, to Helena and Aristos Batsakis, both deceased. In and out of medical facilities since the age of four, when she was diagnosed with an autoimmune disorder that resulted in something I won't even try to pronounce. Attended St. Augustus Parochial School until grade five, then was homeschooled. She earned a degree in social work and family therapy through a reputable online college, after which she got a two-year degree in biology. She's been running Aima for the last three years. No police record. No DMV record. What she does have is a brother. Hector Batsakis. Same birth date, five minutes older. We're running him through the system now."

"A twin," Cole said. "Allie said he'd be a caretaker, a protector."

"I want Dr. Hollister brought in on this," Lieutenant Santos said. "Call her, then fill in the rest of the team. I want our focus on these two."

"Yes, sir." Cole went to his desk and made the call before joining Eden and the rest of the team in the conference room. Laptops, paperwork and scattered remnants of fast-food wrappers and paper cups littered the table. "We've got a name. Hector Batsakis."

"Jenna has a brother." The flash of sympathy he saw in Eden's eyes registered with him.

"A twin."

"Cole...you don't think she knows about this?"

"She knows something. First, I want to talk to Jenna's doctors and find out exactly what her condition is."

"And if what we think the Iceman is honing in on can connect to Jenna's condition," Eden finished. "That's a strong connection, being a twin. Not a lot one wouldn't do for the other."

"You can only break doctor-patient privilege once the

patient is deceased," Agent Simmons said. "Or unless the closest family member agrees. I ran into that issue after Denise died."

"Wait a minute." Eden snapped her fingers. "Didn't Jenna say she was a former patient of Dr. Tanner's?"

"It still wouldn't allow her to break confidentiality." Agent Simmons shook his head.

"No, but it might allow her to talk in hypotheticals," Cole offered. "Allie's on her way in to consult now that we have a suspect."

"Go talk to Dr. Tanner again," Eden said. "We'll try to track down that medical logo on the vehicle I saw."

He didn't like the idea of leaving her behind. His hesitation must have showed.

"I'll keep an eye on her," Agent Simmons promised and earned an exaggerated eye roll from Eden. "I won't let her out of my sight."

"I'll hold you to that." He jogged out of the conference room and tagged Jack. "Let's go, partner. We've got a doctor to question."

"I'm sorry, Detective Delaney, but there's nothing I can tell you about Jenna and her treatment. Her records are confidential." Dr. Tanner's earlier friendliness had been replaced with stoic jaw-locked determination.

"I'm not asking you to divulge her current medical status," Cole said, taking a different route. "What I do need to know is why she's no longer being treated at your facility."

Dr. Tanner's lips tightened. She shoved her hands in her pockets and looked between him and Jack, who had taken up his casual-looking stance in the doorway. Casual, yeah right. That was Jack's pre-pounce position.

"Work with us, Doc," Jack said. "Theoretically, what treatment options are left for her?"

Cole kept his expression passive as his partner looked to confirm Jenna's story.

"In theory?" Dr. Tanner said. "Nothing. Her body can't tolerate—"

"Tolerate what? If there's nothing, that is?" Jack asked. "Look, we get it. You've got a lot to protect here. Believe me, the last thing we want to do is interfere with your work or jeopardize your other patients, but that's what you're doing by not answering our questions. This isn't just about Jenna. It's about the victims, including one we're trying to find now."

Dr. Tanner turned shocked eyes on Cole. "Someone else is missing?"

"Jeff Cottswold," Cole told her. "He disappeared sometime after his appointment here yesterday afternoon."

"Jeff?" Dr. Tanner shook her head. "Oh, no. That can't be right."

"His girlfriend reported him missing after she came home unexpectedly from a trip. When our detectives with Missing Persons asked about his health, she admitted he's been a patient here for the last six months. What is he being treated for? DIOS?" Cole tried to keep his voice even-tempered. Scaring her into cooperating wasn't going to work. "Are his iron levels well above normal?"

"I can't—"

"Can you blink?" Jack asked.

"I'm sorry?" Dr. Tanner snapped.

Jack explained, "Blink once for yes. You won't have said a word."

Dr. Tanner took a deep breath, folded her hands on her desk. And blinked.

"And his suggested course of treatment was...what?" Cole pressed harder. "Medication?" No blink. "Transfusion?" Not a twitch.

"Blood donation?" Jack asked.

She blinked.

"Would that donation have been done at this facility?" Cole wondered.

"It could be, but no. Jeff was on his way to class. He said there's a mobile blood unit he'd seen driving around campus and the surrounding neighborhoods the last few months. He could fit that into his schedule more easily."

Cole leaned forward and looked Dr. Tanner directly in her skittish eyes. "Answer a hypothetical for me, Doctor. If blood that contained an overload of iron were to be transfused into someone with, say, PNH..."

Dr. Tanner's mouth twisted as her eyes sharpened.

"We're just talking theory here, Doc," Jack added. "Could a transfusion of that kind connect in any way to whatever treatment a patient like Jenna needs but can't tolerate?"

"I don't see—" Dr. Tanner broke off, but then said, as if choosing her words carefully, "For someone in Jenna's position, the only option remaining would be a bone marrow transplant. But as I said—"

"Jenna isn't a candidate for that procedure. Because...?" Cole refused to back down. Come on. Surely she had to see this was bigger than one patient's medical files.

"A patient *like* Jenna," Dr. Tanner clarified, "would need to pass certain medical tests, including stabilized iron levels, to make sure she's a viable candidate. The toll a transplant takes on the body, the recovery period... We have to give them the best chance."

"And people with PNH tend to have very low iron levels, don't they?" Jack asked.

"That's why he's taking them," Cole said. "He's using their blood to boost her numbers."

"That's ridiculous," Dr. Tanner protested. "What you're talking about is extreme medicine. Unregulated. Unprescribed. Regular transfusions are one thing, but mostly patients who are low in iron get their numbers boosted from supplements and dietary changes. As far as I'm aware, there's absolutely no evidence..."

"You say that as if we're dealing with someone in their right mind," Jack reminded her. "If all those treatments have failed, what would be left other than extremes or even untested theories?"

"Think this through, Doctor," Cole said sternly, seeking her attention again. "Jenna needs a bone marrow transplant, but you can't give her one because her tests don't pass muster. She needs more blood, better blood, iron-saturated blood, to boost those numbers to qualify."

"There are many factors to take into consideration—"

"She has a twin brother." Cole switched over to Jack since he didn't expect to get any more answers from Dr. Tanner. "Doesn't get much closer than that for bone marrow, does it? Get her iron levels up, she can get her transplant. Except what the good doctor here said is probably right. It's not working. Not the way he needs it to."

"Tell me something." Jack walked over and planted his hands on Dr. Tanner's desk, angling his chin until the doctor had no choice but to meet his gaze. "When did you deny Jenna's transplant?"

"I'd have to check our records—"

"I'm guessing three years ago," Cole said in reference to when the killings had started. "The same time she ceased being your patient."

"The choice to discontinue her treatment was mutual," Dr. Tanner said. "She understood we couldn't help her any longer."

"Yeah, I'm sure she did." Cole got to his feet. "But I don't think her brother agreed with you."

"Why do I feel as if I've taken my life into my hands by bringing you with me?" Tires ground against gravel as Agent Simmons pulled into Cooper's Specialty Vehicles off El Camino and parked. He double-checked his holstered weapon under his suit jacket.

"Look at it this way." Eden eyed the shack-like office surrounded by all sorts of vans, buses and trucks. "You promised Cole you wouldn't let me out of your sight. You're just keeping your word. And besides, it's essentially a used-car lot."

"One of the only dealerships in Northern California that handles specialty vehicles."

"Ah, but they've sold at least a dozen in the last three years. I'll take odds our guy bought here."

"Providing our guy really is Hector Batsakis." His guarded tone told her he wasn't getting his hopes up.

"The evidence is mounting," Eden murmured, glancing down at the file in her lap. "He dropped out of medical school six years ago, citing family issues. Since then he's become a licensed phlebotomist and works as a substitute lab technician all around Sacramento, Davis and Stockton. He also applied for a class B driver's license eighteen months ago." She narrowed her eyes and stared into the face of Jenna Batsakis's brother. She could see the similarity for sure, with the big, wide eyes and generous smile, though Hector had sandy-blond hair. But Allie had suggested the suspect would look pretty ordinary. Although...something familiar poked at the back of her memory.

"All that is circumstantial, including that he can drive a bus. He could be driving a van, for all we know."

"See, this is where you and I can part ways. My hands aren't tied by all those pesky rules and regulations like you and Cole." She shoved open the door to the car. "And I'll bet you twenty bucks he bought a bus."

"Laws aren't pesky and I'm beginning to see why Delaney worries about you." He grabbed her arm when she started to get out. "You're here as a courtesy, Eden. It might just be a used-car lot, but this case is anything but typical. You do what I tell you, understand?"

"Yes, sir." She saluted and jumped out before he could reprimand her. She smelled singed coffee, body odor and gasoline the second they set foot through the cracked glass door that was ajar. Breathing through her mouth, she called, "Hello?"

"Be with ya in a sec!" The telltale sound of a toilet flushing echoed through the thin walls. A paunch-heavy middle-aged man wearing a baseball cap eased through from the back office, wiping his hands. "Help ya?"

"Agent Simmons, FBI." Simmons flashed his badge as he and Eden approached the counter. "This is my consultant, Eden."

Eden gave him points for not using her full name.

"No kidding?" The man's eyes lit up like flares in the road. "FBI, really? Wow, okay. Seth Hammits. Nice to meet you, Agent." He stuck his hand out, not giving Simmons any choice but to shake it. "How can I help?"

"We're looking for information on one of your customers."

"Sure. Which one?"

"We're hoping you can tell us." Eden leaned her arms on the counter and, for good measure, flipped her hair over her shoulder as she smiled at him. Seth's eyes glinted.

"We suspect he might have bought a vehicle from you in the last couple of years. A big one."

"This might help." Simmons plucked Hector's photo out of the file and placed it in front of Seth. "Take your time. It's important."

"Important, huh? Like reward important?"

"If doing the right thing doesn't work for you, sure. We can talk reward," Simmons said before Eden could reach across the counter and smack Seth's greedy little grin. "Information first."

"I might have sold to him. I'd have to check my files. Couple of years, you say?"

"Let's start with three."

"Okay. Okay." He lumbered over to the metal shelving unit and hauled down a weathered accordion folder. "Lucky for you we don't get a lot of business. This one here's for the last five years total." He started stacking up piles by year.

Eden grabbed for one stack as Simmons took another.

"Hey, now, I don't know about—"

"The faster we find what we're looking for, the sooner we'll be out of here. And the sooner I can forget your business license expired seven months ago." Simmons pointed to the crooked framed document on the wall next to the cash register.

"Ah, sure. Help yourself, then." Clearly the threat had also erased Seth's willingness to help.

Eden skimmed each sales slip, name, vehicle type, license and registration number. Photocopied drivers' licenses and proofs of insurance were stapled to the back.

"Why do so many people want old ambulances?" Eden wondered out loud.

"A question for another time, I'm sure." Simmons was almost as quick as her. "Here's one for a 2004 customized cargo van medical vehicle. Sold to a G. Ellington. Part cash, part trade."

"Ellington?" Eden snatched up Hector's file again. "Ellington was his mother's maiden name."

"Glen Ellington," Simmons said. "An alias?"

"Could be. You don't by chance know what this Glen Ellington traded in exchange, do you, Seth?" Eden asked as Seth spun himself around in what had to be a very sturdy chair.

"Course I do. That eyesore is still sitting in the back of my lot. Converted catering van. Said he got it from a former boss when the business closed down a few years back."

"What business?"

"Take a look-see yourself. Make a right and keep going. Can't miss it. Red-and-pink monstrosity. Only gave him five hundred for it and he seemed grateful."

"Do you have a copy machine?" Simmons asked.

"Did." Seth glanced behind him to the dust-covered photocopier. "Broke a few months back."

"Then we're keeping this." Simmons added the sales receipt to Hector's file and followed Eden outside as she greedily sucked in fresh air.

"Turn right where?" she muttered as they clomped through puddles of what she told herself was rain run-off. Most of the vehicles up front were in fairly decent condition. Clearly Seth hoped to actually sell them. But the farther back they went, the more it felt like a junk-yard. "Here it is."

She jogged over to what indeed was a metal eyesore with an enormous pair of hearts mingling on the side panel. "Hearts Aligned Catering. Wait a minute." She skimmed her fingers across the small print under the business name on the side of the vehicle. "It lists three locations, but this address." She pulled out her phone and accessed the notes she kept on the Iceman's killings. "That's only a few blocks from where the third victim was found. Didn't Hector's file say he worked in food service during high school and part of college?"

"Sure did."

"And here." She tapped her finger against the van. "That's a location we haven't seen before. How much do you want to bet that building has an industrial-sized freezer."

"You and your bets." Simmons pulled out his phone and motioned for her to follow him to the car. "Hello, Lieutenant Santos, it's Simmons. Eden and I found—" He stopped, closed his eyes and nodded. "Sure. Okay. Just a minute." He held out his phone. "Cole wants to talk to you."

Eden scowled and braced herself. "Hey, Cole."

"I'm not even going to ask how you talked Agent Simmons into taking you with him."

"Because I told him if he didn't I'd just Uber it behind him. How did things go with Dr. Tanner?" She jumped into the car beside Simmons.

"Productive. I'll be happy to fill you in once you're back at the station."

"We have a stop to make first."

"No, we don't," Simmons said loud enough for Cole to hear.

"Batsakis used to work for a catering company. Up until a few years ago, there were three different locations servicing the Sacramento area. One off Watt Avenue, which is near where both Elliot Scarbrough's and Pam Norris's bodies were discovered. Another was in West Sac—"

"Let me guess," Cole drawled. "The warehouse where we found you."

"Right." She resisted the urge to shiver. "Agent Simmons and I just found a third location off Highway 16 and Sloughhouse. We're headed out there now." She swore she could hear him counting to ten.

"Sloughhouse has its own sheriff's department, Eden," Cole said. "We'll need to coordinate with them—"

"Then coordinate," she interrupted before giving him the address. "We'll meet you there."

"Eden, don't you dare—"

She hung up. "They're on their way," Eden told Simmons. "Better get a move on, Agent. We're losing daylight."

"I'm not going in there without backup." Simmons activated the child-lock button to stop Eden from getting out of the car. "And you're not going in there at all."

"What are the chances anyone is in there, anyway?" she asked. What were the chances anyone was anywhere in the Sacramento suburb known for its extensive property lines and low population?

The deserted single-story warehouse—one of half a dozen scattered up and down the road—had been overrun with anemic trees, weeds and the barest idea of shrubbery. Even from where they'd parked across the highway, Eden could see the parking lot cement had cracked, as had the foundation of the poorly roofed structure. Several broken windows hadn't been boarded up.

Before they'd hit the dead zone that was this section of Sloughhouse, she'd managed to find out on her cell that the property and surrounding buildings had been in foreclosure for almost as long as Hearts Aligned Catering had been out of business. "Seems the perfect place for a serial killer to hole up," Eden murmured. "We could walk around, just to make sure it's empty."

"Could," Simmons said, glancing down the road to where a large truck had pulled into an auto supply warehouse. "We won't. Cole warned me you'd try something like this. He said common sense tends to vanish when you're close to getting an answer—"

"It does not!" She just tended to lose her patience with all the formalities that Cole and his fellow law-enforcement buddies had to put up with.

"Good. Then waiting for Cole and the rest of the team isn't an issue. Besides, I'm not about to put you in any kind of jeopardy, real or potential. The last thing I need is to get into a knock-down-drag-out with your boyfriend." He twisted his wedding band in that nervous habit she'd noticed.

"He's not my boyfriend." Calling Cole that didn't sit right with her. But not for the reason some might have thought. Because he felt like…more. She chewed on her nearly nonexistent thumbnail. Yeah, she'd much rather stalk a serial killer than discuss…this.

"Please." Simmons grinned. "The two of you give off more heat than a nuclear reactor. Everyone in the station is talking about it, so get used to it." He twisted round in his seat to look at her. "He's your boyfriend."

She made a face at him and tried to deflect. "I'm pretty sure I had this recurring nightmare in high school." Her cheeks went hot and she willed Cole and the patrol cars to drive faster. "Except I was naked and giving a speech."

"You know the one thing I miss most since my separation?" Simmons's wistful tone sank into her. "Being happy. Looking forward to going home. Now all I have are boxes and memories."

Eden thought back to her own boxes and memories.

Funny. The instant she heard the word *home* spoken, it wasn't her town house she thought of.

It was Cole's boat.

That unease she'd been avoiding circled low in her belly. "What happened with your wife?" she asked him.

"Denise's murder." It took a moment for him to continue, as if he didn't want to put it into words. "I couldn't let it go. Accessed files I shouldn't have. Pushed where I didn't have a right to, as you well know. My fellow agents lost faith in me. They stopped wanting to work with me. I ended up on a desk. Then in the bottom of a bottle." He reached into his pocket and pulled out what looked like a poker chip. "Six months sober." He twirled it in his fingers. "Figured I'd give it a full year before I tried to fix things with her. If that's even possible." Regret and resignation mingled in his voice.

"What's her name?"

"Suzanna."

"Kids?"

"Never seemed to be time." Simmons glanced over at her. "For me. Biggest mistake I made, giving up. I didn't even fight when she told me to leave, but I couldn't stop thinking here I was, an FBI agent, and I couldn't find the maniac who murdered my baby sister."

Eden reached over and closed his hand around the chip. "We'll find him. And then you'll call Suzanna and go home."

"It's too late for me, Eden."

"You love her. It's never too late to fight for her. So fight. Speaking of fighting..." Even Cole's car seemed angry when it pulled up and parked hood to hood with Simmons's. "Will you let me out now?"

The lock clicked.

"Before you get upset—" Eden called out to Cole as she approached him.

"Why would I be upset?" Cole asked, casting a look as a Sloughhouse sheriff's vehicle parked behind him. "It's not like you're out and about chasing after a murderer who left you strung up in a freezer."

Allie got out of the passenger seat of his car, dressed in a shade of green that reminded Eden of the moss that grew on her roof during the winter.

Suddenly uncertain, Eden managed, "I had protection." Which she was thinking she might need from Cole about now.

"Like I promised, she was never out of my sight," Simmons said as he joined them. Jack brought up the rear as two more patrol cars arrived. "And I locked her in the car until you got here."

"Nice to know you didn't let her drive you completely off the rails. Sorry she talked you into this," Cole said.

"You'd think I was a toddler who escaped the playpen," Eden scoffed. "Allie, tell them—"

"I'm here to keep track of you while they do their jobs." Her friend locked her hand around Eden's wrist. "Should I ask Cole for his handcuffs?"

"Oh, please." Eden laughed. "It's not like he's going to be in there."

"You don't know what is going on in there, Eden. We could find a dozen more bodies or I might get creative and lock you in the deep freeze myself." Cole moved in, loomed over her, and only then did she see the specter of worry hovering in his eyes. She'd scared him. Again. "Now, please get in the car and stay with Allie while we check things out. Do you hear me?"

"Would you like me to bow and kiss your feet before you go?" she snapped.

"In the car," Allie ordered and moved in between them. Eden couldn't remember the last time she'd heard Allie sound so cold.

"Wait—"

But Allie had already shoved her inside the vehicle. The door slammed and she found herself in complete silence. Allie circled around the SUV and got in on the other side, while Cole, Jack, Simmons and the officers finalized their plan with elaborate hand gestures.

"He cares about you, Eden." Allie sounded frustrated; her friend never usually sounded that way. "You should have seen the look on his face when he got to the station and you were gone. It didn't help that you didn't even tell me where you were going."

"It was a last-minute idea." Eden folded her hands in her lap. "And I know he cares about me." She almost wished she didn't. "He said he's in love with me."

"And?"

"And? And what?" How did Allie not see what a disaster this was? How could she not understand that Cole Delaney loving her was the worst-possible news? "That's enough, isn't it? Well, along with the marathon sex session—"

"Do I look like I'm in the mood for girl talk?" Allie's clipped tone did nothing to erase Eden's fear. "Let's pretend for one minute you actually have feelings, shall we? I know I'm usually the touchy-feely one, the one you're afraid will read too much into things and tell you why you feel and think the way you do. But tough. You're pretending that this isn't anything more than a fling with Cole when we both know it's more. Stop. It's cruel. He loves you, Eden. He's in love with you. And you're treating it as if it's a joke."

"I am not." She just didn't want it to be real. Because when things got real...people got hurt.

"Tell me you aren't already thinking of how to drive him away. To convince him what he's feeling is adrenaline. That you're not terrified of being happy."

"How can any of us be happy?" Eden demanded. "We know the evil that's out there, how fast life can be taken away. Simone couldn't be happy with Vince and it's not like you've found Prince Charming even with your cartoon-princess aura."

The silence pressed in on Eden, forcing her heart open in a way she'd tried to prevent for almost two decades. "I'm sorry," she whispered. "You didn't deserve that."

"It's not the first time you've hurt my feelings. It won't be the last. And I'm perfectly happy with my cartoon-princess aura, thank you very much."

Eden shook her head. "Why can't you ever punch back at me? Why do you have to always be so fair and logical?"

"Because fairness, logic and love don't always go hand in hand. Something I'm sure Cole is struggling with at the moment. You need to talk to him about this, Eden. You need to tell him what you're feeling."

"I can't. I can't love him, Allie." How she hated the tears that burned her throat and eyes. They were a sign of weakness, of a loss of control. And Eden needed to stay in control. "Because if I do…whoever I love…they die." Her heart jumped into her throat as she watched Cole and his fellow officers surround the building, weapons out. She looked at Allie, silently willing her friend to understand what she couldn't.

Allie's expression softened beneath her black crop of hair, as if she'd been pushing for just this reaction.

"People leave me," Eden whispered. "Chloe. Mom and Dad. Logan. Everyone leaves me. And I've just found it's easier if I leave them first."

"Easier on whom?" Allie asked. "News flash, Eden. It's been twenty years and Simone and I are still here, so consider that theory disproved. You can push as hard as you want—we aren't going anywhere." She stroked Eden's hair. "I hate to break it to you, but neither is Cole." She scooted toward Eden and drew her head onto her shoulder.

"It's my fault," Eden said softly.

"What? Antagonizing Cole? Well, yeah." Allie laughed. "But you do it with such panache."

"Not Cole." It took every ounce of air in her body to set the words free. "Chloe. It's my fault she's dead." She squeezed her eyes shut as Allie's body went stiff. It was too late to stop now. All these years…all this time, the paralyzing guilt had built inside of her, the fear someone was going to learn her secret—that it was her fault a nine-year-old girl was dead. The truth spilled out. "After we all went to bed, after we thought we were so grown-up because we went camping in Simone's backyard."

"That backyard was over fifteen acres of wild trees and grass," Allie said. "Any one of us could have gotten lost. It's why we had the buddy—"

"I was her buddy, remember? She woke me up so I could go with her to the bathroom, but I told her to go by herself." The sob erupted deep from Eden's heart. A sob that she'd been keeping at bay for two decades. "I was so selfish. I told her to stop whining and just go. And I went back to sleep."

"Oh, Eden." Allie hugged her. "Why didn't you ever tell us?"

"How could I? Every night I wish myself back there. I want another chance to be a good friend. I want to go with her, so she'll come back. So she'll be alive." So she and her friends could live a life that wasn't inundated with killers and darkness.

"We can't do that," Allie said. "I know because I've tried, too. But it wasn't your fault, Eden. We were nine years old. And while you might have cornered the market on it, we were all selfish and bratty. Chloe wandered and got lost, and unfortunately, someone found her. I don't know a lot, Eden, but I am sure of one thing. If you had been with her, Eden, you'd be dead, too."

"I know." Eden hesitated. She'd gone this far. What was one more step? "And sometimes I think I should be."

Bang! Bang, bang!

Eden shoved Allie away. "Cole."

"No, Eden. Wait!" Allie grabbed for her, but Eden was out of the car before her friend could stop her. It wasn't until she reached the front door of the warehouse that Eden realized what she'd done. What she'd always done. She'd acted without thinking.

Heart pounding, she pressed her back against the wall. She could see Allie across the road, gesturing madly for her to come back. Eden shook her head. Better to stay where she was, out of the line of fire. She ducked down and scooted along the wall under the large window to the corner of the building. She could hear shouts and muted orders echoing from inside the warehouse.

Eden's feet crunched in the broken glass strewn with chunks of drywall and concrete. Had they lucked out again? Had they cornered him? Was the Iceman inside? Had they stopped him before he could kill Jeff Cottswold?

Another inch to the left and she'd have cover. Slowly, she gripped the wall and pushed herself up to check around the corner.

Allie screamed her name as an arm locked around Eden's throat.

The few seconds it took for her to realize what was happening felt like hours. She sucked in a breath, smelled sweat and damp, alcohol and filth. She drew her arm forward, jabbing with her elbow. Ten years of self-defense classes had finally paid off. She made solid contact with his sternum as she kicked back with her left foot, catching him in the shin.

He grunted, gasped for air as he threw her to the ground. Glass gouged into her palms and knees. Another figure then leaped into view, coming to Eden's defense.

She couldn't move, couldn't seem to even shout for help. Suddenly, a glint of metal flashed as her attacker extended his arm at her protector.

Something sprayed across her face. Eden had shut her eyes, but now she swiped at her cheeks and heard the distinctive thud of a body hitting the ground.

The hulking hooded figure darted into the thick brush.

Eden pushed herself up. "No." Her heart stopped. Agent Simmons clutched a hand against the blood at his throat. "No, no, no." She scrambled to her feet and ripped her jacket off, pressing it to the gaping wound. She pried his hand free and used all of her weight to stem the streaming flow of blood. "Someone call an ambulance!" she hollered as she spotted people emerging from the building.

"Where did he go?" Jack yelled as he and the others came running.

"There!" Eden jerked her chin over her shoulder as she focused on Simmons.

"Eden?" Cole dropped down beside her, gun drawn, but she didn't give him more than a glance as she stared into Anthony Simmons's eyes. "Ah, man. Bowie! EMTs now! Allie! We need you! Hang in there, buddy. Agent Simmons, can you hear me?"

"Don't you die on me," Eden ordered, dismissing the

glassy, vacant stare that dropped over Anthony's face. "Don't. You. Dare."

"Fight." The raspy gurgle in Simmons's voice was the sound nightmares were made of. "You. Fight." He dropped a hand on Cole's as he added more pressure to Eden's.

"Suzanna needs you," Eden sobbed. "Don't leave her." *Don't leave me.* She couldn't take another death on her hands. Another life lost…

"Suzanna…" His eyes closed.

Not again. Not someone else. Not because of her. *"Where's that ambulance?"* Eden screamed.

Eden sat, clutching Allie's hand in the emergency room's waiting area. She barely noticed Cole and Lieutenant Santos speaking with a scrubs-clad doctor. Ghostly murmurs and solemn nods robbed her of her words. It didn't matter how many times she replayed things in her mind, the result was always the same.

"You should let someone take a look at you," Allie said.

Eden shook her head. The main doors slid open and a flash of white darted toward them.

"I keep telling myself I'm going to get used to getting these calls," Simone said as she dropped down in front of Eden and rested her hands on her knees. "Are you okay?"

Eden nodded. Blood covered her hands, still streaked her face. She hadn't let anyone come near her, not when Agent Simmons should be their focus. She didn't matter.

"It's my fault," she whispered as if nobody else knew. "All I could think about was getting to Cole and I didn't think—"

"You sure didn't." Cole's voice whipped through her.

Eden flinched.

"How's Agent Simmons?" Allie asked as Simone rotated so she could look at Cole.

"He's alive. Barely. They asked about next of kin—"

"His wife's name is Suzanna," Eden said after clearing her throat. "They're separated but..." She pressed a fist against her heart. "He was hoping they'd get back together."

"Let's hope he gets the opportunity," Cole said. His tone shifted. "On the bright side, congratulations, Eden. You were one hundred percent right. Batsakis had turned his previous place of employ into some kind of medical facility, right down to the plastic strip curtains fit for a serial killer. Microscopes, blood bags, IVs, you name it. Given what we found, I'm guessing he's been using it from the beginning."

"And Batsakis?" Eden tried to ignore the detachment in his voice. "Did you get him?"

"The man at the warehouse wasn't Hector Batsakis."

Eden's head shot up. "Then who—"

"Near as we can tell, he's a vagrant Batsakis had hired to keep an eye on the place. Not that we can get a coherent statement out of him at the moment. He's in shock."

"Eden's fine, by the way," Allie said. "In case you were wondering."

"No surprise. Eden always comes through unscathed, doesn't she?"

Simone got to her feet, but Eden quickly reached out, took hold of her hand and squeezed. "Leave it," she whispered.

"What were you thinking?" Cole blasted loud enough to catch the attention of the emergency room staff and waiting patients. "What part of *wait in the car* did you not understand?"

"I—" She what? She'd barreled into a situation she

had no business being a part of because she was scared for Cole? Because she realized she didn't want anything to happen to him before she had the chance to tell him… before she could admit to herself…

Eden took a shuddering breath. For the longest moment of her life, she thought she'd lost him, but here he was. Standing in front of her. Still alive. Furious, but still alive. "I wasn't thinking."

"Well, bravo. You finally get it." Cole's voice didn't dim. If anything, it got louder. "But how many people have had to get hurt or die before you figured out you're not the only person in the world? What was it, Eden? Still chasing your headlines? Needed to get a firsthand look at the connection you'd uncovered? Afraid someone else might get credit for what you shouldn't be doing in the first place? Whatever it takes to catch your killer, right? No matter who gets hit in the cross fire."

"That's enough, Cole." Now it was Allie rising to her defense, but again, all Eden could do was grip her friends' hands tighter. "I know you're angry, but that's no reason—"

"He's right." Eden blinked and sent tears scurrying down her cheeks through Simmons's blood. "This is my fault." Eden realized Allie couldn't argue with her because she knew Eden was right.

"Detective?" Lieutenant Santos called him over as Jack and Bowie entered through the same door Simone had.

"What right does he have to attack you?" Simone dropped into the chair on the other side of Eden and wrapped her arm around Eden's shoulders. "Doesn't he see what you're going—"

"He has every right." Suddenly, she understood what Simmons had been saying back in the car. Suddenly, she realized how little fight she had left in her. "I put them all at risk because—"

"Because you thought Cole was about to get his head blown off," Allie said. "I don't blame you—"

"So I, what? Ran into the line of fire? I ran toward the bullets, Allie. I didn't even stop to think about any consequences." What did that say about her? "Well? Is that guy talking yet? The one you did catch," Eden asked Jack as he headed over to Cole and the lieutenant.

Jack hesitated, cringing slightly as he detoured for her. "Talking, yes. Making sense? Not really. From what we can gather and what we found of his in the warehouse, he's a vagrant who'd been paid to hang around the building. He was also told the government was staking the place out and he should do whatever was necessary to get away should anyone ever try to enter."

"The mentally ill often make for convenient scapegoats," Allie said, as she rubbed Eden's arm.

"True enough. We're processing him now, but honestly, he's not going to give us anything useful. He's already muttering about his archangel and being on a secret mission from the stars." Jack brushed a comforting hand over Eden's shoulders. "Hang in there."

"Easy for him to say," Simone said, dropping Eden's hand. "You want coffee? I need coffee." She searched the signage. "Where's the coffee?"

"Uh-huh, caffeine's what you need," Allie said. "Cafeteria is that way." She motioned down the hallway. "Come on. We'll all go."

"I want to clean up some," Eden said, as she stood on wobbly knees and moved toward the bathroom. She wanted—she needed—to wash the blood off her hands. "But I'd appreciate a cup."

"You got it. Back in five." Allie and Simone hurried

off, but not before, Eden noticed, Simone shot Cole one of the nastiest looks she'd ever seen on her friend's face.

The creak of the bathroom door felt almost welcoming as she went directly to the sink. She turned on the water, braced her hands on the porcelain and dropped her chin. She couldn't get the sound of Simmons struggling for breath out of her mind; couldn't stop seeing, feeling, that spray of his blood as it spilled onto the ground.

Eden pushed a handful of soap from the dispenser, scrubbing her hands so hard they hurt; blood-tinged water circling the drain. She grabbed paper towels and tried to clean her face, saw streaks of thick blood in her hair. Looked in the mirror and saw it spattered on her shirt. A sob caught in her throat.

The door opened and shattered her solitude.

Cole walked in, his face even more stony than before.

Eden felt herself go cold. "Is he—"

"Still in surgery." Cole pushed the door closed and leaned against it. "I'm sending you home, Eden. There's a patrol car waiting to take you back to the town house. They'll park outside, until they're relieved at midnight, at which time another team will take their place."

The town house? Not the boat? Not… "I thought maybe I'd go back to the station—"

"You thought wrong."

"I know I screwed up." The words erupted before she realized she'd said them. "I know this is all my fault." He'd been about to leave, but he froze. She'd wanted to explain, to make him understand, but as he turned and looked at her, it took every ounce of courage she possessed to meet his hostile gaze.

"Screwed up? There's an agent fighting for his life because you couldn't do the one thing I asked. One thing, Eden! Now on top of trying to find the Iceman before he kills his latest victim, we've got the FBI demanding to know why a civilian got one of their agents severely injured, not to mention the start of an internal-affairs investigation once word gets out about the total fiasco at the warehouse. So yeah, you screwed up. And once again, someone else is paying for it."

"Sequestering me isn't going to fix any of it." She'd been wrong earlier. She did have some fight left. If she'd destroyed whatever feelings he'd had for her, fine, but she wasn't going to let their relationship die in vain. "I didn't do this on purpose. And I didn't do it for the fame or for the blog or to even catch the Iceman in flagrante. I got scared for you. I made a mistake. And I didn't for one second believe Agent Simmons was going to pay for it." She didn't think anyone would have to.

"Yeah, well, he's not the only one. We went out on a limb for you, Eden. Me, the lieutenant, Jack and half a dozen patrol officers. Now we'll be lucky if they even let us keep the case."

"Sounds like you're more worried about that than the case." Eden scrubbed a wet paper towel over her shirt. "Guess we're both pretty messed up, then."

"For once in your life, do as I say and go home. It's for your own safety."

"Just because we slept together doesn't mean you get to control me, Cole. As you said, I'm a private citizen. I can go and do whatever I want." And what she wanted right now, more than anything, was to put this case to bed and the Iceman behind her.

Cole stalked over to her. His look of fury she'd never seen before. "Do you have any idea what it felt like for me to hear Allie scream your name at that warehouse after I heard those shots? To realize you'd put yourself in the middle of everything yet again? You're reckless,

Eden. You're dangerous, and after today, I'm convinced you're out of control. You don't care about anyone other than yourself, what you want. What *Eden* needs. You want to do something to help? Then listen to this. You are done with this investigation. You will go home. You will lock your doors. You will bury yourself in that mausoleum of a basement of yours and not poke your head out until I'm convinced it's safe for you to do so. Do you understand me?" He gripped her shoulders hard for a second before he pushed away and walked out of the bathroom.

Eden looked at herself in the mirror, his words ringing in her ears. Yes, she'd heard him. And yes, she understood.

But she wasn't done. Not with this case. Not with the Iceman. And she wasn't about to sit around waiting to hear someone else she did care about—another friend—had died. This wasn't about ego. There was no pride involved. She'd made a promise when hanging in that freezer—to herself and to the victims and their families.

She was going to do whatever it took to find Hector Batsakis and stop the Iceman once and for all.

"McTavish here is heading to the station in a few moments," Lieutenant Santos told Cole when he rejoined them in the hospital waiting room. Cole was wound so tight, one wrong look—from anyone—and he was going to spring apart. "He's getting statements ready about the warehouse incident. He'll hand them over to Internal Affairs. And you should go home."

"I'm staying here." Cole wasn't about to leave until he knew one way or the other. "Simmons took on Eden because I asked him to."

"We all took on Eden," Jack said. "No one could have predicted what happened out there, Cole."

"I could have. I should have." In fact, he never should have agreed to let her on the case, but at the time, he'd needed to keep an eye on her. To stay close to her. Because he'd been terrified of losing her.

Instead an FBI agent could lose his life and the Iceman might claim another victim.

"No wonder you and Eden get on so well. You both suffer the same martyr complex," Jack said.

Allie and Simone rounded the corner carrying trays with cups of coffee.

"Take your pick—it's all bad." Simone started handing out the coffee to the officers keeping vigil. She looked around. "Where's Eden?"

"I sent her home." He frowned when Allie snatched his cup away.

"How very gallant of you," Simone said, in a tone that had him wanting to protect his man parts. "Make it a habit of kicking a girl when she's down, do you?"

"Maybe if she stayed put we'd have fewer problems like this." Simone with her claws out. Great. The day just kept getting better.

"Right. I'm going to leave before this turns nasty." Jack gave them all a salute with his coffee and headed out. "See ya back at the station."

"Do you think Eden doesn't know what she's responsible for, Cole?" Allie asked him. "Or were you not paying attention? She's devastated by what happened."

"I can't care about that right now." He had to focus on what he could control. His job. The case. His team. Then he'd worry about Eden's hurt feelings.

"Well, you should." Allie poked a finger hard into his

chest. "You should have seen her face when those shots rang out from inside the warehouse. She thought you were hurt, Cole. You were all she cared about."

Cole froze. "What shots from the warehouse?"

"Yes, what shots?" Lieutenant Santos moved in, as did Simone. "You said none of you fired your weapons."

"We didn't. Bowie? Nelson?" Cole waved the two uniforms over. "Did any officers fire their weapons inside the warehouse?"

"No, sir." Nelson, ginger hair shining under the hospital lights, held his cap in his hands. "Near as we could tell, they came from outside."

"That's where we headed when we heard them," Bowie confirmed. "Simmons got there first."

"I want everyone who was on that call to turn their weapons in for testing," Santos said. "I want this by the book for when IA comes to investigate."

"Wait a minute." Simone held up her free hand. "You're saying that someone outside the warehouse fired shots to make it sound like they were from inside? Who would do that? And why?"

"It doesn't make any sense. I was there, and if you'd asked, I'd have agreed with Eden. Those shots came from inside. I can't even remember seeing anyone around. But now…" Allie trailed off.

Every word Cole spewed at Eden slammed back on him with a vengeance. "This wasn't an accident. And it wasn't a mistake. Somebody wanted Eden in the line of fire. They wanted her there when we drove Batsakis's watchman outside. Someone who knows Eden. Knows how she'd react."

"This wasn't Eden's fault," Allie said. "Not *all* her fault."

Simone pointed a finger at him. "We all know what Eden does when someone she cares about is in trouble. She leaps first and worries about the fall later. So I ask again...where's Eden?"

"Ma'am, our orders from Detective Delaney were clear. We're to drive you directly to your house and stay until we're relieved."

"Officer Pearson, isn't it?" Eden scooted forward in the back of the patrol car. She should feel honored. Most officers didn't have partners, but somehow she'd managed to warrant two escorts. "And, Castillo?"

"Yes, ma'am." The young woman in the passenger seat gave her partner an uneasy look from beneath the visor of her cap. Her nose had a light dusting of freckles that added to her youthful appearance.

"Tell you what's going to happen if you do as Cole told you," Eden said. "You'll drive me home and I'll go in the front door. Wait a few minutes and after which, I'll go out the back door, get into my car and drive to the station myself. At some point, someone in the department is going to notify Detective Delaney that you didn't do what you were supposed to. So." She rapped her knuckle on the metal divider. "We can either do this together or me on my own. Your choice."

"Nothing at the academy prepared us for this," Castillo muttered. "I say get her to the station and let the detectives in Major Crimes deal with her."

Pearson gave a curt nod.

"Smart." Eden sat back and pulled out her phone as it buzzed for the fifth time in as many minutes. Allie again. No, Simone. She flicked through her missed calls. Nope. Not going to happen.

She wasn't putting anyone else at risk.

Eden turned off her phone and rode the rest of the way in silence.

"What do you mean she's not answering her phone?" Cole demanded, as Allie hung up again.

"Gee, I can't imagine why she might want some alone time," Allie mused. "It's not as if the one person she trusts more than anybody embarrassed her in public and then dismissed her."

Cole shook his head. When was this nightmare going to end? He glanced over to where the lieutenant was on his phone. "She doesn't—"

"Why do you think she flew out of that car? I swear, Cole, for someone who's as bright as you are, sometimes you have the brain of a gnat. Because she thought you were hurt. Because she was afraid she wouldn't get the chance to tell you how she feels about you before you go and die on her. Which is what she thinks everyone she loves is going to do, by the way. And who can blame her, with everyone she's lost?"

"Hallelujah. You actually got her to talk about it," Simone said. "That's going to entail a couple of bottles of the good stuff. So where would she have gone?"

"I had two patrol officers drive her to the town house."

"Terrific. We'll head there. You go—" Allie waved her hand in the air "—wherever you think is best."

"Passive-aggressive," Simone said. "I'm impressed."

"I'm not." Cole frowned. "Look, even Eden isn't crazy enough to..." Now it was his turn to trail off as her two best friends turned disbelieving expressions on him. "Yeah, never mind."

"Detective Delaney? Lieutenant Santos?" Dr. Inari, whom they'd spoken with earlier, approached and waved them over. "Agent Simmons has been stabilized for now. He'll need more surgery, but given the amount of blood he's lost, we want to wait until he's stronger before we proceed. We've put him into a medically induced coma."

"He's going to be okay, then?" Cole felt as if a two-ton boulder had been lifted off his chest.

"He's done better than we expected. That's all I'm comfortable saying at this moment."

"His wife is flying in from New York," Lieutenant Santos said. "She'll be here by morning. You." He pointed at Cole once the doctor left. "Tammy called from the warehouse. She found something she thinks you need to see. Since you're insisting on not going home, this seems like the perfect option for you to clear your head and deal with whatever anger you've got going on. Detectives Sutherland and Ramirez should be on site in the next hour. You can then turn the scene over to them."

"Yes, sir." As anxious as Cole was to make things up to Eden, the lieutenant was right. He wasn't in the best frame of mind. He hoped Allie and Simone would still help him out. "Would you two—"

"We'll meet you at Eden's." Allie nodded.

Clearing his head involved Cole rolling down the windows and turning the radio's volume up to full blast. Classic '70s rock blared through his head like a scouring brush.

He was closing in on the Sloughhouse warehouse off Highway 16 when his phone rang. "Delaney, go."

"Detective Delaney? It's Jenna Batsakis."

"Jenna?" Cole strained to hear her. Stupid dead zones. He made a right turn and sped up. "What's going on?"

"It's…out…my…rother."

His brain filled in the blanks. Even though he knew

about the siblings, he said, "Your brother? But you told us you don't have any relatives, Jenna." He yelled in case she couldn't hear him. "I don't like being lied to."

"I...sorry. But he's...family...left. Scared, Detective. Hector's in...basement, where...told me...treatments... approved. I—I think he has someone with him. I...yelling. Can...come?"

He quickly pulled over so he could make a U-turn. "You're just off Zinfandel, correct?"

"That...our mother's house. I moved downtown... closer to the community center. It's off B Street." He barely caught the street number.

"I'm on my way, Jenna. Can you get out of the house?"

"He'll know...wrong if...do. Might leave."

Who knew what her brother would do if he felt backed into a corner. "Okay, keep your phone on you. I'll be there as soon as I can." He waited until he was back on 16 before he dialed Jack. Flipping the siren on in his car, he barreled through a red light, ignoring the horns and screech of tires as he headed downtown. "Yeah, Jack. It's me," Cole shouted into the voice mail. "Jenna Batsakis just called. Said her brother's in the basement doing something weird. I'm going over to..." He recited the address. "Send a couple of backup units and have an ambulance standing by. I think he's got Jeff Cottswold with him."

"What are you doing here, Eden?" Jack's exhausted voice bounced off her adrenaline-boosted system. "I thought Cole sent you home."

"Don't worry, I kept the bodyguards." She sorted through stacks and stacks of receipts and paperwork from the various victims. Nothing like having two pairs of eyes watching every move she made. "There has to be something here with that logo I remember seeing on the bus."

"The logo again?" Jack set his coffee down and circled the table. "You don't think we're past that now, since we've got Batsakis's warehouse in lockdown?"

"That's my point. If you guys have run him to ground, he doesn't have many places left to hide, does he? And that bus, coach, mobile blood bank thingy he drives around in is the best place to start."

"I must be getting used to you because that actually made sense. Tell me what you're looking for."

Frustrated, Eden smacked the stack of papers on the table. Nothing with Pam Norris's records. "Medical receipts, vouchers, lab results, something that ties our victims to his mobile unit. I usually just chuck mine into a bin on my desk and sort them later."

"Castillo, Pearson?" Jack called. "Front and center."

"Sir?" The two officers moved as one, glancing uncertainly at Eden. "We can explain."

"You don't have to," Jack said. "It's called the Eden St. Claire effect." He pointed to the papers and receipts. "Each of you take a stack. We're looking for any kind of medical paperwork, especially if it has a blood-related logo or any related information."

They each set their caps down on the table and got to work.

"What's this?" Eden asked two cups of coffee later, when she still hadn't found anything. A lone worn cardboard box sat on a chair; there were odd scribbles written on its side.

"The hotel Eric DeFornio was staying in kept that box in their storage room when he didn't come back. Someone made an inventory list, but that's as far as we've gotten so far," Jack said. "Might want to wear gloves if you're going to go through it. Lot of meth heads live in that place."

"I think we're beyond tetanus concerns at the moment." Eden dragged the box over to the table and flipped open the lid. The stench of sweat and other things she didn't want to think about hit her first. She tossed the clothes to the side after going through the pockets. Next, she reached for the coat underneath… "Hang on." She pulled out a folded-up piece of paper. Computer printout. "Got it."

"What?" Jack rounded the table.

She smoothed the printout flat, jabbed her finger at the blood drop with a caduceus through its center. "That's what I saw on the side of the van." Now that she saw it again, the image crystallized in her memory. "Aesclepius Blood Donations. This address is near Zinfandel Drive. I know that was listed…" She grabbed Hector Batsakis's file. "Sure. Here it is. The house belonged to his mother."

"Hold up." Pearson snatched a photo off one of the boards. "Elliot Scarbrough had a receipt for a mobile blood unit in his office when they searched it." He tapped his finger against the image of the receipt on Scarbrough's desk.

"Search every photo from each victim's home," Jack ordered. "I want as many of those receipts noted as possible. Castillo, pull up that house on street view." He leaned over her chair and watched the image come onto the screen. "Single-story structure, center of a cul-de-sac. At least five homes for sale on the same street. No one around to pay much attention to them. I'm calling the lieutenant."

"I'm going with you, Jack," Eden said.

"Did today not teach you anything?" Jack blasted. "Seriously?"

"What was I supposed to do when you guys started shooting? Just sit in that car and—"

"When *we* started shooting?" Jack's brow knit. "What are you talking about? Those shots came from outside."

Eden's brain slowed. "What?" That didn't follow.

"Hang on." He held up a hand as he spoke into his phone. "Sir, I need units over at the following address as soon as possible. If Hector's not there, it might still give us an idea of where he's gone. Yeah, I'm going there now." He hesitated and then winced. "Yes, sir. Eden will remain here at the station." He hung up. "That was from the top, Eden. You stay put."

"What about Cole? Have you heard from him?" Eden deflected.

"Right." He punched up his voice mail and listened, worry and irritation flashing across his face. "I can only make out half of what he's saying. I swear he finds every dead zone in the city. I'll try calling him on my way."

"Ma'am?" Castillo started organizing papers once Jack had left. "Can I get you anything?"

Eden sank into the chair, feeling elated at having found the Iceman and possibly saving his latest victim. "I guess I'm stuck here, huh?"

"Or we could take you back to your place," Pearson offered. "As we were originally ordered."

"No." They'd need as much evidence as they could get to use against Batsakis when they finally brought him in. She may as well put her true talents to use and give them a hand with more research. "I'll help you get all this put into some order, okay? I just want to look up one thing first, though." She logged in to the nearest laptop and brought up Aesclepius Blood Donations. Then, with a fresh cup of coffee in her hand, she settled in to read every word on their website.

Cole screeched to a stop in front of the dilapidated house on B Street. Single story, weathered porch, crooked shutters. The lack of activity sent his heartbeat racing.

He was used to silence, but this dead-end street held an odd vibe that had every nerve in his body tingling. Why on earth would a young woman like Jenna live here? Keeping his ears open for the sirens—that would be his backup—he got out of the car, unlatched the snap on his holster and headed up the narrow, neglected walk.

The house was old. Creaky, rickety old. The hair on the back of his neck prickled. Something wasn't right. He didn't see any sign of a handicapped ramp or railing on the stairs to the porch. Nothing about this house said special needs, and given what he'd seen of Jenna Batsakis, she was in need of help.

Reason battled with concern. He should wait for Jack, but if Jenna was in trouble—

Yeah. Doubt niggled at his mind and he stopped walking.

If she was in trouble. His phone rang.

Cole took a step away. A twig snapped behind him.

He spun, ducking at the last second, as a plank of wood came for his head. It missed. But before he could move again, he felt the smash against his back. He went down, hard and aching, and tried to roll as he caught a glance of a frail young woman in a bright yellow dress. Jenna's hands trembled around a splintered two-by-four. "Jenna—" he managed before a third swing turned everything black.

"What's this?" Eden murmured as she scrolled through the last bit of information on the about page.

"What's what?" Pearson asked as he finished loading Eric DeFornio's belongings into the weathered box.

"I pulled up an old newsletter Aesclepius mailed to subscribers…" Her voice trailed off as she opened a new window and typed in the address. "This newsletter has an address I don't recognize from the case. Huh. It's an old church."

"Which one?" Pearson leaned over the back of her chair as Eden clicked through various articles on-screen. "Oh, sure. St. Augustus. One of those full-service churches. Used to have a soup kitchen for the homeless. It was a grammar school at one time, too. Kindergarten through eighth grade. I remember my grandmother talking about it."

Eden continued to scroll. "According to this article from five years ago, they often hosted blood drives, as well." That certainly couldn't be a coincidence.

"St. Augustus closed, what? Three, four years ago?" Castillo wheeled her chair over to them. "There was a rash of assaults in the area. Then a couple of the regulars went missing. City got involved, shut the place down. Wasn't much holding it together anyway, after Father Gregory passed on."

Eden and Pearson both looked at the wide-eyed brunette.

"What? I'm Catholic. Churches work as a kind of homing beacon for us." She grinned. "What's it got to do with Aesclepius?"

"Don't know. Did the vehicle Batsakis bought have tracking capability on it?" Eden asked. A coach like that would have a pretty substantial power source.

"Um." Castillo dug through some documents. "Capable, not activated," she confirmed.

"Is it something you can activate remotely?"

"Only with a court order through the manufacturer," Pearson said. "And there's no one here right now who can call for one."

"Can you contact Cole and see if he can apply for one?

If he needs a DA's help I can get that." Eden reached for her phone to call Simone.

"I'll give him a try," Pearson agreed.

"Great. Hey, Simone."

"Where are you?" Simone demanded. "Cole said you were at your house."

"Change of plans. I'm at the station."

"Oh, thank goodness." Simone let out a big sigh. "Allie, she's at the station with Cole. She's fine."

"Wait. No." Eden gripped the edge of the table. "Cole's not here. I thought he was still at the hospital with you all."

"We're not at the hospital. He sent us to your place. Where you're supposed to be."

"Then where's Cole?"

"His lieutenant sent him back to the warehouse to look at some evidence Tammy found. He was going to come by after." She hesitated. "I have to admit, I thought he'd be here by now."

Eden's stomach dropped. She hung up and dialed Tammy, squeezing her eyes shut even as she hoped she was wrong.

"Go for Tammy." The normally cheery voice had definite dulcet tones.

"Hey, Tam, it's Eden. Can I talk to Cole? He's not picking up his cell." Not that she'd tried to call, given how they'd left things. A problem for another time.

"He's not with us," Tammy said. "We've got evidence here of a jacked-up electrical system, though. Like Batsakis tried to bypass the regular power source. Maybe he'd hooked up to a portable generator. I wanted Cole to see—"

Eden hung up again, making a mental note to buy the lab tech another bottle of tequila. Or maybe a case. She made one more call. "Jack? Where's Cole?" she blurted the second he answered. She could barely speak past the catch in her chest.

"Last I saw him he was at the hospital—"

"He's not. And he's not at the warehouse, either, and that's where Simone said he was headed. You can't decipher the message on your phone?"

"Total loss. Why? What's going on, Eden?"

"What about the Zinfandel house?"

"We hit an accident on 50. We're still about five minutes out. I'll let you know when we—"

Eden shook her head and disconnected.

"You hang up on everyone, or just your friends?" Pearson asked.

"Something's wrong." Eden dialed Cole. It went straight to voice mail, as she expected it to. "Even when he's angry at me he takes the call." Except this time she'd pushed him too far.

"Now his phone, that I can get a read on," Castillo said. "We can track all department—"

"Do it," Eden whispered. Unease gave way to panic. "Where's Batsakis's personal file?" She plowed through what was left on the table.

"Here." Pearson handed the file to her. "I left it on top."

"Yeah, great." She flipped the file open and scanned the contents. "Where's that name…? There." She jabbed a finger under where it said "education." "He and his sister attended St. Augustus grammar school on B Street for second through fourth grade. Right before she got pulled for homeschooling."

"Place is pretty decrepit," Castillo said. "Street view, here."

Eden cringed at the crumbling structure. "Is that current?"

"Doubtful," Pearson replied. "That part of downtown's pretty dead, so to speak. Can't imagine they've installed cameras."

"Soup kitchen. Grammar school. Did…?" Eden's mind raced. "It had a working kitchen, didn't it? Maybe even a walk-in freezer?"

"I'd imagine so. Not that it would be working now."

"Hook up a decent generator, though, it wouldn't be so hard to get it working again," Castillo said.

"Or you could hook it up to a coach with its own power source," Eden said. "Tammy told me they suspect he was using a portable power source at the warehouse. Guys, before you say no, I want you to listen to me."

Castillo and Pearson glanced at each other. Then at her.

"No," they said in unison.

"Fine," Eden grumbled as she reached out with her foot to draw her purse closer. "Did you find Cole's phone yet?"

"No, but if he turned it off, it wouldn't register anyway."

"What about his car?"

"He's been using his personal vehicle the last couple of weeks," Pearson said. "We don't track those."

Eden resisted the urge to scream. She couldn't explain it, but she knew Cole was in trouble. And there didn't seem to be anything she could do about it, not as long as these two had her under lock and key. An idea caught. A bad—very, very bad—idea. She reached out to grab a bottle of water and twisted off the cap.

"One of you needs to call your lieutenant and tell him about this church. It's off the radar, it's abandoned, but it's the best lead we have. If I'm wrong, I'm wrong." But she wasn't. She knew it. "Go!" she said to Pearson and then opened a new document after taking a long drink of water. "I'll get all my notes down and printed out, so you can add them to the file."

"O-kay..." Pearson looked uneasy before he turned and walked over to the bull pen to make the call from Cole's desk.

Eden watched him leave. Her heart pounded in her chest. One down, one to go.

"You know," Officer Castillo said and scooted her chair closer to the table, "I have to admit, you being a reporter isn't such a bad thing. You've got a good brain. You think like a cop."

Maybe, Eden considered. But she certainly wasn't about to act like one. She inched the bottle of water toward the laptop.

"Let's see if we're wrong about that street-view camera at the chur— Oh, jeez!" Eden leaped out of her chair as water flooded across the keyboard. "I'm such a klutz!" Sparks exploded from the computer, followed by a hideous pop and sizzle.

"Move!" Officer Castillo pushed Eden out of the way, shoved the bottle across the table and plucked the laptop out of the growing, massive puddle. "Oh, that's not good." The smell of smoke permeated the room, making the officer's eyes water.

"I'll get paper towels." Eden scooped up her purse and darted for the door. She scurried the long way around to avoid Pearson in the nearly empty bull pen. She didn't dare look behind her as she raced for the back exit.

Reckless or not, she wasn't leaving Cole out there on his own. He had always had her back. Now it was her turn to have his.

* * *

Cole pried open his eyes. His mouth felt dry, his throat raw. His head… Oh, man, he felt as if he had a ten-bottle hangover before the bottles had been smashed over his skull. The distant hum of a generator buzzed in his ears. He felt cold and shivered.

Where the—

He attempted to sit up, but he couldn't move. Tucking his chin into his chest and straining up, he saw he'd been strapped down onto a gurney with leather restraints. He tried to pull free, but he only managed to rattle the steel railings trapping him. His breath escaped in bright white puffs. He arched his neck, shifted his torso as far as he could, only to realize he'd been hooked up to what he could only describe as a distillery. Blood was being pumped out of his body, through the tube in his arm, faster than he could have liked. A gurgling echoed in the otherwise silent room.

Cole took a long, deep breath. The temperature bit into his skin. He'd been plunged into Eden's nightmare. And like Eden…he wasn't alone.

An identical gurney on the opposite side of what looked like a freezer held the prone form of a familiar face.

Jeff Cottswold.

And his container of blood was almost full.

Cole swore and arched again, biting back a scream as pain shot through his head. The door snapped open.

Jenna, along with a male, sandy-haired version of herself, stepped inside.

"Detective," Jenna said. The friendly, innocent expression of the woman he'd met at the community center had faded behind cold, stark detachment. "I suppose you're hoping for an explanation."

Cole shrugged. "Really couldn't care less right now." There wasn't any need to explain bat-crap crazy, and Jenna's pupils were definitely spinning in that detached-from-reality look.

He glanced at Hector. "I know you." He searched his memory. He'd seen this guy before. *But where?*

"Might not recognize me without my tool kit." The smile did it.

"Glen." The lab tech who took Eden's blood in the hospital. He frowned. That made no sense. "Why were you there? Why take the risk?"

"A test," Jenna said. "When we heard Eden had been found alive, we needed to know how much she remembered. Hector's worked off and on in that hospital for years. No one pays him any attention." She smiled. "He's invisible."

"And what if Eden had recognized you?"

"He'd have blamed it on the drug, of course. But we didn't have to."

"She never even blinked as far as I was concerned," Hector said.

"What's with the IV?" Cole wished the pain in his head would subside. Maybe then he could think clearly enough to see a way out of this mess. Instead his concentrating on the pain was only making things worse. "It's not like I'm your type."

Jenna buttoned her thick coat and shivered. "No, you're not. But you and your team were getting just a little too close. We decided it was time for them to be focused on finding you, instead of us. We'll let this go another couple of hours. By then, you'll be too weak to do anything to save yourself and we'll be out of the state."

"Don't suppose you'd like to tell me where you're headed?" He twisted his wrist one way and then the other, but the restraints weren't budging. "You know, in case I surprise everyone and live." Like Eden had. *Eden.*

"Suffice it to say we've found a clinic that's not nearly as restrictive when it comes to experimental treatments." Jenna wandered over to Jeff and trailed a finger along the length of tubing.

"Why did you take Eden?" His teeth began to chatter. The cold was sinking into him as quickly as the blood was draining from him.

"She wouldn't leave us alone. She wasn't supposed to learn a lesson. She was supposed to die."

"Then why call me and tell me where to find her?" The band around his left wrist loosened a bit. When neither Jenna nor Hector responded, he craned his neck to look at them. "Finding her alive, along with the other bodies, reopened the case. You have to see that."

"The cold must be getting to him," Hector muttered. "That's the stupidest thing I've ever heard."

"Why on earth," Jenna asked with amazement shining in her eyes, "would we have called the police?"

"Because—" There was no *because*. It was the one thing in this case that had never made sense and now he knew why.

He and Eden had it wrong. These two weren't proud of their killings. They didn't care what anyone else thought about what they were doing. This was all about getting what they wanted: their victims' blood. Eden was an inconvenience. One they'd attempted to get rid of. "So you're not show-offs."

"Do we look like we need a good ego stroking?" Jenna asked. "Eden St. Claire ruined a perfectly fine plan with her endless whining about the victims. They served a greater good. They helped to advance science. They died for a purpose."

"I'll be sure to share that with their families," Cole said with as much sarcasm as he could muster and thought of Agent Simmons's sister. The agent might end up with closure, if Cole lived, but would an explanation be enough? It wouldn't be for Cole. Now, as the horror of what these two people had inflicted on their victims was made clear, he began to understand Eden a little bit more. "Your mother would be so proud."

"Our mother understood the importance of sacrifice," Hector blasted. "And so did Jenna eventually."

"So this wasn't your idea, Jenna?" Cole glanced at her in time to see her flinch. "Weren't in any rush to become a vampire?" He had to keep talking. Had to stay awake. Had to keep hoping Jack would come bursting through those doors at any minute.

"I admit the idea took some getting used to." Jenna looked lost in the past. "But I couldn't deny that the program my mother started gave us the means to find what we needed. It was a sign, you see. From her. She'd provided the avenue to find the right donors. People no one would miss. But then they closed the church and we had to find another way."

And there Cole followed, around the last bend to insanity.

"Then you really didn't call the cops so the bodies would be found." But someone had wanted Eden found. Alive. Someone with a vested interest in her future, someone who knew her every move, knew about Chloe and cotton-candy perfume and flowers…

The return of Chloe's killer hadn't started with Simone and the violets.

This had all started with the phone call that led him to Eden.

Which meant Eden—and Simone and Allie—were still in danger.

He pulled harder against the restraints. He had to get out of here. He had to get out of here in one piece; at least long enough to warn Eden.

"Whatever you're babbling about won't matter much longer." Jenna smiled. "You were so understanding, so compassionate." She walked over and touched his arm. "Thank you for that."

"Why? Why all of this?" He needed to stall. To let the air in the freezer continue to drain free through the open door. "Why the freezer? Why the cold?"

"We like as pure a donation as possible," Hector answered. He checked Jeff's line and gave his sister a nod. "The Propofol is enough to knock you out, but the cold temperatures keep our donors sedated longer without tainting what we need."

It was like being lectured by Jekyll and Hyde.

"But what about the reason behind it all? I don't get it." Cole twisted, trying to keep them both within view.

"Is it so wrong to want to live?" Jenna asked.

"It can't be that simple."

"Why can't it be?" Hector demanded. "We came into this world together. I wasn't going to let her leave without me."

"I guess that would have been too much to ask." Cole imagined the lives that would have been saved.

"Didn't you hear me? I said I wanted to live," Jenna spit.

"Your life isn't worth any more than the lives of your victims," Cole said. His mind spun again. His vision was going gray, as if he was losing consciousness. Quick—a flash of color. He saw a figure by the freezer's open door. Of red-tinged blond hair and sparkling blue eyes. Eden.

He closed his eyes. He was seeing things. "What gives you the right to decide who deserves to die?"

"I'm alive," Jenna said, as if it explained everything. "I should have died when I was a baby, I was so sick. But our mother prayed and prayed and I was saved. And we, or rather Hector, was given the knowledge he needed to keep me alive. I'm only the start, Detective Delaney. Once we prove this treatment works, it'll help hundreds, thousands of other patients. And they'll have us to thank for it. All those people won't have died in vain."

"No offense, but I'd love to see the faces of the vics' relatives when you share that theory with them."

"Yes, well, we don't always get what we want," Hector said. "Jenna, step back. I need to crank up this pump and put the good detective out of his misery. It's time we moved on with our plans."

The second Eden entered the broken-down church, she knew she'd found them. There was a charge in the air, an energy, something she could feel surrounding her. That and the fact she'd seen the bus parked out back, motor running.

The various hoses and electrical wires that were connected to the bus led via the rear door of the building into the kitchen, which had been another tip-off.

She held her phone out, record button on as she heard voices drifting through the echoing freezer. She'd made her way quietly around the counters, past the refrigerator and the ancient stove that looked to be housing a family of rats.

The lights were dim, but bright enough for her to see. There were still no sirens. She'd been counting on Castillo and Pearson to raise the alarm sooner rather than later. The fact that she'd boosted a patrol car, with GPS, from the parking lot should have increased their response time. With everything going on, the station was operating with a skeleton crew. Still, now was as good a time as any to put her increased faith in Cole's fellow officers to the test.

"But I haven't finished interrogating you yet." The sound of Cole's voice surged through her, warming her heart. She exhaled in relief. He was alive.

Eden pulled her stun gun from her waistband as she tried to follow the conversation. She bent down outside the walk-in freezer and set her phone on the floor, microphone aimed toward the occupants.

She peered around the metal door, waiting for Jenna and Hector to turn their backs to her. Eden, stun gun at the ready, waited for her chance.

Out of the blue, she heard car doors slammed outside. Voices yelled. In the distance, sirens blared.

Eden closed her eyes. Worst timing ever.

"Go see who that is!" Jenna ordered her brother.

Eden tensed, thumb on the button. The second she saw Hector's foot cross the threshold, she stepped out and plunged the prongs into his stomach. The sound of lightning times a thousand crackled in the air.

She counted to five before she dropped her arm, enjoying the smell of ozone as it mingled in the icy air. She shoved Hector hard and sent him sprawling backward into the freezer.

He landed, twitching, at his sister's feet.

Jenna backed up as Eden moved in. All these months, all the people they'd killed, the terror they'd inflicted... but nothing sent the anger washing over her faster and stronger than seeing Cole—the man she loved—strapped down.

"Eden—" Cole's voice lacked its normal strength. "Be careful."

"You won't hurt me." In the blink of an eye, Jenna had shifted into some kind of pathetic poor-me character. "I'm sick."

"You got that right," Eden replied.

"Get me out of these things." Cole rattled his restraints against the bars, a mix of fury and humiliation crossing his handsome face. She rushed to his side.

"Careful. You'll break your wrists," she said as she unbuckled him and lowered the railing. She looked over her shoulder at a pathetic Jenna, who stood, silently, huddling into herself.

"And here I thought you'd be needing *my* help." Cole shook his head, obviously trying to clear his mind. "They pumped me full of that sedative."

"I know." She touched his face. "Cole, I'm so sor—"

He kissed her, hard and quick, holding on to the back of her neck with disturbingly weak fingers. Then he stared into her eyes. "I'm the one who's sorry. Loving you means loving all of you. You wouldn't be who you are if you hadn't done what you did."

Eden grinned. "I should drug you more often. That sounded so nice."

"Eden! What the…?" Jack arrived first, followed closely by Lieutenant Santos and Pearson.

"I'm thinking about getting my name changed to that." Eden sighed and backed away from Cole to let the others in. "Eden, what the— has a kind of ring to it. Did Castillo catch on to my ruse, or did you track the car?" she asked.

She locked her eyes on Jenna and amused herself by hitting the Taser's on button every so often. Funny how she could make the woman twitch without even touching her.

"Give me that." Jack ripped the stun gun out of her

hand. "Both. Honestly, Cole, if you don't marry this woman we're going to have to lock her up somewhere. She's an absolute menace." But he hugged Eden tight nonetheless.

"Like the state can afford it," Lieutenant Santos said. He pushed his officers aside to let the EMTs in.

"You want to marry me?" Eden called out to Cole as she was dragged backward out of the freezer and engulfed in two pairs of arms. "Hey, where did you guys come from?"

She would have known Simone and Allie's embrace anywhere.

"Where we always are," Allie sob-laughed. "Right behind you."

"You owe me a case of wine," Simone said. "For all the years you've scared off me this last week. And I want the expensive stuff."

"Yeah, whatever. Where's Cole?" Eden craned her neck to peer around them.

"Jeez, one minute they're on, the next they're off. It's like a reality show with these two," Allie joked.

"Do you think he really would marry me?" Eden found herself falling into a dream she'd given up on decades ago.

"Well, I sure don't," Simone said. "But why don't you find out." She pushed Eden toward the freezer, Eden's onetime nightmare. Now a place that held the most promise.

She looked on as Bowie and Pearson hefted Hector off the floor and cuffed him, hauling him out of sight.

The EMTs bandaged Cole's arm after disconnecting him from the Batsakis siphoning machine. Eden reached for Cole's hand. "Is he okay?" she asked one of the paramedics.

Jeff Cottswold's stretcher was being carefully wheeled

from the freezer, the monitor they'd hooked up for his vital signs beeping loudly. A good sign.

"He's got a possible concussion, various contusions and severe loss of blood," one of the EMTs said. "And he's definitely been drugged with something. We'll get him into Emergency."

"I'll go with you." Eden wouldn't let go of Cole's hand.

"No." Cole shook his head, the lack of color in his face more disturbing than she would ever admit. "No, you hate ambulances as much as you do emergency rooms."

"True." Eden nodded, but she stepped closer and clutched his uninjured hand against her chest, took a deep breath and embraced the fear. Because Cole would be there to catch her. "But I love you."

Epilogue

Two weeks later...

"I can't believe you quit your job, Eden." Simone straightened the platter of turkey-and-Swiss pinwheel sandwiches for the fifth time in as many minutes, before moving on to rearrange the napkins and plastic forks. The Major Crimes squad room had been transformed into party central with balloons and streamers in an effort to celebrate Agent Simmons's release from the hospital.

"I can," Allie piped in as she entered with a pink bakery box overflowing with doughnuts, a line of officers trailing behind her as if in a trance. "What choice did she have when the Sac PD offered her a consulting gig?"

"It's not official yet." Eden didn't want to get ahead of herself. The chief still had to sign off on it, but with Cole, Jack and their lieutenant joining forces to recommend she work with the group of detectives overseeing cold cases, it was a sure thing. The only caveat? The blog had to go. But she'd be given a new one, an official one, sanctioned by the police department.

She thought it'd be harder to let her blog go, but when she thought about it, what she'd be able to do in return made the loss worth it. "If it happens, they're going to give me rules."

"In writing," Cole said as he strode in. "Preferably in triplicate. It's all part of my evil plan to be able to use her brain at a moment's notice."

"That's why he's marrying me," Eden joked and rolled her eyes in mock contempt. "For my *brain*."

"So it's marriage, is it?" Allie glanced over as the officers and detectives began flooding in to sign the oversize card for Agent Simmons.

"That depends." Cole wrapped his arms around Eden from behind and rested his chin on top of her head, asking, "What are you doing next weekend?"

"Next weekend?" Simone angled a look at him. "You didn't get her pregnant, did you?"

"No, he did not," Eden replied, although an odd hitch caught in her chest. "But we did make plans to get married in Tahoe. I need bridesmaids."

"Us?" Allie gasped.

"Who else would she ask?" Simone knocked her hip into Allie's. "Of course we'll be there. Cole, you have groomsmen, I assume?"

"I've got Jack, the best man, who's already planning the bachelor party, right?" He looked over his shoulder as Jack joined them.

"I was thinking about renting a party bus with a stripper pole." Jack grinned. "What do you think, Eden?"

Eden smacked his hand when he reached for a sandwich. "I think it depends on how comfortable you are in a G-string."

That earned a round of guffaws from his fellow officers.

Cole and Jack went to greet their guest of honor, Agent Simmons, who was in a wheelchair for the next few weeks and accompanied by his beautiful wife, Suzanna. She and Eden had become friends.

Eden had decided she wasn't betraying a confidence by telling Suzanna about her conversation with Agent Simmons before he'd been attacked. Besides, she wasn't about to give him an out when happiness was closer than he realized.

Eden drew Allie and Simone into the far corner. "What's going on with you?" she asked Simone. "You've been jumpy lately."

Simone shrugged and folded her arms across her chest, a gesture that spoke of uncharacteristic uncertainty. "You mean other than the fact that our friend's murderer seems to have gone back into hibernation?"

"He'll pop up." Eden kept her voice low. "All the more reason to have an entire police department at my disposal." Making light of Simone's point was the only way she could cope for the time being. "When Chloe's killer comes forward again, we'll be ready for him."

The doubt in Simone's eyes had her shifting uneasily on her feet. "You didn't think I'd forgotten about it, did you?"

"Absolutely not." Ever the peacemaker, Allie rested her hands on theirs. "But Eden's right, Simone. You've been acting strangely for a while now and it's not as if we don't have a lot to be grateful for."

Last Eden had heard, the Batsakis siblings had been locked away for good. However, it was doubtful Jenna would live to see a trial. Her condition had taken a serious downturn and she was currently under twenty-four-hour guard in the state's leading mental hospital. Personally, Eden had been hoping for a long, painful death. Yeah, she was still working on that becoming-a-nicer-person thing, but at least the victims' families finally had their answers. "And you've got the Denton case coming up…"

"Bingo," Allie said, when Simone's eyes narrowed. "You're having problems with the case?"

"You could say that." Simone shook her head and her blond hair cascaded around her shoulders. "Our main witness is getting nervous. It'll be a miracle if she holds it together until the trial starts. But listen, today's about celebrating life." She gripped Eden's chin in her hand and squeezed. "You're happy. It looks good on you."

"Are you talking about the fact that she doesn't get that deer-in-the-headlight look anymore whenever Cole mentions the *M* word?" Allie smiled.

"There is that," Simone agreed. "Maybe you've finally put some ghosts to rest."

"Maybe," Eden said. The anger, the grief, all the emotions she'd never been able to process about her parents, about Logan, even Chloe, had settled down, along with that monster inside her. "Some, anyway. There are big changes coming. For all of us."

"Speaking of changes, where are you and Cole going to live?" Allie asked.

"On the boat, for now," she told them. Allie almost choked.

"You're going to live on a boat?" Simone stared. "Well, if that doesn't prove life's completely unpredictable, I don't know what does."

Eden caught Lieutenant Santos gesturing at her through the window. She nodded, and he motioned for Allie and Simone to join him.

Cole caught up to her as she was walking. "Where are you going?"

"Delaney, you, too." Lieutenant Santos waved all of them into his office and closed the door behind him. "I know this isn't the time or place, but I have the three of you here, and this one—" he pointed to Eden "—is going to find out anyway. Detective Henry Carter's widow brought this by the chief's office this morning." He lifted a large padded envelope off his desk.

Cole moved in behind Eden and rested his hands on her shoulders.

Lieutenant Santos continued. "The envelope was addressed to her husband, and when she opened it, she realized what it was."

"And what is it?" Eden asked. Icy dread, unwelcome and all too familiar, overtook her. This time, however, she had Cole to deflect the chill.

Lieutenant Santos tilted the envelope. A child's tennis shoe dropped onto his desk. Turquoise. With pink flower laces.

"Chloe's missing shoe," Simone whispered.

"The one they never found." Allie's voice trembled before she cleared her throat.

"Given the other deliveries that have been made, and the fact that very few people were privy to certain aspects of the case, the chief, the DA and I are all in agreement." Lieutenant Santos looked at each of them before he went on. "We're reopening the Chloe Evans murder investigation."

Eden didn't know whether to scream or cry. She stared at her friend's shoe as memories of that night, of the mistakes she'd made, the things she couldn't change, flooded back. She wouldn't wallow in them anymore. She wouldn't use them as excuses or walls to hide behind.

"You were right, Eden," Allie said in a low voice. "He's back."

"He is." Eden reached up to her shoulder and gripped Cole's fingers in hers. "Only this time we're going to bury him."

* * * * *

The next gripping installment of
HONOR BOUND *will be available May 2017*
from Harlequin Romantic Suspense and
USA TODAY *bestselling author Anna J. Stewart!*
Don't miss Simone's story!

Widow Penelope Barrington never thought she'd speak to Reid Colton again, as he's the man she holds responsible for her husband's death. But when she finds evidence incriminating her father in his *father's disappearance, she's forced to team up with her teen crush to find the truth...before it's too late.*

Read on for a sneak preview of Beth Cornelison's COLTON CHRISTMAS PROTECTOR, the final book in ***THE COLTONS OF TEXAS*** *miniseries.*

"Reid..." she rasped.

He raised his head to look deeply into her eyes. "I want you, Pen. I won't pretend otherwise any longer. But if this isn't what you want, you can tell me to go to hell, and I'll respect your feelings."

She opened her mouth to reply, but so many thoughts and emotions battled inside her, she could only stare at him mutely.

When she didn't reply, his expression darkened. He levered farther away from her as if to leave, and she tightened her grip on his shirt.

"Pen?" He angled his head, clearly trying to read her.

"I...need more time." Her heart thrashed in her chest like a wild animal tangled in a snare. She felt trapped, caught between loyalty to Andrew and a years-old lust for Reid. Factoring in the mind-numbing twists her life had taken, her father's deceit and the foggy road that was her future, how could she know what was right? For both her and Nicholas, because she had to put her son's needs at the top of her considerations.

Reid bowed his head briefly, his disappointment plain. "More time. Right. Because we've only known each other for fifteen some years. Been friends for seven."

"Andrew—"

"Has been gone for over a year," he finished for her, his voice noticeably tighter. Pain flashed in his eyes, and he shoved away from her. "All right. I promised to respect your choice, and I will."

Freed of his weight and warmth, a stark chill sliced through her. Confusion or not, she didn't want to be without him. She did desire him, value the protection he offered, appreciate his friendship.

"Wait!" she cried before he could rise from the couch. She sat up, shifting her legs under her to kneel on the cushion beside him. "Reid, I'm still sorting out my feelings, but I want..." Her throat tightened. "I need..."

He arched an eyebrow to indicate he was listening, waiting.

She drew a slow breath, her body quivering from the inside out. She threaded her fingers through the hair near his ear before cupping the back of his head and drawing him close. "This..." she whispered as she slanted her mouth over his.

HRSEXP1116

HARLEQUIN®
A Romance FOR EVERY MOOD™